Accolades for *Finding Harmony* and the *Katie & Annalise* Mystery Series

2011 Winner of the Houston Writers Guild Novel Contest
2010 Winner of the Writers League of Texas Romance Contest
2012 Winner of the Houston Writers Guild Ghost Story Contest

"An exciting tale that combines twisting investigative and legal subplots with a character seeking redemption...an exhilarating mystery with a touch of voodoo." – Midwest Book Review Bookwatch

"A lively romantic mystery that will likely leave readers eagerly awaiting a sequel." – Kirkus Reviews

"A riveting drama with plenty of twists and turns for an exciting read, highly recommended." – Small Press Bookwatch

"Katie is the first character I have absolutely fallen in love with since Stephanie Plum!"

– Stephanie Swindell, bookstore owner

"The characters are completely engaging, and the story catapults us into action, adventure and mystery. Hold on to your hats!" – Hanna Dettman, voice actor

"Corrupt island police and a Mexican drug cartel make a fast-paced, fun read that will make you laugh, hold your breath, and maybe even say a little prayer for a character or two. I couldn't put it down—great read!" – Sandy Weaver Carman, radio personality and author of *The Original MBA—Succeed in Business Using Mom's Best Advice*

"Engaging storyline...taut suspense, with a touch of the jumbie adding a distinct flavor to the mix and the romance perfectly kept on the backburner while dealing with predatory psychopaths." – MBR Bookwatch

'Clever, funny, and a page-turner from the very beginning." – Rebecca Weiss, attorney

Finding Harmony

Katie & Annalise Series, #3

Pamela Fagan Hutchins

e

SkipJack Publishing books may be purchased for educational, business, or sales promotional use. For information, please write: Sales, SkipJack Publishing, P.O.B. 31160 Houston, TX 77231.

First U.S. Edition
Hutchins, Pamela Fagan

Finding Harmony/by Pamela Fagan Hutchins
ISBN: 1939889103
ISBN-13: 978-1-939889-10-2 (SkipJack Publishing)

Foreword

Finding Harmony is a work of fiction. Period. Any resemblance to actual persons, places, things, or events is just a lucky coincidence.

To Eric
(always)

Acknowledgments

My editor is a goddess. Thank you, Meghan Pinson, for making me sound like me, only better.

To my dear darling baby brother, my thanks for all advice aero and nautical.

The beta readers who enthusiastically devote their time—gratis—to helping us rid my books of flaws blow me away. The love this time goes to Ginger, Hanna, Rebecca, Rene, Rhonda, Sandy, Sonja, Staci, Stephanie, and Susie.

The biggest thanks, once again, go to my Cruzans: husband Eric, friend Natalie, and house Annaly. They are the ones who inspired me to dream up stories in the islands.

Eric gets an extra helping of thanks for plotting, critiquing, editing, listening, holding, encouraging, supporting, browbeating, and playing miscellaneous other roles, some of which aren't appropriate for publication.

Kisses and a pageant wave to princess of the universe Heidi Dorey for fantastic cover art. I love each one more than the last.

To each and every blessed one of you who have read, reviewed, rated, and emailed/Facebooked/Tweeted/commented about the Katie & Annalise books, I appreciate you more than I can say. Stephanie, Rhonda, Liz, and Rebecca stand above the rest here. It is the readers who move mountains for me, and for other authors, and I humbly ask for the honor of your honest reviews and recommendations.

Ashley Ulery, you gorgeous creature, thank you for giving voice to Katie and friends in the audiobooks.

Finally, my eternal gratitude to Eric, Marie, Stephanie, Heidi, Liz, Clark, Susanne, Allie, and Susie for keeping me alive and reasonably sane on the 60-Cities-in-60-Days book tour as we built the audience for Katie & Annalise one town and one reader at a time.

Table of Contents

Chapter One

One hundred pounds of squealing pig juked left and went right, and my husband fell for the fake. Mud splashed over his head and splattered our three-year-old on the other side of the fence. A coconut palm did the wave in the distance, lending support to the swine, one island local to another.

"More, Daddy, more!"

Taylor hopped up and down, his hands gripping the middle rail above his head. He looked like the 102nd Dalmatian in his muddy white shirt, a poor choice in retrospect. Even a year after Nick's sister's death had left Taylor in our care, I still wasn't quite up to speed on motherhood.

A loud *chuptz* sounded behind me as the pig's owner sucked his teeth derisively. The Pig Man shaded his eyes from the sun and peered over at Nick past a rusted-out Buick and some wandering chickens. His voice belied faith in the pig-catching abilities of a mere continental.

"You got to get your arms around the neck and behind the shoulder, meh son. Lock your hands around your wrists. Like this." He demonstrated with his hands clasped over his head. "Then you slip the rope over he head." Then he turned his back and went about his business of doing nothing—limin', as they say on St. Marcos. Strains of Jimmy Cliff singing "The Harder They Come" spilled from his radio. Nick caught my eye and rolled his.

"Yes, sir. I think I've got him this time." My husband stuffed the length of twine back into his waistband, smearing what may not have been mud on himself in the process. Luckily, we had driven separate cars.

Not for the first time, I wondered how I had gotten from there to here so quickly. "There" was my old life in Dallas as a single attorney with a penchant for Bloody Marys; "here" was my new one as a mother of three, married to Nick Kovacs on a Caribbean island.

I looked back at Nick. The pig still had the upper hand. Maybe he knew his fate; tomorrow he would be the main course at a christening party for our three-month-old twins, Jessica and Olivia. On St. Marcos, it wasn't a party without a roasted pig. That meant a visit to the Pig Man to buy one—but first, you had to catch it.

Nick appeared closer to doing just that. Taylor, the little traitor, was cheering on the pig, which looked like it was getting tired. Nick lunged like the Pig Man told him to and finally slipped the halter over our swine's head.

"One hour and seven minutes," I called out.

"I spotted him the first half hour," Nick replied.

I stifled the smirk tickling the edges of my mouth. The alternative to Nick catching the pig was me in that pen—supportive, appreciative, and awestruck seemed the way to go. "Woo hoo, Nick, I am so impressed. You caught the baby pig. We're roasting Wilbur!"

"Daddy caught Wilburn," Taylor announced. He turned to me. "Can we keep Wilburn?"

I wondered what Charlotte would have spun in her web if she'd heard that. "Wilburn" had a nice ring to it.

"Now you've started it, Katie," Nick said as he moved in for a kiss. Despite the pig muck smeared on his shirt and caked on his pants, I let him. I patted him on the behind, too.

The Pig Man nursed a rum and Coke and continued limin' while Nick wrestled the pig into the small trailer we had borrowed for the day. I applied some spit and elbow grease to Taylor's smelly spots. When Nick closed the trailer's door with a clang, the Pig Man roused himself. "That be one hundred and fifty dollar." He held out his hand. Nick filled it and we bid him good day.

The Pig Man lived even farther up in the rainforest than we did. We pointed our SUVs back down the one-lane dirt road that ran the ridge over the island's northwestern shore. The cliffs fell away to crashing blue waves below, where the sea was whipped into a meringue against the rocks. Home, rugged home.

Nick's banged-up maroon Montero pulled to a stop before a small wooden barricade that hadn't been there earlier. Neither had the wild-eyed man who appeared from the bush, a Heineken in one hand and a machete in the other. His hair stood away from his head in a patchy Afro and his camouflage pants and ragged jam-band t-shirt hung on his bony frame. This should be good. I rolled down my window.

"Dan-Dan, how are you doing?" Nick said.

"You got to pay the toll to pass," Dan-Dan answered.

"No problem. I'm paying for the lady in the next vehicle, too."

"That two beers. One for each. You got to pay me two beers."

Nick pulled out two of the four beers he had stashed in his console for just this reason. Dan-Dan must have been sleeping off yesterday's collections earlier; we had made the round trip for half price today. "Here you go." Nick handed him the beers and the sack lunch of fry chicken and johnnycake we had picked up earlier at the Pig Bar. As a recovering whatever-I-was (I refused to say alcoholic), I insisted we give him food, too, even though I honored the requirement of beer. Hopefully Dan-Dan would eat it. "You take care of yourself, now," Nick said.

Dan-Dan pulled the barricade aside just long enough for our vehicles to pass and then hustled it back into place. I waved at him as I drove by, but he gave no sign that he had seen my gesture.

Taylor waved and shouted, "Hi, Dan-Dan!"

This brought the man's head up. He smiled, showing his snaggly teeth, and motioned me to stop. I did; Nick kept going. Dan-Dan ran into the bush, then back to my truck. He was not one to waste effort on the niceties of small talk.

"Who that man in the bush at your house?" he asked.

"You mean my husband Nick? Or maybe my father-in-law, Kurt? Kurt is older but he looks like Nick, and you know Nick, right? The one who just drove off, Taylor's dad."

He shook his head. "Not dem men. A man like me, a local man. A man who talk about dead people dem." Pluralization, West Indian-style: them, after a noun, pronounced "dem."

I swallowed. "Well, I don't know, but if you see him, tell him to go away." I tried a laugh. It came out flat.

He pulled a wooden figure out of his pocket and handed it to me. A pig. "For the boy."

How in the world had this man carved the perfect gift on the perfect day for Taylor?

Taylor strained against his seat belt. "He made Wilburn for me. I want Wilburn."

I handed it to him. "What do you say, Taylor?"

"Thanks, Dan-Dan!"

I turned to thank Dan-Dan myself, but he was gone, back from where he'd come. Some people feared the old guy, but he was all bluster and had never harmed anyone. He was just one of the ragtag personalities that made St. Marcos unique—and one of the reasons that tourists and snowbirds avoided this part of the island. I considered that a good thing.

My phone rang: Nick calling, although we had caught back up to him. "I'm headed into town to the abattoir," he said.

"I'm so glad it's you and not me," I replied.

"I have my uses."

"Yes, you certainly do." The tone of my voice left no doubt as to his other uses.

"Hold that thought for later," he said, and clicked off.

Nick turned left at the next fork and Taylor and I stayed to the right to head back to Annalise. We bounced down the dirt road under a canopy of green vines and pink flowers, past the ruins of an old sugar plantation and up to her gate. A wild tropical orchard lined her drive, and I often slowed down here and rolled down the windows to breathe them in. When the trees parted to reveal her, Annalise stood tall and proud on the crest of a hill, overlooking a forest of mango trees on the valley floor.

We lived in—I might as well just say it and get it out there—a jumbie house in the rainforest. Jumbie as in voodoo spirit.

Yeah, right. I know. I didn't believe it either at first. I promise I'm not some crazy woman who needs her head shrunk. Living at Annalise just showed me there's more out there than our first five senses can detect. On St. Marcos, I'd discovered a sort of sixth sense that made me aware of things. Things that were almost undetectable back in Dallas, like someone had hit the mute button. But on St. Marcos, by the sea, I could feel them. I could feel her. Annalise.

The crazed barking of our pack of dogs broke my reverie. We had started with six of them but were down to five after one succumbed to a swarm of bees; the rainforest could be as brutal as it was lovely. Our dogs served us well as security force and welcome committee, and they did both jobs well. Today they alerted my live-in in-laws to our presence, and Julie met us at the door.

"Hi, 'Lise. Hi, Gramma," Taylor said to the house and Julie before shower-ing our German shepherd with the full force of his attention. Poco Oso and Taylor were best pals.

"Shhh, Kurt is putting the girls down for their nap," Julie said. "Did you get a pig?"

"Wilbur is on his way to slaughter. And I'm a recently converted vegan."

Julie and I shared a grimace. No matter how abhorrent the thought of cooking Wilbur was to me, the girls came into this world on St. Marcos, and their christening deserved the full island wingding. Except for the roasted pig, all the food would come from Miss B's Catering, which we had ordered for delivery two hours earlier than we needed it, in the hope that it would then be on time. Life ran at a slower pace here.

I tiptoed into my daughters' room. If you closed your eyes and sniffed, you'd know you were in a baby girl's room: powder, lotion, baby wipes and new diapers. I loved the scent. Not that it always smelled this sweet; with twins, there's double the diaper issue, but I'm slightly OCD and we took care of stinkers fast. Kurt was rocking Liv in our yellow and blue plaid glider; Jess was already sleeping in her crib. Soft mewling sounds slipped from her lips as I kissed my fingertip and placed it on her cheek. She'd better hope those dainty mewls didn't become the growly snores of her father someday. I stroked her head, enthralled by the fuzz of the hair she almost had.

Kurt, Julie, and I spent the next few hours preparing Annalise for the party while Taylor had lunch and a nap. Annalise loved a good party, and we could feel her energy level throttle up, but mine began to throttle down as the hours passed and Nick didn't return. How long could a butcher take, anyway? Maybe it was delayed postpartum depression talking, but it occurred to me that whatever was in town must be a lot more appealing than a wife who still needed to lose ten pounds of pregnancy weight. But I pushed the thought out of my mind. Not my Nick.

At dusk, he drove up to the house, pulling the trailer behind the truck. Kurt, Julie, and I each grabbed a child and ran out to greet him. It's not every day Daddy brings home a big dead pig.

"Hi, Daddy," Taylor yelled.

Nick grinned at us and turned off the ignition. He stuck his head out the window. "Who wants to help me bring in Wilbur?"

"Wilburn!" Taylor said as he hopped from one foot to the other.

"Nick . . ." I pleaded, but he ignored my hint to ix-nay the ilburn-way. OK, I'd started it, but ewww.

Kurt handed Liv to Julie and helped Nick carry the dressed pig—swathed in innumerable layers of plastic wrap—to the dining room.

"Oh, no, fellas. Not my dining room table. No way," I said.

"It's here or the coffee table," Nick replied.

"Neither! How about the garage floor?"

"You really want to leave a slaughtered pig on the floor of the garage over-night, up in the rainforest? Really?"

I thought of the traps we kept baited for the rodents of all sizes that ventured in looking for food. The monthly visits from the exterminator. The mahogany birds known in the states as roaches. "Maybe not such a good idea," I admitted.

"Ya think?" Nick said.

Before I could think of a snappy comeback, someone knocked on the kitchen door. I answered it with Liv poised on one hip. We didn't get many visitors up here. I opened the door onto a complete stranger who was standing outside the span of light in total silence. No sound or sign of our dogs. Weird.

"Good evening," I said.

Nick appeared and stepped in front of Liv and me. "Good evening to you. May I help you?" Nick said.

The scruffy local stepped forward and looked around Nick to the baby and me. "I here to see the missus."

"Go ahead," Nick said.

"It private business." He ducked his head forward in an attempt to indicate respect.

Private business? What in Hades could anyone want to talk to me about that Nick couldn't hear? How odd, I thought, but I wanted to know what the man had to say.

"No offense, but—" Nick started to say.

Uh oh. Nothing good ever came out of Nick's mouth after "No offense, but." I interrupted. "It's OK, Nick. You'll just be a few feet away in the kitchen. I'll call you if I need you."

I immediately regretted my words. This man had an unsettling vibe. I didn't want to talk to him alone, but it was too late. The look my husband gave me would freeze the blood in the veins of a lesser redhead. He stalked to the kitchen, his footsteps drumming his displeasure in a deep bass tone. I suspected I would have some making up to do later. I almost called out for him to come back, but I pushed my nerves aside. *Don't be a wuss. He's only twenty feet away.*

"You Ms. Katie that buy this house?"

"I am."

"I here about the dead."

"The dead pig?"

"I don't know nothing 'bout no pig. I here about all the dead people dem under the house."

Liv whimpered. "Shush, love." I bounced her lightly. She was falling asleep; not me. This man had shocked my system like a triple espresso. I wasn't the only one wide awake, either; I could feel Annalise rise up. She didn't like this man any more than I did. The dogs reappeared in the yard. Where the hell had they been? They kept their distance but formed a rough perimeter around the stranger.

"Excuse me?" I spoke loudly, hoping to draw Nick back to me without scaring my visitor away until I'd heard him out.

"All the dead men and women dem buried under this house," he said. "I work here, long time ago, building the house. I see skeletons dem with my own two eyes. The boss man—the bad man—he try to cover it up so nobody know. But I know. He put this house on sacred ground. He disrespect the dead."

Eerie night music filled my ears as thousands of bats' wings beat the air, vacating Annalise's eaves to begin their evening hunt. "I'm not sure I under-stand what you mean," I said to him.

"This house built on a slave graveyard. The law say you can't go digging up the dead."

Was it built on a graveyard? Against the law? I had no idea about either point. He went on.

"Maybe I think you don't want me talking to the government about this. Give me a little something for disrespecting my people dem, and I won't say nothing. I going now for a time, but when I reach back, maybe you have something you want to give me and my family."

He turned on his heel and walked off toward the bush, but as he crossed the yard, the light above the door exploded, showering glass in a wide arc that left Liv and me untouched. Glass flew at him and the sound chased his back, but if he was hit, he didn't flinch.

Only I could see the tall black woman with the knotted headscarf standing two steps away from the porch. A scowl puckered her young face, and her calf-length plaid skirt whipped around her bare legs as she slowly disappeared. *Well done, Annalise!* I could have told him not to piss off my house.

The dogs gave way to him, growling low and I felt an urge to whisper, "I see dead people dem," in my best local accent. This guy was spooky. What if he was telling the truth? My mind reeled from the possibility. It was highly unlikely, though. I felt Nick's hand on my shoulder and relief surged through me.

"I'm sorry, sir, what did you say your name was?" I called after the old man as his black skin disappeared into the black night. He didn't answer.

Chapter Two

Nick and I shared an incredulous look. I hugged Liv close and pressed my lips against her fine red hair. Suddenly, a thunderous crack whipped our heads around. Nick and I ran to the driveway after what had clearly been gunfire, my feet pounding the hard-packed dirt as Liv bounced up and down on my hip. I held her neck with one hand and wrapped her body tight with my other arm. I was running blind, and the night was fading from charcoal to jet ahead of me. The night sounds magnified; the sickeningly sweet evening air made it hard to breathe.

Nick pulled away from me and crossed the distance fast. Over his shoulder he shouted, "You and Mom stay in the house with the kids. Send Dad. And lock the doors behind us."

I could hear the pounding of my heart as it pulsed in my burning ears. I stopped to catch my breath. Words of retort automatically formed on my lips but I bit them back. What kind of brain-dead idiot runs toward a gunshot holding her baby anyway? Two long beats passed before I spun around. I walked double-time back to the house and Kurt met me on the way.

"That sounded like a gunshot," he said.

"Yes! Nick asked you to please come—and hurry," I said.

Kurt didn't bother to answer. He sprinted into the night after Nick.

Julie was frozen in place holding Jess. I patted Taylor's shoulder and herded him onto the couch in the great room.

"Taylor, how about some Disney Channel?" I clicked it on, knowing that it would be a miracle if it was enough to hold this busy child still. I looked back at my mother-in-law, who still hadn't moved. I needed her help, so I gave her a gentle prod. "Julie, I'll take care of the doors and windows. Could you find a place for the girls?"

Julie hesitated, eyes wide, then nodded and arranged a blanket for the babies on the great room rug. She spoke soothingly and was soon entertaining the kids.

I sprinted from door to window to door, closing and locking. Unless the weather was bad, we usually left all of them open, letting the trade winds cool the house. Today we had opened them as far as they would go. I cursed Annalise's design: seven doors and thirty-seven windows. This was not a "just go deadbolt the front door" type of undertaking.

"Annalise, I would really appreciate it if you would learn to do this your-self," I muttered. No response; none expected. Her quietude was encouraging; normally, if she sensed a threat, she transmitted her agitation with vibrating cups and saucers and snaps of electricity.

I had no sooner finished locking up than I heard three raps at the kitchen door.

"Who is it?"

"It's us, Katie," Nick said.

I unlocked the door and opened it wide for Nick and my father-in-law. Kurt's face was ashen. This couldn't be good.

"We need to call the police," Nick said.

I stared at my husband. Nick is a private investigator by trade, but in my opinion, he's a Lone Ranger and borderline scofflaw. And that's when he worked in the states. Here on St. Marcos, no one called the police if they could help it. Cops and perps were nearly indistinguishable. The *St. Marcos Daily Source* featured bad-cop stories on its front page several times a month, with crimes by officers ranging from drug trafficking to kidnapping and murder.

On top of that, our local friends had advised us that as non-natives, we must never harm an intruder; if the police got involved, they would always side with the local, even if he was armed. Some gave even stronger advice: don't just "not harm" the would-be burglar/rapist/murderer/kidnapper—kill them instead, then dump the body offshore past the Wall, a 6,000-foot drop less than a mile off the northern edge of the island. Nick and I had agreed that if we ever had an intruder, we would call our friend Rashidi for help, not the police. Our protection consisted of five dogs, an aluminum baseball bat, a flare gun, and a jumbie house, and we had not had a single incident since we moved back to St. Marcos a year ago. Until today.

"What is it?" I asked.

"There's a car parked near our gate, out on the road," Nick said. "With a very dead body inside. Fresh dead."

A million questions warred with my restraint, but I held them back and handed Nick the phone. He explained the situation several times to the officer on the other end of the line.

"We live off of Scenic Road on the north side of the rainforest. We heard a gunshot near our house."

"No, I didn't know that it was a gunshot, but it sounded like one. I went out to see what it was, and I found a car parked outside our gate."

"OK, well, I found a dead person inside the car."

"No, I don't know who it is. No, I'm not one hundred percent sure it is a 'he,' but the dead person is large, I'd guess over six feet and more than two hundred pounds, and doesn't have a woman's shape."

And on and on it went, my questions answered as he answered theirs. I twisted my gold wedding band, which had been my mother's, and my grandmother's before her.

Nick looked whipped when he finally hung up the phone. "God, I miss Jacoby, " he said, referring to a police officer friend of ours who had been murdered in the line of duty. "But they're on their way. I'm showering before they get here—it could be minutes or hours."

I followed him into our bathroom.

"Are you all right, Nick?"

He turned on the hot water full-blast and stepped into the shower. We were entering the dry season, and a full water-pressure splurge when you are dependent on a cistern is a sign that you are either very foolish or very upset. Nick was not foolish. The bathroom filled with steam and I traced "I love you" in the mirror while he soaped up.

He said, "I'm exhausted from chasing that damn pig around, and now we have to deal with this. You know how it will go with the cops."

"I do," I said. "Oh my God, I forgot about Wilbur on the table."

"Can you put him on ice? I'm sorry I won't be able to help you much—but I bought several bags of ice on my way home."

"Ice. I hadn't even thought of that. Wilbur is decomposing on my brand-new dining room table." My shoulders and voice tightened.

"Katie . . ."

"There's a dead pig on the table, a dead guy in the driveway, and a legion of dead people dem ready to swim up through our cisterns into the house. It's the freaking *Day of the Dead* up here."

"He's not really in the driveway," Nick said, turning off the shower. "And you know there are no dead people under the house. That guy was just looking for a quick buck." He wrapped himself in a towel and wrapped his arms around me. "And we are having a wonderful party tomorrow for our two perfect daughters."

I used the back of my wrist to hide a smile. "I hate it when you ruin a good tantrum. I was just winding up."

He kissed my lips. "Are you going to put that nasty stuff on my face or not?"

I adopted a serious expression and pulled out the expensive moisturizer Nick secretly loved. I performed my ritual of massaging it into his face with my own just inches from his, humming "You're So Vain."

Nick crossed his eyes. "That's better. I could feel wrinkles like the fjords of Norway forming."

"OK, Methuselah." I gave his cheek a firm pat when I had finished. "I'll go take care of Wilbur while you deal with St. Marcos' finest."

"Sounds like a good plan."

Nick didn't look like Methuselah. He looked damn good. I looked down at my Sloop Jones knit dress, my standard uniform. I loved the painted-on colors and the blousy shape of the sleeveless mini, and I owned it in seven different patterns, one for each day of the week. Was I a match for my sexy husband? I wondered. Nick got better-looking every year, and he hadn't given birth to twins three months ago. I sometimes forgot about the flabby body underneath my baggy dresses, but I knew I didn't look like the same woman he had fallen in love with. She was an attorney who wore Donna Karan and St. John knits with three-inch slingback heels to work, who rocked the beaches of St. Marcos in a string bikini, her freckles so sun-kissed they almost counted as a tan.

I had to keep my thoughts off this track.

I walked out and found Julie and Kurt feeding the three youngest Kovacs, one from a box of Cheerios and two from a bottle. No, I did not breastfeed. I was a giant La Leche fail.

"Thank you for taking care of the kiddos earlier," I said to my mother-in-law.

"I'm sorry I panicked, Katie," she said. "I'm better now. Although I'm very disturbed about the dead man."

"Me, too." More than I dared show or admit. I wondered if the murderer had sped away or was still hiding in the forest. Or had the man died at his own hand? Either way, a dead body in the driveway was seriously bad karma.

When Nick and Kurt went back out to the body to meet the police, I went to the dining room to study the Wilbur project. Beanie-baby-type stuffed animals snuggled "Wilburn" on all sides; Taylor had been busy. The sweet boy had placed a stuffed pig nearest the dead swine's head. Those toys would be taking an antibacterial dunk in the washing machine, stat.

My tabletop was made of glass. I had come so close to buying a mahogany-topped table, but mahogany would have been a disaster now. I worked a waterproof tablecloth underneath his plastic-sheathed body and tucked rolled towels around him, then laid bags of ice over him and wrapped more plastic around everything to hold it all in place. I ducked into the kitchen to jot myself a note to buy more plastic wrap, then stepped back into the dining room to inspect my work.

"Ah, you have mad skills, Katie Kovacs, mad skills," I told myself, then went into the kitchen to make our very late dinner.

When Nick finally dragged himself back into the house two hours later, he looked like he needed another full-water-pressure shower. He joined me in the kitchen while I made him a plate of leftovers.

"How'd it go?" I asked.

"The cop in charge of the police investigation, George Tutein? He's not a nice dude," Nick said.

"Dude?" I laughed. "You sound like a teenage surfer from Port Aransas, Texas. And with that hair," I ruffled the brown waves that always seemed a bit too long in the most perfect way, "you look like one, too."

He pretended to ignore me, but I saw he enjoyed it.

I continued. "I haven't met him, but I've heard of him. In fact, he's the officer who signed off on my parents' deaths, then had Jacoby send me to hire their murderer as my private investigator on the case. And I read about him in the paper recently. He won the St. Marcos Police Officer of the Year award. There was a picture of him with his kids and wife. It said she's a pediatrician."

"Huh. Well, maybe he got up on the wrong side of the bed today. Did Kurt tell you they identified the body?"

"No. Who was he?" I asked. I stuck his plate in the microwave under the island countertop.

"The guy's a Petro-Mex employee named Eddy Monroe."

The Petro-Mex Refinery ranked second only to the local government as the largest employer on St. Marcos. The Mexican government owned Petro-Mex, a multinational oil and gas company, which in turn owned 100% of the refinery.

"You mean one of the employees escaped the compound?" I regretted the quip almost instantly. "I'm sorry, that's not very nice of me; he's dead, after all." I set Nick's plate in front of him and handed him silverware, then decided to go all out and got him an O'Doul's out of the refrigerator.

"Thanks, babe," he said. "It's true, though. That is the most insular group of people I've ever seen. They're like a cult, almost."

The refinery ran a housing compound of 750 homes. Inside the barbed-wire-topped fences lived nearly 3,000 people. They had their own restaurant, pool, church, recreation center, grocery store, and gas station. Residents offered services like day care and hairstyling from their homes, and their children even went to school within the gates. They didn't have much reason to leave the compound, and when they did venture out they seemed confused to find themselves on a beautiful tropical island. Who was I to judge, though? I would feel like Rip Van Winkle if I were locked behind a barbed-wire fence beside a roaring industrial plant, too.

Nick continued. "It took all I could do to keep Tutein from marching into Annalise and interrogating all of you. I'm not so sure he won't."

I gave the countertops a good wipe-down and surveyed my kitchen's smooth green and tan granite countertops, mahogany cabinets, stainless steel appliances, and striated porcelain tile. The "colors of outside inside" palette usually soothed me. Not tonight.

"I could handle him," I said.

Sometimes I wondered if my husband forgot I was not only a trial attorney, but also a black belt in karate, thanks to my cop-father's obsession with self-defense. I moved to the sink and began scrubbing dishes. I had a dishwasher, but hand washing used less water.

"Seriously, Katie, I would prefer you and he never even cross paths."

Nick rarely had such visceral negative reactions to people. I made a note to stay away from Officer Tutein.

And of course that's when Tutein walked in. Or tried to.

I heard someone attempting to open the door, really throwing his weight into it, but it stayed shut like it was locked. It wasn't, which meant it was someone Annalise didn't like.

"Who's there?" I asked.

"Detective George Tutein. Let me in, please."

Knocking would have been nice. I opened the door and stood aside. He had pulled his unmarked car all the way up to our front door and parked on the grass. Someone in the front seat was staring at me, with only the whites of their rounded eyes clearly visible in the dark.

"I can't get cell reception. Let me have your phone, please," Tutein said without a greeting or asking my name. He held out his hand.

"We don't have landlines up here, but you're welcome to try my cell," I said. I took my battered old iPhone out and offered it to him.

He stared at it. "Never mind, then."

He wheeled around and walked out, and the door slammed shut behind him of its own volition. It was easy to love Annalise. She was our oversized guardian angel.

I turned around to find Nick watching me.

"You're right," I said. "He's an ass, and very odd. Why wouldn't he want my cell phone?"

Nick tapped his lip with his index finger, then said, "Maybe he didn't want you to have a record of his call in your log. Hey, speaking of asses, guess who showed up out there, babbling about dead people?"

"Our wacko from earlier?"

"Yep. Went right up to Tutein with his story. Tutein asked me about it. I told him the guy was crazy and that there were no skeletons, but Tutein stuck him in the back of his unmarked to give him a ride to town."

So much for not telling the authorities. The white eyes staring at me from Tutein's car must have belonged to him. At least Nick had a chance to explain our side of the story to Tutein. I looked up from rinsing dishes at Nick, who had finished eating and was texting someone.

"Who's that?"

Nick looked at me with blank eyes. "Huh?"

"Who are you talking to?"

"Oh. The head of security for Petro-Mex. You know how I've tried to get their business for a year? Well, I called him as soon as I saw the dead guy's Petro-Mex uniform. He retained me to help them determine the cause of death. They don't trust the police. Tutein already informed them that it's an open and shut suicide. But Petro-Mex says it can't be."

This was a lot to take in. Alarm bells rang in my head, far away but getting louder. "Why?"

"He just got married. No one believes he was the type to kill himself, and especially not now. Supposedly his co-workers think he was stupid happy."

"Why does Petro-Mex even care? I mean, isn't this a family matter?" I had started the process of drying and putting away the dishes now, and realized that in my consternation, I had dried the same plate three times.

"They don't make much of a distinction between family and company, really."

Ah, right. The cult. I held out my hand for his dishes, but Nick stood up and took them to the sink himself. And washed them. It was nice of him to help, finally. When he was done, he pulled a chain attached to his belt loop and flipped out the gold pocket watch we found hidden in the walls of Annalise. I'd had it repaired for him as a "Congrats, Dad" present when I learned I was carrying the twins. It still read "My Treasures" on the front as it had when we first discovered it, but now it held pictures of the three kids and me, instead of the family of Annalise's previous owner.

"Ten o'clock," he said.

I was beat. "Wanna finish this conversation in bed?"

"Sure." He followed me to our bedroom, saying, "I think this is going to be a big one for us. It would be nice to have more on-island clients."

Nick worked almost exclusively for stateside clients. But he also primarily did computer-forensics-type investigator jobs. Not potential murders.

"I don't know, Nick. I've got a bad vibe about this one. You're the only you I've got. I'd like to keep you safe and sound."

"Worrywart."

But that was the funny thing—I wasn't. I rarely worried about Nick. Now, I felt uneasy. It felt like this investigation would make every day a Day of the Dead until it was over. We were so isolated out here. We relied on each other. I couldn't lose Nick, and I hated this foreboding.

The words blurted out of my mouth. "Nick, don't take this job. Please. My sixth sense is talking to me." I held out my hand and he took it. "I can't explain it, but I'm scared."

He sighed deeply. "I'm sorry, I have to take it. I need you to support me on this. If it goes sideways, I'll drop it. OK?"

I stared off into the distance, fighting the dread inside me. It seemed I had no choice. But I knew. I knew something was off with this investigation. Or did I? I could be making something out of nothing. My sixth sense wasn't *always* right. But why take the chance? I didn't want another dead man at our house. Especially not this one.

I realized what needed to happen. I would have to be the one who kept him safe, that's all, and I knew how to do that.

"When do we start?" I asked.

Once upon a time, Nick and I had worked together at the Dallas law firm of Hailey & Hart. Later, and up until the twins were born, we had partnered at his private investigation company, Stingray, when I wasn't working for peanuts as the twangy Texas-born half of a singing duo with Ava, my exotic local partner. It made sense for me to volunteer for this case.

"Whoa, cowgirl. There is no 'we' on this one. This is a death case—way too dangerous. And you have a lot going on up here, with the babies and all. I'll get Rashidi to help me if I need it."

I'd met my friend Rashidi around the time I met Ava, when I first moved to St. Marcos. He was the one who had introduced me to Annalise. Nick had since co-opted him from me, however. I felt heat creep from my collarbone up my neck and ears and over my head until my scalp flamed. I knew I didn't technically push my brain out when I was in labor with the girls, but some days it felt like Nick treated me that way.

Nick whistled something tuneless as he sat down at the small writing table in our bedroom and jotted notes into a spiral notebook.

"Nick—" I started to say.

His head swiveled around, yanked by the tone of my voice, but my iPhone rang.

Ava. Maybe talking to her would give me time to back away from the ledge. Because I was about to jump off of it and all over my husband.

"Later," I said to Nick. Did I hear a muffled exhale from him?

"Hi, Ava," I answered, and I walked into the bathroom for the call.

"Hello, Katie. I got a call for a gig. When you start singing with me again?"

Ava's question felt sudden, even though I had expected she would ask it at some point.

She continued into the pause I did not fill. "We could make it work, even with the kids—like only book daytime gigs if you want. I still get calls from places wanting afternoon beachside entertainment for the tourists." Ava's daughter was only one month younger than my twins.

"Let me ask Nick," I hedged.

"Then you tell him 'no' is not an acceptable answer. Monday night we invited to perform a set at a Yacht Club party. You need to dress nice—none of your bag dresses—and do something with that hair. I'll swing by Monday afternoon, and we rehearse."

I feigned nonchalance but a thrill ran through me. I would sing tomorrow night! That beat the heck out of worrying about dead people or how to keep my husband from becoming a dead person himself.

I hung up and went back into the bedroom, where Nick was still working his pencil. I decided to hold off on the news about the Yacht Club until after the christening party. I dressed for bed. I pulled back the covers. I cleared my throat noisily.

When he finally looked at me, he asked, "What's wrong?"

I sucked oxygen in to displace the space in which my words were hiding, and pushed them out on the exhale. "I don't know what's wrong with me. At least not completely. But there is one thing I want that is very, very important to me. I need you to say yes to it."

"Oh yeah, what's that?" he asked.

"I want to work with you on the Eddy Monroe case for Petro-Mex."

He didn't look happy about it. He kicked the bed frame into line, stalling for time. I kept my face neutral while he wrestled it down inside himself.

He spoke slowly when he got around to answering. "Yes, on one condition."

"What?"

"That we start with an emergency meeting of all Stingray Investigations personnel assigned to the Dead Guy In The Driveway case."

I considered his proposal and found it acceptable. "Let the meeting begin," I said, beckoning with my finger. He swan-dived onto the bed.

Technically, what came next might be called sexual harassment in some companies, but it was the most effective teamwork session of my career. When the ceiling fan came on of its own volition, we met eyes and laughed.

"Thank you, Annalise. I think we're going to need that," Nick said.

"She takes good care of us. But I can assure you, she will turn on you like a feral pig if you ever do me wrong." I know it sounds strange, but my jumbie house was my best friend. We had each other's back.

He bit the back of my neck and I groaned—in a good way.

"Feral pig? You've got Wilburn on the brain and your Texas roots are showing." He nibbled some more. "I will never do you wrong, but not because I'm scared of some big voyeuristic jumbie house built on a graveyard."

A picture of Nick toppled over on my bedside table with a firm thwack. One by one, every picture of Nick in our bedroom fell on its face.

"That's kinda disparaging, honey. And we don't really know whether she's built on a graveyard or not. But I think those pictures are what Navy types would call a shot across the bow. An apology would be good before she fires off a real cannonball."

"I'll consider myself warned. My sincerest apologies, Annalise. Although you are a big jumbie and a voyeur, I mean that in only the most respectful and complimentary way. I'll withhold judgment on the graveyard part."

My house fell silent. Nick gave his full attention to the nape of my neck and the heat between us grew from a sizzle to bonfire.

I smiled again, and let myself go.

Chapter Three

"Katie, I'm taking the morning off today," Nick said when we woke up on the day after our christening celebration.

What a terrific idea. Our daughters' soiree was lovely, but we had worked so hard between guests and babies and whatnot that we had hardly said boo to each other the whole time. I pushed the light satin coverlet aside and rolled over onto my adorable husband, considering how best to reward him for this gesture.

"So, I'm thinking I'll head over to the airport and get a few hours up in the plane, then put in an honest three hours' work before I meet Rashidi for his surfing lesson on the North Shore. Maybe you and the kids could meet me for dinner afterwards before your gig with Ava?" he said.

I rolled back off him. Thank goodness I had not gotten any further into the reward process. Honestly, ever since he and his father bought that Piper Malibu airplane, he had been obsessed. He had that tendency: planes, surfboards, bass guitars, and whatever case he was currently working on, Nick had a lot of enthusiasm for his pursuits. Apparently, I hadn't made the list that morning.

I bit my lip and thought *One should never speak hastily in anger.* One should instead plot carefully and act strategically. So first, one should lull her target into a false sense of safety.

"OK, if that's what you want to do, baby, that's fine with me. I'll just be here with the kids and your parents. Is there anything you would like for me to do for you today while you're out, honey?"

Was the last "honey" too much? Did I give myself away?

"Are you sure?" he asked. "Because if you are, it would be great if you'd pick up some wax for me and meet me at the beach with my board. That would save me a ton of time, because you know I can't leave my board in the hot car or all the wax will melt off." He nuzzled the back of my neck. "What did I ever do to deserve you? I can't possibly imagine."

Nope, I obviously had not shown my hand. So, step two: after a gentle approach to the target, go for the jugular.

"Let me get this straight: instead of spending time with the kids and me, you are going to go fly and surf half the day, and then fart around on the internet and Twitter?"

Nick's dark eyes said "oh shit" but his mouth did not form any words.

"And on top of taking care of your children, you would like me to run your errands so you can maximize your fun time without us?"

In my experience, the target usually makes at least one defensive move.

"I did suggest we meet up for dinner," he said.

"Well, I guess I would have to agree with you, then."

"What do you mean?" Nick's pupils dilated to their widest setting.

"I can't possibly imagine what you ever did to deserve me."

My work was almost done: I would allow the target to recover and find its way back into my good graces on its own.

Nick studied my face. "Katie, I didn't mean to hurt your feelings."

"I know." Deep sigh. "I know you didn't."

I let the silence work its magic.

"How about we take the kids on a picnic into Ike's Bay, just the five of us? We can put the girls in the snuggle carriers, and I can carry Taylor in the backpack."

I resisted, but not too much. "No, that's OK, you go fly and surf."

"I want to be with you guys. We can give my parents a day alone. They won't know what to do with themselves."

"Really?"

"Really."

"I would love to, Nick."

Amazing how easy it was for me to make everyone in the family happy. Truly, I have a gift.

Of course, the actual trip wasn't the idyllic family outing I'd envisioned. All three kids squalled as if we had dipped them in acid instead of the ocean. But it would make for funny memories someday.

At seven o'clock that night, I was standing offstage beside Ava, a spot at once familiar and disturbingly foreign to me. My nerves jangled like the silver bangles on Ava's arm. I would not throw up, though; that would be very bad.

Ava and I pretended not to glare at each other, but we spoke through gritted teeth under our smiles.

"Where you been?" Ava asked.

"What do you mean, where have I been? I'm here right when you told me to be. In fact, I'm early," I retorted.

"I leave you a voicemail! They change our time. I give you the new time and our song list in my message."

My bad. I'd forgotten to listen to my voicemail. But Ava had been a no-show for practice, which was why I'd come early: to hook up with her for a quick run-through of whatever songs she intended us to perform.

"If you had shown up to rehearse today, it wouldn't be a problem," I said.

"Something come up and I can't make it."

Lord help me. With Ava, something came up more often than not. Last year, when she house-sat Annalise while we were off-island in Corpus Christi, she'd left to meet a record producer in New York without telling us. Then, when the producer was only interested in our duo, not Ava's solo, she ran off on a whim to Venezuela with her (now) baby daddy. Burglars stripped Annalise bare with her gone and our friendship had never quite regained its footing. Ava still resented me for messing up the record deal with my absence, and I couldn't get over her casual abandonment of Annalise.

"Well, I'm here now, and it's our turn to sing next. So what are we going to do?"

"Do you think you can start with 'It's My Party'?"

I looked out into the audience at the Yacht Club's annual Memorial Day Fling fundraiser. Most of the partygoers were continentals in the sixty-plus age range, so it made sense to perform something they could relate to.

"Of course," I said.

"If you not comfortable, I can do it by myself."

"I'm fine with it," I snapped.

"Good," Ava snapped back.

Time to chill. I concentrated on Ava's best qualities and fast-forwarded through "It's My Party" in my head.

Ava handed our background music to the young guy manning the sound system, who looked like he was barely out of his teens. His youth only served to emphasize my age to me, although I could still say I was thirty-seven for a little while longer. Luckily, I exuded youthfulness in comparison to the Yacht Club's patrons tonight, most of whom were probably so liquored up they wouldn't be able to tell if I was nineteen or ninety. From their forte rumble and staccato peals of laughter, it seemed they were well on their way. I watched a woman of about my mother-in-law's age teeter toward the bar, listing dangerously to one side. If her stagger didn't give her condition away, the fuchsia lipstick she had applied unevenly to her mouth did. Not a pretty sight.

I had grown accustomed to singing to drunken tourists with Ava when we performed together, pre-babies. Ironically, it did not bother me to be around all this alcohol. Sure, the smell turned on my central nervous system, but the buffoonery turned it right back off. I never wanted to be like these people again.

I searched the room for Nick. We had left the kids with his parents and driven the winding island roads for forty-five minutes to get here, and he'd dropped me off at the door before going to park the car. I picked my way around the big stones that littered the dirt lot, trying not to break my heel or twist my ankle in my dress-up shoes. I wore a figure-hugging blue and purple dress with spaghetti straps and a deep V neckline. It had been a favorite of mine before I had kids, and tonight I added Spanx power panties to achieve the right "hot enough to wear in front of a crowd" look. If people had compared me to Nicole Kidman before, I would count myself lucky if I rated Lucille Ball tonight.

Upon making my grand entrance, I had caught the frantic "get over here" gestures of Ava and gone straight to the stage. She, of course, looked sexier than me in peep-toe leopard print shoes trimmed in red and a scarlet stretch-wrap dress with caplet sleeves. I did the best I could with what God gave me; God just gave Ava more.

So, here we were, ready to kill each other and ready to go on. When the musicians before us had finished their set, Ava and I walked onstage and adjusted the microphones. Nick appeared just in time on stage left, talking to possibly the only woman in the room under forty besides Ava and me. Of course. Nick was not traditionally handsome, but he was sexy, and he had a magnetic appeal that attracted women to him like he was true north.

I was glad he'd come tonight, though. He hadn't protested the gig, which made me suspect an ulterior motive; he'd frowned on me performing since my last trimester. Fatherhood brought out his paternal side—only I wasn't his kid.

The sounds of our music played through the massive Klipsch speakers around the room. This East End club allowed the platinum-and-diamonds set to enjoy themselves without leaving their safe homogeneous community. The only black faces in the room belonged to Ava, the sound guy, and the servers. When we finished our first set, we got such an ovation that the sound guy asked if we would do another.

"So, your next act a no-show?" Ava asked.

"For true," the kid admitted.

"What you do for us if we help you?" she asked in a tone I could never have pulled off.

"What you want?" he asked.

"I want you to get us some afternoon gigs."

"Yah, I hook you up. No problem."

"All right." She handed him another CD. "Here our music."

"Ava, what the hell are we singing?"

"Now we sing what we like. All our old stuff. The crowd too drunk to notice if we mess up, but if you don't remember one, just make up a background part. Or bend over, show some cleavage, and shake your bana."

"Irie," I said in my best local accent, using the West Indian word meaning "it's all good."

"Stick to the Queen's English, girl. You awful," she said, and stuck out her tongue. Our tension eased.

An hour later, we left the stage to accept the adulation of our new fans. Who was I kidding about the joy of song being enough? I drank in the compliments like I used to down Bloody Marys. Nick sauntered up to us, a drink in each hand: sparkling water with lime for me and a rum Painkiller for Ava.

"I would not believe you guys took six months off if I didn't know it was true. You sounded great," he said.

"Shucks, Nick," Ava drawled in her best Texas accent.

"Stick to Calypso, girl," I told her. "You're awful."

Ava ignored me. "Look like some well-fed and very large fish swimming here." She referred to the Rolex- and Tag-Heuer-wearing men trolling the waters around her.

"Is Rashidi with Laurine?" I asked.

Rashidi and Ava shared a house. They occasionally shared a bed, but Ava did not let that constrain her enthusiasm for men.

"Yeah. I can't stay out too late, but there enough time for me to do some damage."

"You're incorrigible."

"I wouldn't be if you pass that sexy husband of yours along to me."

I had no doubt. Nick grinned. I didn't know which of them I wanted to punch more. While this joke had run between Ava and me since she'd first met Nick, it had less luster now that I felt fat and frumpy and knew my friend's history with married men.

"Never," I said, and she disappeared into the crowd.

I gave myself a ten-count to relax. The Yacht Club's exterior walls rolled up on all sides to create an open-air interior, and the view seaside stretched out over a maze of docks that was lit with strands of yellow Christmas lights. The masts of sailboats rocked to and fro like twiggy poltergeists in the dimly lit night sky. Even over the odor of alcohol and sweat, I could smell fishiness and seawater.

"There's someone I want you to meet," Nick said to me as Ava strolled off, vamping for her admirers. He led me through the room to a group of men at the far end of the space.

"Who am I meeting?" I asked.

"Petro-Mex bigwigs," Nick said.

Aha.

Nick and I stepped up to the men, and before he could introduce me, they turned to us with half bows and applause. Ah, shucks.

"Here she is, gentlemen, my wife Katie. Chanteuse by night, my assistant at Stingray by day."

"Katie Kovacs," I said, stepping forward onto Nick's foot and shifting my weight onto it. He flinched. I added, "Nick's partner at Stingray."

They all spoke over each other at once.

"Mucho gusto, Katie."

"Congratulaciones."

"Buenos noches."

They overwhelmed me with their good wishes and testosterone. I notoriously fell for dark macho men, my husband being the prime example, so I enjoyed the attention. A lot.

"Nice to meet you all. I look forward to working with," and I was careful to say *with* and not *for*, "my husband on your case."

"I am the director of seguridad, of security. We will be meeting tomorrow, no?" The speaker towered over his counterparts; he was Mexican, but much taller than I would have expected. He wore a powder-blue guayabera shirt with pressed ivory linen pants. His teeth sparkled. Very handsome.

"Sí, mañana," I said.

"Tú hablas español. Es muy bueno!" the security director replied.

"Gracias, señor."

I could feel Nick roll his eyes. Served him right for calling me his assistant.

After a few more minutes of small talk, we bade each other farewell.

Nick took my arm. "Are you ready to go, Señora Coqueta?"

"Coqueta?"

"I thought 'tú hablas español'? I called you 'Miss Flirt.'"

"Oh Nick, please." I batted my eyes. "I was just practicing my client relations."

"Let's go before you get too good at them."

"Sí. Just let me run to the bathroom first."

I pushed my way through the crowd and into the stifling bathroom. The Yacht Club did not use air conditioning, which was mostly fine in the open-air areas. It was not fine in the cramped bathroom. No windows equaled no airflow. Two metal stalls and fifteen square feet of standing room in front of rust-stained porcelain sinks and a Formica countertop. No likey.

As I stood in line, two women in their mid forties shoved in behind me. Youngsters in this crowd, probably on the prowl. Unfortunately, they recognized me.

"Oh honey, you were so great. Can we buy you a drink?" the taller woman asked. She had pencil-thin legs topped by a paper-flat butt and had encased herself in a sequined sheath that accentuated her thick torso and cut into her cleavage. Her ample cleavage. So very ample that I worried she would tumble over with only her spindly legs to support that weight.

"Yeah, we just loved you and that black girl," her companion said. She'd obviously spent her money on hair and false eyelashes, as opposed to Olive Oyl's expenditure on her breasts and liposuction. She blinked rapidly and I wasn't sure whether she was batting her eyes or trying to see out from under the clumpy mascara. Or maybe a strand of her bleached hair had gotten caught in an eyelash when she'd teased her bouffant into place.

I cringed with Texas shame. Before I could do more to reply than smile and say thanks, they went on.

"I hope this line moves fast, because I have the worst case of sand fleas," Hairdo said in what I think she intended to be her whispery-secret voice. "You would not believe."

I had lived on St. Marcos for three years and had never heard of sand fleas. I was quite sure I did not want to hear about them now, but something told me I had no choice.

"I know! I brought a hairbrush to scratch mine with, but they're in my un-mentionable place, so it's not ladylike to do it out there," Olive Oyl said.

To my horror, she pulled a blue-handled hairbrush out of her purse. I turned away quickly. If I were Catholic, I would have been chanting and counting my rosary beads right about then. I stuck my hand in my purse and caressed my package of Clorox wipes.

One of the stall doors opened and Ava walked out, not bothering to hide her fleeting grin.

I motioned the two women ahead of me. "Y'all go on ahead. I know how badly you . . . itch."

"Why thank you, sweetie. Now don't forget—we want to buy you a drink."

They disappeared into the stalls, chatting loudly. We stayed quiet until they left.

"Now you see where locals get their bad impression of continen-tals?" Ava said.

"Oh my, oh yes, God yes," I said, but I was thinking, "Just so y'all know, I am ashamed these women are from Texas," à la Natalie Maines circa 2002. So many statesiders brought their worst, most drunken behavior to the islands.

When I escaped the bathroom, I found Nick texting madly at the bar. A fake thatch roof topped the mahogany bar, giving it a cheesy look that would have worked fine on the beach, but inside the Yacht Club, not so much. Clear bottles of Cruzan Rum with colorful labels for each flavor lined the wall behind it. The popular rum was made on St. Marcos, and you could buy it cheaper than milk. The bartender poured drinks like he had taken one too many sleep aids; his throng of patrons was lined up three-deep before him.

One of the many nice things Nick had done for me since we first got together was to give up alcohol. He had an O'Doul's by his right hand. When he saw me, he stuffed his phone into his pocket and replaced it with the beer.

The insecure teenage girl in me couldn't help herself.

"Who were you texting?" I asked.

"Oh, no one. Work stuff," he said.

"Which is it? No one or work?"

"Umm, work."

"Our work?"

"No, a different case."

Why didn't this make me feel any better? I scanned the room for some giggling hotty reading a sexy text from my husband, but saw none. I needed to get a grip. I tugged at my dress to cover the bulges of post-baby fat.

"Are you ready to take me home, Mr. Kovacs?"

"I thought you'd never ask, Mrs. Kovacs."

When we exited the club, I slipped off my heels. Without warning, Nick swept me into his arms and marched us to the car.

"Wow, this is nice. Will I get the kind of treatment tomorrow at work that I'm getting tonight?" I asked.

He chuckled and deposited me in the passenger seat.

"Tomorrow we are back to business, Mrs. Kovacs."

"All business?"

"All business. But that's tomorrow. Tonight we get to pretend that I am the geeky kid who picked up the hot singer after her show."

"Excellent. And the next morning the geeky kid goes to work only to discover the hot singer is his new boss?"

My husband laughed aloud as he turned the Montero to the right and out onto the highway. No blinker. Nick often didn't bother with the details. Was a blinker technically required when leaving a parking lot? I didn't know. I hoped he piloted his plane more carefully than he drove.

"Keep dreaming, Katie."

"What? You think I couldn't handle running the business?"

He snorted. "Let's hope the world never has to know."

Chapter Four

Nick and I arrived at the gate to the Petro-Mex Refinery at nine a.m. the following morning, a little bleary but upright. The geeky kid/hot singer game plus a wake-up with the twins had kept us up past our bedtime.

I looked down to admire my outfit. Thank the Lord I had invested in chocolate Spanx pants that let me pull off a professional look without squeezing into my old-life work clothes. The money sunk into my lawyer wardrobe was another reason that losing the rest of my baby weight was a necessity.

"Nicholas Kovacs and Katie Kovacs, here to see José Ramirez," Nick informed the guard, handing him our driver's licenses.

"Nicholas?" I whispered. "Is that your secret agent name?"

"Nicholas" did not show any sign that he'd heard my question. Some people had no sense of humor.

Several uniformed guards emerged from the small gatehouse and surrounded our car. Harry Belafonte sang "Day-O" through the distorted speakers of a boom box beside the door. I couldn't help but notice the guards carried guns, canisters of what appeared to be pepper spray, and knockout batons. Holy cripes, were they expecting an invasion of the body snatchers?

"Nick, are we in trouble?" I asked.

"Huh?" he asked. "Oh, you mean the guards?"

"Uh, yeah. I mean the armed guards swarming our vehicle like paratroopers."

"No, this is normal."

"I don't think this is very normal." Maybe in Iraq or Russia it was normal, but last I checked, St. Marcos was a territory of the United States of America.

"Normal for them. They get a lot of threats. Some of it's post-9/11 hysteria, but Petro-Mex is a weird hybrid. They're here in the U.S., so they attract terrorists who oppose the U.S., but they are also Mexican, and that means Mexican politics comes up. They have problems with crazy locals occasionally, too. And they've had attacks in Mexico by the drug cartels, which lean on them pretty heavily for payola in their territories. It's so bad they have a humongous

standing reward for information leading to the apprehension of anyone involved in terrorist plots against them."

"What do drugs have to do with oil?" I asked.

"It's a geographic relationship. The cartels in Mexico operate regionally.
Their reach extends far beyond drugs, although drugs are their focus. I pulled
up an article about a couple of attacks on Petro-Mex in Mexico by the Chihuahua cartel. It's in the orange folder in my briefcase. You should read it."

While the guards continued to sweat us, or conduct the slowest ID check of
all time, I pulled out the article and skimmed. The Chihuahua cartel had hit
three Petro-Mex sites in north central Mexico this year. The cartel, run by a
former Mexican federal agent named Ramón Riojas, claimed that Petro-Mex
owed them a percentage on oil production in their region, and that Petro-Mex
had refused to pay. The government had done nothing, and the article suggested it was powerless against the cartels. They sounded like mafia to me.

Now Petro-Mex was building a pipeline through the same area. The article
quoted an "impeccable source" as saying that the cartel had promised a strike
on Petro-Mex if it didn't comply with their demands for payment on production
and the pipeline. But Petro-Mex was stalling, because to do so would embarrass
them internationally and hurt them financially. The author listed some of Petro-
Mex's global operations, including the refinery on St. Marcos, and opined that
the cartel would target operations in the countries that could put the most
pressure on Petro-Mex if an attack occurred on their soil.

It sounded to me like the Chihuahuas' bite would hurt worse than their
bark. I put the article back into Nick's briefcase and looked out the window at a
holstered gun with a brown hand resting atop it.

"I think I just peed my pants a little," I said.

"Toughen up, old girl. I think we've landed a dream client. Think of the
long-term potential for Stingray here."

Old girl? Before I could smack my business partner around, the guards motioned us through the gate and over a speed bump that resembled a small
brick wall.

"Shit!" Most of the coffee from the mug in my hand splashed onto my lap.
Lukewarm coffee with loads of sugar-free hazelnut Coffee-mate in it (the
pouring kind, not the clumpy powder kind). Another reason to be thankful for

the brown Bod-a-Bing pants, which would camouflage the spill while smelling like coffee for the next hour, and reek hideously of spoiled milk after that. This would give me incentive to end the meeting before my pants turned into a pumpkin and the Petro-Mex folks discovered a stinky Cinderella in their midst. A Cinderella fast asleep with her head on their conference room table because she hadn't had enough coffee after a late night with Prince Charming.

My lips vibrated from the roar as we passed a large piece of equipment on the other side of an interior fence. My nose curled, too.

"This place smells like poo," I said. "Do they have a cattle feedlot in here?"

One corner of Nick's mouth lifted. So maybe his sense of humor had returned; the man did not function well on less than eight hours' sleep. "That's mercaptan. No feed yards."

Smells like cow shit anyway, I thought.

I said, "This place is freakin' huge."

The five-minute drive to the administration building ended at a surprising oasis. I counted thirty-two majestic palms tickling the skyline, their trunks encircled with nodding elephant ears. A manicured green lawn stretched from the road to a brown stucco building edged with beds of Ginger Thomas, the official flower of the Virgin Islands, bright yellow in a tangle of green bush. To the left of the entrance, tiny waterfalls cascaded over the rock ledges of four ponds, one into another, barely disturbing the black, white, and orange koi swimming between the lily pads at the bottom. Why had Petro-Mex gone to so much trouble?

The industrial plant was spread out over 3,000 coastal acres and included the housing communities, the refinery proper, an enormous tank field, and a deep-water marine harbor. Nothing stateside compared to it in size, although there were larger similar properties elsewhere in the world. The relative isolation of this particular refinery, though, made for unique challenges and characteristics. The lack of pipelines connecting it to its markets led to the necessity of the big tank field and robust harbor, and because emergency services on St. Marcos were practically nonexistent, the refinery maintained a fire-rescue-emergency response organization bigger than that of a small city in the U.S.

At the front desk, we had to register our laptops and phones. Jiminy Crickets, I thought, they really do mean business. Finally, a young local woman escorted us down the utilitarian halls to a windowless conference room at the center of the building.

We entered the room and five dark-haired men rose in unison, their chairs rolling back silently over the hunter-green carpet. Like the previous night, the men spoke over each other in effusive greetings that were mostly directed at me. I obligingly presented my cheeks for their kisses and shook hands all around.

Nick and I took a seat at the oval table and I eyed its thick mahogany top and glass cover. *Damn, I'm going to get fingerprints all over it.* I acknowledged to myself the difficulty of this Transformers moment, back from island wife/mommy/musician mode to the professional I'd been less than three years ago. *Steady, girl.*

"Welcome, Nick and Katie. Katie, my name is José Ramirez," said the one man I recognized from the Yacht Club the night before. The tall handsome one. He introduced the others. "We are so glad you have moved to St. Marcos and can help us. One quickly finds that the police here are of little help in matters such as this one."

"Nice to meet you all," I said.

"Happy to be of assistance," Nick added, the formal at-work Nick I hadn't seen since the days we had slaved away together at Heygood & Hart in Dallas. *Hey, this guy is kinda sexy.*

"I hope that you did not have too much trouble getting here this morning? The security can be overwhelming to those not used to it," Ramirez said.

I agreed. "The security was intense. But so was the traffic. An eighteen-wheeler nearly took us out coming around the corner to the plant. It all but tipped over."

Nick shot me a look. What? It was true. I heard my mother's voice in my head: "Katie, if you can't think of something nice to say, don't say anything at all."

Ramirez clucked. "It is a problem. We open our jet fuel rack at nine a.m. each day, and the local drivers race to get in line. If they are first to fuel up, they have the greatest chance of fitting in repeat trips to the airport during the day. A matter of commerce. And not a good one."

Nick said firmly, "We understand." I got the impression he didn't want me to open my mouth again about the trucks.

Ramirez said, "As you know, our employee, Eddy Monroe, died of a gunshot wound to the head several days ago." Um, yeah, in our driveway. "The police ruled his cause of death a suicide. We are not convinced this is true. These things you already know. Nick has been kind enough to take the case and do some preliminary work. I have brought in some of my co-workers," he said, including the others with an elaborate flourish of his long-fingered hand, "and would like to update them on what Petro-Mex hopes to accomplish, and your results so far."

Six heads nodded in acknowledgement, mine one of them.

"I appreciate everyone's discretion with some of the comments I will make, and would remind you that we are all subject to confidentiality agreements."

Nods again.

"Several factors are at play. One troubling issue is that we experience a higher than normal rate of suicide in the refinery community. Not just among our employees, but among their family members as well."

One of the other men broke in. "We cannot accept the police's quick judgment about Mr. Monroe, if for no other reason than the emotional strain the label of a suicide puts on all of us. It's too easy, too convenient, and at the same time too damaging. And it hurts our ability to keep valuable employees and replace those we lose. It's already hard enough for my people in human resources to attract people to work here."

Wow. This was news. Truly, they kept the suicides in the family. Very Stepford Wives of them. Maybe that explained the overly Zen gardening outside.

Another Petro-Mex employee interrupted in Spanish. This sparked a heated discussion that I could not follow, other than the words "terrorista" and "muerto." Terrorista didn't need an English translation, and my limited Spanish vocabulary included muerto, the word for "dead." I dug my fingernails into Nick's thigh but he just sat there like a drugstore Indian.

Ramirez held up his hand and interrupted the other men sharply. "Enough. We can discuss this when our guests are not present." He turned to Nick and me and added, "My apologies for the lack of manners of my colleagues. It will not happen again." Said colleagues averted their eyes, and I heard an audible expulsion of breath. Hot prickles marched up my neck.

"Now, where was I?" Ramirez asked. "Ah, yes, the other factors necessitating your inquiry. While Mr. Monroe was from the United States, his wife is from Mexico. She has requested the investigation, and we want to honor her wishes. Mr. Monroe does not present a classic case for suicide . . . too many signs point us in another direction." He placed his hands on the table in front of him and laced his fingers together. Done.

What signs? I didn't ask aloud.

Nick spoke. "Thank you, José. After our telephone conversation on the night of Mr. Monroe's death, I secured the police report. I've also spoken with Detective Tutein again." He swiveled his head toward the other Petro-Mex employees. "For those of you who didn't know, Katie and I were already involved in this case before Mr. Ramirez called me. Mr. Monroe died right outside the gate to our home. Detective Tutein interviewed me as a witness for the investigation by the police." He looked back at Ramirez. "Suffice it to say, Tutein did not appreciate my visit. I didn't get anything from him except a few subtle chuptzes."

"Not unexpected," Ramirez said.

My turn. "We have scheduled an interview with the widow, Elena Monroe, this afternoon. Also, we will need access to the hard drive of Mr. Monroe's computer, or computers."

Ramirez said, "I will arrange—" but he was interrupted by the same man who had spoken up about the impact of the police's suicide finding. He was speaking loudly in Spanish this time, and Ramirez raised his voice in return, then turned back to Nick. "We will have to get back to you about the computer." Then he spoke to everyone in the room. "Any questions for Nick and Katie, gentlemen?"

The four other dour-faced men said nothing, and Ramirez concluded the meeting. What the hell was going on here? I was pretty sure it wasn't my pants that were stinking up this case.

As we stood up in the stifling silence, Ramirez kissed me goodbye. A mere five minutes after it had begun, and with nothing accomplished as far as I could tell—unless you count me being creeped out even more about this case than before—our meeting ended on a resounding minor chord.

Damn.

Chapter Five

Nick and I swung by the Petro-Mex compound straight from grabbing a quick bite of lunch at the BBQ Hut, a ramshackle building across from the boarded-up shell of Fortuna's, which was once a popular restaurant run by an ex-boyfriend of mine who now lived in a maximum security prison in Puerto Rico. I hadn't always made the best of choices in my personal life, but I'd changed all that with Nick. Or I had changed a lot of it, anyway. Oh, hell's bells, I was still an occasional mess and I knew it, but I was trying, and I was proud of him and how Stingray Investigations was growing. I relished working our first official case together.

In order to speak to Elena Monroe, we had to clear the security gauntlet again. Would I feel more or less safe living behind this type of protection? I suspected it would make me paranoid. Certainly it explained some of the us-them division between the refinery's residents and the rest of the islanders.

The houses inside the gates stood in perfect rows, like little toy soldiers with green berets. Each one wore the occupant's name like a lapel insignia, although the only thing indicating rank was architecture. Privates lived in modular homes, captains in concrete, and the superior officers boasted individualized concrete and stucco dwellings.

Elena Monroe lived in a modular home on the far side of the compound. As we drove through the neighborhood, I gaped at my surroundings. I had lived on-island for two years and had never seen the interior of the Petro-Mex community. On St. Marcos, people lived indoor/outdoor. Most of our homes did not have air conditioning, and heaters were unnecessary. We all spent as much time on our patios, decks, and balconies as we did inside. Not so, at Petro-Mex. Not a soul entered my field of vision.

When we parked in front of Elena's house and got out of the car, industrial noise pummeled our ears. Although the refinery was almost a mile away, it sounded like we were in the middle of an avalanche. They should hand out earplugs at the guard gate. We walked to the door together and I almost reached out to hold Nick's hand, but it didn't seem professional. Patting his butt, then, was out of the question. Rats.

A tiny woman opened the door before Nick could ring the doorbell, the scent of Calvin Klein Obsession preceding her. She looked twenty-one, maybe twenty-three years old, tops. Her lustrous hair hung in a sheet of black steel to her waist, which was tiny between a double-D rack and a bootylicious bana. Whoa.

But it was her eyes that arrested me. She had the sultriest brown eyes I had ever seen. I'd expected puffy flesh, dark circles, spiderwebs of redness, but if I didn't know she'd lost her husband a few days before, I would never have believed it.

I decided to hold Nick's hand after all.

"Meester Kovaucks?" she asked.

Was it just me, or did the two of them exchange a "let's pretend we don't already know each other" look? My eyes turned greener.

"Hello, Mrs. Monroe. Yes, I'm Nick Kovacs and this is Katie."

"I'm his wife," I interjected. *Oh criminy, where did that come from?* And then it hit me: I was being a jealous bitch, and this woman was a grieving widow. My husband loved me, even if I still had leftover bulges from the twins. I resolved to control myself and forced a toothy smile.

Mrs. Monroe said, "Sí, yes, hello, very nice to meet you. Call me Elena. Please come into our living room and find a chair," she said. Her accent was heavy on the "eeeeez" and rolled R's. Sexy talk.

We entered a darkened room full of Mexican women. Sisters? Friends? Neighbors?

"Mamá, por favor vas a la cocina?" Elena said to an older woman who bore a striking resemblance to the Charo of "cuchi cuchi" fame in the 1970s.

Elena's mother rounded up the other women and herded them reluctantly into the kitchen, where they hovered by the door closest to us.

A knock sounded at the front door. Elena walked to it, her steps a slink slink slink motion, and greeted a man who spoke to her in rapid Spanish.

I put my lips on Nick's ear to whisper, "I feel completely out of my element." I hoped not only to get my message across to him, but also to tear his eyes away from Elena as she raised her arms to rake her hands through her mane of hair, exposing her concave brown midriff and about a quarter inch of the underside of her unrestrained breasts. I was pretty sure I might vomit at any moment.

Elena began her shimmy back toward us and the visitor followed her. I recognized him immediately. He had attended our meeting earlier and had really pissed off Ramirez during the heated interchange en español about Eddy Monroe's computer. What was he doing here? I looked at Nick and saw fury on his face.

"Mr. Kovacs," said the visitor, "we met earlier today, no? I am Antonio Jiménez, the manager of Human Resources for the refinery. I will be sitting in on your interview with Mrs. Monroe." His smile did not reach his eyes.

"I wasn't informed that you would be present, Mr. Jiménez. This is very irregular," Nick replied. His tone lowered the temperature in the room by five degrees.

"Pero, it won't be a problem, no? Petro-Mex cares so much about Mrs. Monroe, and I think she would like for me to be here." Another five-degree chill.

Nick looked at Elena. "Is it your wish that Mr. Jiménez be present, Elena?"

She looked at Mr. Jiménez, and then at the floor. "Ahhh, sí, sí, yes, it is OK," she said. She put one hand over the other.

We took a seat, but Mr. Jiménez chose to remain standing behind Elena. So we began our interview, sandwiched between the whispering females and the glowering Petro-Mex HR manager. Nick and I had planned that I would interview Elena, one woman to another, so I took the lead now. He would add any questions he thought I missed. I had conducted countless depositions and questioned hundreds of witnesses in court, but this strange scenario flummoxed me a bit. I cleared my throat and pulled out a yellow pad.

"Elena, we are going to record our meeting. Will that be OK?" I asked. Nick set his iPhone on the arm of the chair and pulled up the audio recording app.

Elena turned around 180 degrees to seek permission from Mr. Jiménez. Not a good sign. He nodded.

"Sí," she said to me.

I started softly with her. "I am very, very sorry about your husband."

"Gracias," she said.

"Tell me, how long had you and Mr. Monroe been married?"

"Six months."

Shorter than I'd imagined. "How did the two of you meet?"

Once again, her head rotated back to Mr. Jiménez, whose face this time was impassive. She turned back to me and fumbled over her words. "Eddy, my husband, well, I met Eddy through friends. Friends here at Petro-Mex on St. Marcos." Her eyes remained dry, but her face looked tight enough to crack.

Everything about her answer said it was not *the* answer. Should I push her on the question? I decided to let Nick be the hammer if he wanted to.

"Elena, the police said Mr. Monroe may have killed himself. What do you think happened? Do you think he killed himself?" I cringed as I said it; I had never had to ask such painful questions as an employment attorney. Embarrassing, à la "did you grab the plaintiff's ass," but not painful. At least I knew the answer to this question, as Ramirez had told us she'd requested the investigation precisely *because* she didn't believe her husband had killed himself.

Before, her answers had puzzled me. This time, her reply astonished me.

"Yes, I think he did. I think he killed himself. He was very depressed."

Mr. Jiménez all but lunged forward at her. "But Mrs. Monroe, you told us you did not believe he killed himself. And how could he? You are so beautiful, and he was a newlywed. You are mistaken. All of his co-workers know how happy he was—with you, with his job, with everything. You are grieving and confused, and that is why you say this terrible thing, no?"

Elena gave no explanation for changing her story. She didn't cry. She simply sat with her hands gripped together and her knuckles white. Her mother appeared and sat beside her, stroking her anxious daughter's hair and speaking to her in words I could not understand, not for lack of trying. I sat stock still, taking it all in, the two women, the large silver and bronze crucifixes hanging behind them, the heavy wooden furniture, the black leather upholstery. Jiménez shoved in next to them on the couch and the conversation grew animated.

Nick whispered to me, "This is a clusterfuck, Katie. We're not getting anywhere with Lurch standing behind her. We should get the hell out of here, and come back at her later with a different approach. I have some ideas."

"Yes," I said, "Let's get out of here."

I stood up. "Elena? We know this is a very upsetting time for you. Thank you for talking to us. If you have anything else you want to tell us, here's Nick's card." He handed it to her. "But for now, we will leave you with your family and friends. So sorry to intrude."

Elena rose. She turned toward Nick and extended her delicate hand. He took it. She did not shake, simply stood with her hand in his, and looked up at him from below her lowered lashes. "Thank you, Nick." Neeeeeeek. "On your card, it says you are a pilot?"

Nothing about her demeanor said grief. Yet she was radiating an emotion so strongly that it permeated the air around her: fear.

"Yes, I am also a pilot."

"Bueno. I have your card, so I may call you, no?"

"That would be great," he said, her hand still in his. "Oh, and could we trouble you to let us look at the files on your computers, to look for people who might have wished Mr. Monroe harm?"

Mr. Jiménez stood up beside Nick and faced Elena. "Mrs. Monroe, you do not have to give him anything you do not want to," he said.

"Yes, sir," she said to him. Then, "I am sorry, Nick, but there is nothing on our computer that will help bring Eddy back."

Nick and Mr. Jiménez locked eyes. Neither looked away, but Mr. Jiménez spoke.

"So that's it, then. Buenos días, Mr. and Mrs. Kovacs," he said.

His squinty-eyed expression of distrust was getting old.

"Nice to see you again, sir. Good day to you," I said, and I grabbed his hand and shook it harder than I should have. If he noticed, he didn't show it.

We bolted out the front door from the dark interior of the house, away from the dark meeting. The brilliant light burned my eyes. I'd turn into a vampire if I lived in there.

I was rattled. Elena's weird come-on to my husband, if that's what it was, had knocked me back a step. I didn't get it. And try as I might to sympathize with her, I didn't like it.

We walked briskly to the Montero without a word. Nick sucked his top lip into his bottom one. Then he ran his hand through his hair, a sure sign of consternation.

I spoke first. "That was a freak show. I want to get as far away from this place as possible."

He said, "Let's just head straight back up to Annalise then, and we can talk about this on the way, OK?"

"Fine by me. But don't forget, we promised Taylor we would take him to the Agricultural Fair this afternoon." I looked down at my iPhone. "Your mom texted me about an hour ago that she has the kids ready to go, and she said Taylor has been asking when he gets to go see Wilburn approximately every forty-five seconds."

Nick pursed his lips and exhaled at length. "All right."

He looked down at his phone and scrolled through a text. He muttered and I caught the word "Elena." *Elena?* As he typed a quick response he said, "You know, it probably wasn't such a great idea after all to bring you in on this case. I'm worried about your safety. I think you're going to have to sit this one out, after all. I'm sorry, Katie."

I saw flashing strobe lights and a siren went off in my head.

Breathe, Katie, breathe.

My emotions were still in such a tangle that I decided to hold it in for now—an act of monumental will. Because what I wanted to tell Nick was that he was a patronizing boob and could kiss my ass. It's possible that my sudden personal growth and maturity might have had something to do with our proximity to Playboy's Playmate of the Year, the one who had held Nick's hand and refused to let go.

Or maybe it was because I was scared, too.

Chapter Six

Two hours later, Nick was pushing the twins in our all-terrain double stroller beside me as I walked hand in hand with Taylor through the crowds at the Ag Fair, carefully avoiding the eyes of my recently former boss. Taylor coughed. We hadn't had a good rain in weeks and the throng had kicked up quite a dust cloud. The girls slept peacefully, despite the noise and smells.

"Mama, I want cotton candy," Taylor said.

"Soon, but first let's eat dinner. Cotton candy on an empty tummy will make you sick."

"Daddy, I want to go see the pigs. I want to see Wilburn."

"We're headed there now, champ. Walk faster and we'll see them sooner."

I preferred the smell of fry chicken and johnnycakes to the odor of the barnyard, so I chimed in. "We have to eat some dinner first, though."

The food smelled great. St. Marcos residents love their parties, and Carnival in January, monthly Jump Up festivals, and the annual Ag Fair were the big events of the year. The Ag Fair featured an exposition of plants and animals, but it also boasted a carnival and the best food the island had to offer. I knew what I wanted to eat: sizzling hot beef patés—spicy ground beef inside fried pastry, doubly greased up. Heaven.

We stopped at the food tents and I got in line for the fried things with Taylor while Nick stood in a separate queue for roti, a tortilla-like wrap made from ground lentils wrapped around curried chicken. And I was the one trying to lose the baby weight. Bad Katie.

I kept Nick in my line of vision. I was still flustered. Everything from the surreal interview with Elena and the lurking presence of Mr. Jiménez, to the weird exchange between the grieving widow and my husband, to getting fired on the way out the door—all of it unsettled me.

"What do you want to eat, Taylor?" I asked.

"I want to go see Wilburn," he insisted.

"Sure, but before we go see Wilburn, what food do you want?" Taylor had turned toward the barns and was shifting from foot to foot as he swung my arm and heaved toward the pigs. "If you don't answer me, I'm getting you dirt and bugs, OK?"

"Noooooo, Mama. No dirt and bugs. I wanna see Wilburn."

"You can, after you eat your dirt and bugs." I looked around for Nick and saw him and the girls. Good.

Taylor started to giggle. "I'm not s'posed to eat dirt. Daddy said so. And bugs are yucky. I want rice and peas."

There's my little island boy. "Rice and peas? Are you sure? Because they have dirt and bugs if you want it."

"I want rice and peas."

"Oh, good. I thought it was weird that you wanted dirt and bugs," I teased. Maybe I could keep his brain occupied with silliness long enough to feed him.

Just at that moment, the local man ahead of us in line turned around with his food in hand and our eyes met. His, black and unnerving, drilled into mine, startled and green. I knew him. And he certainly acted like he knew me. He walked toward me and my pulse thumped in my ears like a bass drum. His strides ate the ground between us in giant gulps, then he broke eye contact, stepped around me, and walked past.

The timpani drum kept beating until my ears burned. I heard something else now, too.

"Mama, Mama, MAMA."

Pull it together, crazy lady. "Yes, honey," I said with the appearance of complete sanity.

He pointed at the food server. Oops.

I gave my order, I think. Or I gave *an* order. And I paid and took the food. But my mind was whirring like a messed-up hard drive. Missing sector alert, data corruption error, total system failure imminent. Who was that man? Why did he stare at me like that?

When Nick and the girls returned, I realized I had lost sight of them for a while.

"Honey?" Nick peered into my vacant eyes. "Are you OK?"

"Mama's quiet," Taylor said. "She wouldn't talk to the lady."

"Oh, Taylor, you silly. I'm fine. Mama got distracted. That's all."

Nick lifted his chin and looked down his considerable nose at me. I tried with some success not to like him.

"I'm serious! I'm fine," I lied. "Let's grab a table and eat."

We sat at a picnic table that only took five Clorox wipes for me to render usable and ate our meal. "Take You There" blared from giant speakers at the corners of the tented area, and the local youth danced; the songwriters hailed from the neighboring island of St. Thomas. I didn't enjoy my paté as much as usual. Taylor ate one tenth of his rice and pigeon peas and announced himself full and in need of a bathroom.

"Let's go, buddy, I need to use the loo, too," Nick said. "We can leave the ladies here to eat the rest of our food while we're gone."

Off they went. Lanky dark Nick and squatty dark Taylor. Taylor was bound to be olive-skinned like Nick, since Nick's sister bore the same genes, and Taylor's father—his nasty drug-dealing father, from whom we'd won custody after Teresa died—also had brown skin, hair, and eyes.

As I watched, Nick stopped to talk to a Latino man that had stood up to intercept him. His neck bling flashed gold from between the sides of his shirt, which was unbuttoned too far down his chest. And he had a mustache. Open shirts, gold medallions, and mustaches travel in threes. The man motioned to his left, and Nick and Taylor followed him until they disappeared from my view.

That was perplexing. The closest bathrooms had been right in front of them. It agitated me to lose sight of them, but Liv woke up and whimpered.

"Little red, come to Mama," I crooned. It turned out she needed a stealth diaper change and a quick bottle of formula. I cradled her in my arms to feed her. Every time I held one of the girls, they felt heavier. They were growing so fast. Jess timed her wake-up to coincide with Liv polishing off her bottle, so I propped Liv up in the stroller behind her bar of squeaky toys and started on Jess.

A name popped into my head. George. George something or other.

That was it. George Tutein. The cop who investigated the dead guy in the driveway. The one who had barged into our kitchen. The one who had given a ride to the wacko babbling about dead people under Annalise. The one who had signed his name to the crap police investigation into my parents' deaths. He was the man I had seen in the patés line. Well, damn. He remembered me, too. And he didn't flash me a winning smile. Great, just great.

A mop of tousled hair entered my vision and pulled me away from my thoughts.

"We're back, Mama," Taylor said.

I bounced Jess on my knee to burp her. "I thought you guys must have fallen in. What took you so long?"

"We weren't gone that long," Nick said.

"Pretty long. I lost you there for a while. Who was that guy you were talking to?"

"What? No one. We went straight there and back. There was a line."

You're lying to me. Nick's lying to me.

"Really?" I asked in a voice that said I knew he was acting dodgy. "Whatever, Nick." Difficult as it was, I decided to drop it until we weren't in front of the kids. I knew he'd gotten my meaning. I changed the subject. "Well, who's ready to go see some pigs?"

"MEEEEEEE!" This, from Taylor. Of course. Off we trundled toward the livestock barn. I pasted on a smile and forced Nick's lie out of my head.

In the barn, Taylor begged and begged for a piglet. Nick and I remained stalwart in our no's. When he didn't win the pig war, Taylor sulked and suddenly wanted every small creature we saw. As in, "If I can't have Wilburn, can I have a bunny? A chickie? A duck? A calf?" We repeated "no" one thousand times until he threw a tantrum, snuffling and wailing. The joys of parenthood.

When Taylor had finally worn himself out, we left the Ag Fair. This time I pushed the stroller and Nick draped our sleeping boy over his shoulder. Taylor's body stretched half the length of Nick's, his pudgy legs dangling to Nick's waist.

Nick must have checked his text messages twice for every one time Taylor asked for an animal friend. The joys of marriage. He checked them again now.

"What's up, Nick? You've had your eyes glued to that screen the whole time we've been here," I said.

"Work. Sorry."

"Work?"

"Yeah, work."

"Was the guy you walked off with earlier 'work,' too?"

"What?"

"You know. When you took Taylor to the potty? And you guys walked off with some guy, all cloak and daggerish?" *And then told me you didn't?*

Nick kept walking, but he didn't look at me. "I don't know what you're talking about. We went to the bathroom, that's all."

Only the sleeping babies stopped me from yelling "Liar, liar pants on fire" at the top of my lungs. As it was, I muttered it just loud enough for him to hear. Who was this man, and what had he done with my perfect husband?

I ignored him and strapped the babies into their car seats for the ride home.

Chapter Seven

When our alarm went off the next morning, I asked, "What time is it?" without opening my eyes.

"Five a.m. I'm leaving to go interview some witnesses."

"Witnesses for what?" I asked. As if I couldn't guess.

"Petro-Mex."

"Are you going to fill me in?"

"Katie, I told you already, you aren't working on this with me anymore. This feels too dangerous. I have to do this one alone."

Alone. As in, without his wife around. On the heels of meeting the Mexican Sexpot, lying about meeting a strange man at the Ag Fair, and texting his fingers off, he had to do this alone, without his fat brainless wife who'd just had two babies.

"That's bullshit, Nick," I said, my voice low but hard.

"No, it's the right thing to do," he said, matching my volume.

"Well, I obviously have no say in this. So, whatever."

"Don't be like that, baby. Please."

"What, you mean like pissed? Too late." I turned to face the wall and wrapped my arms around a long pillow.

"I love you. I'm sorry I've made you mad."

He slipped his arms around me from behind and molded himself against me. My body responded without considering how mad I was. If a woman's personal parts could pout, mine did. *Traitors.* His cold nose prodded my neck, looking for warmth. He didn't find any.

I held firm, and he slipped out, whisper-quiet. I tensed, my body ready to run after him and relent, but the part of me he'd lied to overpowered the impulse. *I showed him.*

I made myself stay in bed until I heard him drive away, then I got up to use the bathroom and saw that in my brightest, sluttiest red lipstick, Nick had written, "SMILE, I'm a sucker for you," on the bathroom mirror. A Blow Pop lay on the counter beneath it. Where had he found the candy? As if that even mattered. He was pulling out all the stops.

Well, I was still upset. He was sorry for making me mad? I hated nothing worse than a non-accountable non-apology. How about sorry for being a big fat Pinocchio? How about being sorry for treating me like a child? He could stew in it for now.

By six a.m. the morning had entered warp speed. I ran around the house with my in-laws and Taylor as the twins took turns crying and the cat and dog wove in and out of our feet. The doorbell rang in the midst of the rush. The last time I had answered this door, it was Officer Tutein. Thinking of him made me think about the wacko who thought Annalise was standing on dead people, which made me think about the dead guy in the driveway. Which made me think about Nick. Nick had not texted me, and his silence was grating on me.

I tried to wipe the crankiness off my face before I threw open the kitchen door, and was relieved to find Rashidi on the porch.

"You," I said.

"Me," he replied, holding out his arms for Jess. I handed her over without a word. Jess cooed and her fat little hand reached up toward the Rasta beads in the dreadlocks that swung at her eye level. "Uncle Rash here, Princess, and I'ma spoil you good." He walked past me into the kitchen.

"Come in," I said to his back.

All but a few of my friend's long dreadlocks were tied back into a tail today. This was his formal look, so I knew he must be teaching later. He taught hydroponic farming and other topics I didn't understand at the University of the Virgin Islands. He gave botanical tours of the rainforest, too, and it was on one of those that he had first introduced me to Annalise. He also ran a lucrative side business as a tour guide to the stars. His Rasta-man looks drew continental women to him like albino bees to dark honey.

"Hi, Rashidi," my father-in-law said.

"Hello, Kurt. How the old man of the sea today?" Rashidi answered. Kurt had had a long career as a ship pilot back in Corpus Christi Bay in Texas.

Kurt gave his stock answer. "Just another crappy day in paradise."

"Yah, mon. Where the missus? I wanna feast me eyes on some beautiful women this morning, so I come here first."

"I hear you, Rashidi," Julie called out, appearing in the kitchen with Taylor at her heels and Oso at his. She fussed over Rashidi as he kissed her cheek. "Have something to eat. We just finished breakfast and there's leftover whole-wheat blueberry pancakes. Better hurry before Kurt gives them to the dogs. And we have coffee."

"Hi, 'Shidi," Taylor said, head-butting Rashidi's leg.

"Hey, tough stuff, watch me leg." To Julie, Rashidi said, "Pancakes? Better for me than those mutts." He grabbed a plate and fork like family. "Katie look in need of the coffee, for true. May I brew me some tea instead?"

"No, no, you eat, I'll brew," Julie said, putting a kettle on the stove. Julie and Rashidi had a love fest going that would have made Kurt jealous if Rashidi were twenty years older. Kurt just smiled and wandered into the garage to putter with his tools. He had set up a carpentry shop in there when they followed us from Texas to St. Marcos, and he was working on mahogany side tables for the great room.

Rashidi managed to serve his plate and eat with Jess tucked adoringly into the crook of his left arm. Jess took after her grandmother where Rashidi was concerned. Taylor ran off behind Julie, who had promised to color with him, and I fetched Liv from her bouncy seat and sat down beside Rashidi with another cup of coffee. Immediately Liv twisted her head to fix her eyes on Rashidi.

"Your popularity with the ladies is enough to make me queasy, Rash," I said.

"Yah, I'ma ladies mon. That why I come here today," he said between bites.

"Oh yeah? Why's that?"

"Nick tell me all about your Day of the Dead, and that old guy who saying Annalise built on a graveyard. I got some information for you, from a pretty lady who work in the gov'ment." The kettle began to whistle and he jumped up to turn off the burner. He returned to his chair with a cup of chamomile tea.

Nick had told me that Rashidi was working his contacts for information. "Thanks," I said. "What did she say?"

"She say the boss man at the Department of Planning and Natural Resources the one over antiquities and such, and he make the rules and do what he like. She say he not got enough to do, and he like to stick he nose in other people business." He shoveled in the last of the pancakes.

"Born and raised in the St. Marcos tradition, it sounds like."

"Yah, and she say if he hear 'bout old bodies underneath a house he all over it. Last time something like this happened, he haul a continental guy off in handcuffs. But a week later, the boss man show up at work driving a new car, and problem solved. No digging, no jail, no fines. So my advice keep quiet 'bout the skeletons."

I hated my continental status in situations like this one. "If there even are any skeletons. But I expected as much. Maybe we'll never hear a word about them again, but I think your information means 'plan for the worst.'"

"Where Nick?" Rashidi asked. He had taken his plate to the sink and rinsed it. Better than family.

"Interviewing witnesses on that Petro-Mex case. You know, the dead guy we found in our driveway." I checked my iPhone; it was already 10:45. "I haven't heard from him since before dawn."

I texted Nick quickly: "Rashidi came over to update me on DPNR vis a vis Annalise/graveyard. Can you please check in and let me know your plans?"

Rashidi, meanwhile, had taken Jess over to the bouncy seat and buckled her in. She immediately kicked and chortled. Her hand shot out and whapped a spinning duck. "Bye, baby doll. Good day, Kovacs family."

"You're off?" I asked.

"Yah, mon, I head to the university to romance some more beautiful women. I see you later. Good day, Annalise," he said, patting a stout masonry wall as he exited.

"Thanks, Rashidi. Have a good one," I said.

Later, after Julie and I fed the kids and settled them in for naps, I retreated to the upstairs office and Julie went downstairs to the rooms she and Kurt had moved into six months after we came here from Texas. Their bottom floor apartment opened onto the patio and swimming pool and had a view of the west-end beaches and ocean beyond. The main floor housed the kitchen, master suite, great room, music room, and a guest bedroom, and upstairs Annalise had three bedrooms and a library. One bedroom belonged to Taylor, one was a nursery for the girls, and one we had converted into an office.

I loved the office. While my computer booted up, I threw open the balcony door to let in the breeze and stood at the railing. The view transported me. I imagined myself looking out over this same vista a hundred and fifty years ago, when the sugar mills and plantations were thriving. I could almost hear the creak of leather harnesses in the distance as horses turned the crushers inside the mills, grinding sugar cane into sugar. The scent of fermenting mangoes floated up from the orchard, making me think about the homemade mango ice cream in the freezer—snack for later. I scanned the road through the thick canopy of trees for my husband's car. No luck.

Nick rarely went this long without contacting me. He'd left so early, though, maybe he'd forgotten to charge his phone. I looked down at mine again, and there was a message light. It was from him.

"Busy. Going well. Home for dinner."

Wow, that was super informative. I checked my inner pulse and it appeared I was still mad at Nick. I didn't want to spend the evening fighting, but the odds weren't looking good for me to become the bearer of sweetness and light anytime soon.

In the meantime, I had work to do, and apparently Nick had piled a bunch of crap on my desk before he left. I started to move the stack of paper to the floor but stopped when I recognized maps of the refinery. This was no longer my business, since he had dismissed me from the Petro-Mex case "for my own safety," but I began to study the pages one by one. They were printouts of the harbor and the huge field of tanks, shipping schedules from the Petro-Mex harbor, and a stack of emails to and from Eddy Monroe. I read every last word of them, but nothing held any significance for me. I set Nick's papers on the floor and logged into my email at exactly 1:00 p.m. I loved catching a clock with double zeros.

As I browsed my inbox, the power suddenly cut out and my screen went black. *Damn, another power outage?* I looked up as the ceiling fan's blades slowed. The digital display on the clock was black. I waited a few beats for the generator to kick on—nothing. I walked to the second story landing and leaned out.

"Kurt? Can you hear me?" I called.

"Ye-ah," he shouted. His Maine accent drew the word out into at least two syllables.

"I think the power is off, but the generator didn't kick on."

Silence for several seconds. "Umm, no, the power is working fine down here." Hee-yah, I heard.

"Weird, because everything lost power in the office."

"I'll check the breaker." Bray-kuh.

As I stood at the railing, galloping my fingers and thinking about Kurt's Maine accent instead of the oogie things that kept happening in my house, Oso slipped out of Taylor's room and lay down at my feet.

Kurt returned. "Nope, breaker's fine."

"OK, let me re-check. Thanks."

"Yup."

I went back into the office with Oso and flicked the light switch on and off. Nothing. The fan was motionless. All screens displayed black. And then I heard the whine of a computer coming to life. That was more like it. I walked over to my computer, but the noise wasn't coming from there. I looked over at Nick's desk and my throat constricted as I saw the Windows logo come to life on his screen. *What the hell?* His computer hadn't even been on before the power went out. And, still, nothing else in the room had powered up yet. I fell back into my chair hard. White spots on a black background danced before my eyes, then thinned out as my focus returned.

I stepped unsteadily over to Nick's desk and pulled his chair under me. His screen glowed in 256 colors and his Outlook email auto-loaded in its startup sequence. I typed in his password, katie18annalise, and his inbox filled the right-hand side of the screen. Unread after unread message, ten in total, all from today, and several read messages from the Petro-Mex security manager, José Ramirez, last night. I opened each one, looking for a clue to my husband's whereabouts. The messages from Ramirez were the source of the printouts from Eddy's computer. Nothing about the site of Nick's interviews today.

And then his screen went black, and his computer died.

I sat in the silent, dark office with the wind blowing through my hair. Oso whined and I reached down to pet him. The fur on his back stood on end, and that's when I finally understood.

Chapter Eight

I would regret the sharp tone of my voice, I knew. "I am still waiting to see Detective Tutein. I've been here since seven a.m."

"Have a seat, miss. Detective Tutein very busy today," the female officer manning the front desk explained again.

"My husband is missing! I spoke with Detective Tutein last night. He is expecting me!" Sharp became shrill, and my fellow sufferers in the crowded waiting room turned to watch me. "Have you told him I'm here?"

"I sure he come by soon."

"Is Officer Morris here?" I said, referring to Jacoby's former partner. He would help me. I knew he would.

"Morris move down island Easter last. His wife homesick." She sniffed. "Please have a seat, miss."

I flopped back into the hard chair I had been sitting in for the past three and a half hours. Tears pushed the limit of my eyes' fill capacity but did not spill over, and I stared at the wall plastered with memos, announcements, and fliers without seeing any of it. I clasped my purse hard with both hands to still their shaking. I needed food soon to absorb all the coffee in my stomach or I would vomit. The slightest bad odor at this point could trigger the nausea response.

A baby screamed with gusto while its mother ignored her and continued filling out paperwork on a clipboard balanced on her knees. For the love of God, I thought, stick a bottle in her mouth, woman.

I ran to the bathroom and heaved black bile into the toilet. Better. I got up and splashed water from the faucet on my face. I wiped my face and neck with a scratchy paper towel, then trudged back to my seat in the waiting room. The baby had quit screaming, thank God.

The wall clock's second hand mocked my impotence. Tick. Tick. Tick. Nick. Nick. Nick. Gone. Gone. Gone. *Shuddup shuddup shuddUP.*

After I had finally realized the day before that Annalise was sending me a message, I'd filled Kurt and Julie in on my concerns. Nick didn't show up for dinner, and when we'd had no word from him by seven o'clock, I called the police.

The officer I spoke with rebuffed me, explaining that the police did not consider an adult missing until twenty-four hours after he'd disappeared—if then. A frantic discussion with my in-laws led to an idea: maybe I could convince them that Nick's disappearance was related to the Eddy Monroe investigation. It probably was, after all. Or it could be one of a million any-things, none of them good. Like the long reach of Taylor's father Derek, or Derek's little brother Bobby. Nick had sent Derek to jail and gotten Bobby shot. Both were pretty good reasons for revenge I found Detective Tutein's card in Nick's Petro-Mex file and called him. I got the same twenty-four-hour rule response, but he agreed under pressure to see me if I came in to the station today.

So here I sat. I had filled out the Missing Person Report three hours ago, and no one had called me in for an interview. Tutein had not acknowledged my repeated requests to see him. Every second that passed was another lost second of search time for my husband.

Damn.

Kurt and I had combed the island looking for Nick all night long. I hung out the window with a flashlight, searching for signs of Nick's Montero along the sides of the main roads between our house and town, but my beam barely penetrated the dark. Rashidi and Ava had organized searchers to cover the neighborhoods, even a contact in the Petro-Mex housing compound who would look there, and between all of us we'd blanketed the island, searching for any sign of his SUV in parking lots, driveways, roads, anywhere.

Nothing.

Except a painful dream in the few hours of sleep I caught before dawn, in which I chewed out my husband for not coming home on time. In my dream Nick said, "I wouldn't ever choose to spend a night apart from you. Shame on you for thinking I would."

Ouch.

Double damn.

My phone rang. Julie.

"Anything?" I answered.

I could barely hear her over the scream of the baby across from me. "Kurt found Nick's car. I don't know why we didn't think of this sooner. He parked it inside the hangar." She paused. "The plane's gone."

Oh. Oh, Nick. He'd left the island and told none of us. Where were the witnesses he had went to interview? *Baby, what have you done?*

"Katie, are you there?"

"I'm here."

The officer behind reception finally called my name at that very moment. "Mrs. Kovacs, Detective Tutein will see you now."

I stood and moved toward her, juggling my purse and coffee while trying to keep my phone to my ear to hear Julie.

"Kurt's going to update me after he finds out more. He's at the airport. I'll call you as soon as I know something," Julie said.

The reception officer returned my sharp tone from earlier to me. "Mrs. Kovacs? You no longer wish to see Detective Tutein?" Hard to believe, coming from a public servant, but the woman chuptzed me. Very softly.

I held up one pleading finger as I said, "Thank you, Julie. I'm heading in to meet with Detective Tutein now. I love you. Bye." I clicked off.

"My apologies. The call related to information about my missing husband. I am very eager to meet with Detective Tutein. Thank you, miss."

She lumbered to her feet. Fifty pounds too many would slow me down, too. In fact, it had, not too long ago. The officer's extra poundage clung to her hips, thighs, and bosom, but there was no sign of a baby on board. Her uniform fought to hold her in. As she walked ahead of me with a roll-jerk-hesitate rhythm, her thighs swished against each other. We moved slowly. Achingly so.

Several minutes later, after passing a number of interior offices and cubicle pods, we arrived at an office with an exterior wall. Big shot office. She knocked—tap tap—on the gunmetal gray door, then opened it without waiting for a response and stepped inside, blocking me from doing the same.

"Mrs. Kovacs to see you, sir, about a missing person she believe related to one of your cases."

A bass voice so deep it vibrated my chest wall said, "Come."

"Thank you again," I said to the retreating back of my escort. No response.

I rubbed my wedding ring for courage and stepped into the office.

The imposing charcoal-skinned figure standing before me would rattle most people. But the sight of Detective Tutein affected me in a singular way: I plummeted.

He hated me. He positively radiated it from every pore.

"Mrs. Kovacs," he rumbled. "Sit."

I sat.

"I believe we meet before," he said.

"Yes, sir, we have, when you came into my house looking for a phone. We spoke last night, too, and I believe you know my husband, Nick Kovacs."

"Yes," he said, making the word shorter than three letters.

"As I told you on our call, he's disappeared. I filled out a Missing Person Report this morning."

"Good. Someone will get back to you to assist you. Will that be all?"

Shit!

"Oh, no—please. I hoped you could talk to me. Nick was investigating the death of Eddy Monroe on behalf of Petro-Mex. Yesterday he left our home at five a.m. to interview witnesses on that case, and he never came back."

"Yes, well, if Petro-Mex want to throw their money away and mock the results of my investigation, they free to do so. But it sound as if your husband on a fool's errand. Monroe clearly kill himself. I doubt Mr. Kovacs' disappearance anything sinister, and I see no reason it relate to a suicide."

His sour tone curdled my blood. I tried to reason with him. "I met with the widow. I can't believe any newlywed man would kill himself with her waiting for him."

"What? You mean the mail-order mamí that his refinery friends give him as a retention bonus? Please." He flipped his hand away dismissively.

My jaw opened and fell an inch. Oh. That was certainly relevant, at least. And appalling.

"I understand your position, Detective Tutein, but—"

He cut me off. "There no 'but,' Mrs. Kovacs. An officer will call you in to process your Missing Persons Report. You should wait in the lobby until this happens. I cannot help you."

"I've waited for four hours already. My husband is missing!"

"You continentals all the same. You expect special treatment. You think we locals stupid and incompetent."

The memory of Olive Oyl and her redneck friend at the Yacht Club made me cringe. This was what locals thought of us. But I was not like that. Nick was not like that. "Detective Tutein, I'm—"

"Enough! It not the concern of the police when a man cat about."

That did it. Red hair trumped common sense. "*Cat about*, Detective Tutein? You have no right making accusations about something you know nothing about. And I assure you, you know nothing about me or my husband."

"I know you, I know your husband, I know your parents, Mrs. Kovacs. And you should ask why Eddy Monroe kill himself in front of *your* house. Good day." He flipped his fingers to shoo me away.

I couldn't process his words. How did he "know" my parents? And how should I know why Eddy Monroe died in front of Annalise? I gulped air. Could I do nothing to enlist the help of this man? I stood with my purse and coffee in hand, staring at the top of his close-cropped head, ready to put my anger aside and beg if necessary, but no strategy came to mind. I turned and walked to the door.

He stopped me. "One more thing, Mrs. Kovacs."

Hope. "Yes, Detective?"

"About the dead bodies under your house. I hate to think you haven't reported this to the proper authorities." He tapped his pen three times on his desk.

No. Please, no. All the saliva in my mouth dried instantly and I couldn't swallow. I couldn't answer.

He continued, "I think I have to look into this matter of desecrating a graveyard myself. You hear from me soon." At that, he resumed reading and marking the papers on his desk as if I was not standing before him with my very existence in his hands.

My steps echoed down the barren halls as I returned to reception. Sweat beaded my forehead. I stepped back into the waiting room, and the receptionist pointed me to an open door to her left. I obeyed and with my last reserves of strength propelled myself into another hard-backed folding chair at a small table in a windowless room. My head landed on the table with a thump. I closed my eyes and left it there.

"Good day, Mrs. Kovacs," a woman's voice said.

I jerked my head up, out of the habit of island manners, and replied, "Good day."

For five minutes, Officer Ferber worked with me to take down the Missing Person Report, professionally, kindly even. Between my stress over Nick's disappearance and the meeting with Officer Tutein, I was operating with minimal brain activity, but if she thought me a simpleton, she didn't show it.

Halfway through our conversation, Julie texted me: "No one at the airport knows where Nick went. Kurt still working on it."

Questions ricocheted through my head. How could no one know where he went? Didn't he have to file a flight plan? *What if someone else took the plane?*

I told Officer Ferber that Nick's plane was missing, too. The news discombobulated her, and she informed me she would consult with a superior officer on protocol for handling missing persons cases for individuals who had left the Virgin Islands.

"But we don't know if he left St. Marcos," I said.

"No, but just in case, I will ask. He could be anywhere, you know," she said.

Yes, I know.

I left the station drained and numb. Even in the worst days of my battle with alcohol, I couldn't remember feeling this emptied out. *Nick.* I pointed my truck toward home and somehow, half an hour later, made it back to Annalise and pulled to a stop in my own driveway.

Inside, Julie had just put my kids—Nick's and my kids—down for a nap. We hugged each other, dry-eyed and exhausted, and traded meager updates.

"Kurt told me he's calling the FAA to let them know the plane is missing," Julie said.

"Oh, thank God. I had no idea what to do, and the police were no help," I said.

"Kurt made me promise we would both sleep now, Katie. Take something, rest, and we'll be refreshed so we can work again when we wake up. I'm going to see if I can fall asleep in Taylor's room. Maybe Kurt will have more information when we wake up."

I retreated to the master bedroom. She was right, I had to sleep. But I had to do something, anything, first. I sat at the writing table and flipped open one of the spiral notebooks Nick kept in a stack there. Across the top of the page in strokes so firm the pen ripped the paper, I wrote "To Do List." Just to make myself feel better, I wrote Search on the top line and Call Police on the next line, and then drew a line through each. Airport. FAA. Line. Line. *Now move it forward, Katie.* Call Ramirez. Check Nick's email. Ransack files. Go through his clothes pockets from yesterday. Search Montero. Although Kurt had probably already done that. I chewed on the pen cap, but I couldn't come up with anything else.

Quickly, fading from exhaustion, I found Ramirez's number where I had programmed it into my speed dial. No answer. Shit. I left a voicemail. "This is Katie Kovacs. Call me as soon as you can. Nick left the island yesterday morning to interview witnesses on the case for Petro-Mex. I don't know where he went, and he never came home. The police are not helping me. I need to talk to you." I left my number and hung up, then crossed out "Call Ramirez" and closed the notebook. I pressed my hand into its blue cover, hoping for an epiphany. Nothing.

I went into the bathroom for a Unisom and put both hands on the mirror outside the lipstick *SMILE* Nick had scrawled for me yesterday. *Come home, Nick.*

I stumbled back to our room without washing my face or brushing my teeth, without taking off my two-day-worn clothes, and huddled in our bed, alone.

Chapter Nine

The sound of footsteps on our bedroom floor woke me.

"Hey babe, what's up?" Nick asked.

"Where were you? I've worried myself sick about you!" I said.

"Silly. I went to buy you presents. I found so many wonderful things for you that I just lost track of time, and then I didn't finish in time to leave last night. I stayed over, and today I bought even more gifts for you."

Now I noticed the wheelbarrow in front of him. He pushed it closer to the bed. Presents on top of presents crowded its belly, each one wrapped in crisply folded bright paper and festooned with a white bow.

"But it's not Christmas. It's not even my birthday!" I exclaimed.

"It doesn't have to be. I said I'd put a smile on your face every day for the rest of our lives. I missed a few days, so I bought you a present for each of them. Go ahead, open them."

How to choose? A box near the top of the pile in shiny red paper seemed to cry out, "Pick me!" I grasped it and pulled it toward me. Underneath the presents, the wheelbarrow turned into a rubber life raft.

I looked into my hand. My iPhone was buzzing. Waking me up. *What time is it?* Five thirty—I'd slept for at least four hours.

In the middle of the day? What?

Oh.

Nick.

My tears started. I let it out. I sobbed. I thrashed and wailed. I moaned. I screamed. I cried all my tears. And as I rolled around on his side of the bed, I discovered the t-shirt he had worn yesterday before he left.

I buried my nose and face in the worn black cotton, breathing in his scent, dragging him into my lungs, searing my husband into my olfactory memory. I held up the shirt. "Heygood & Hart," it said, and below that, "Legal Eagles Softball Team."

My iPhone buzzed again with a text message from Ava, who was with Rashidi, checking in for news. I dropped the phone onto the bed without answering her.

A knock sounded on my door. "Katie, are you awake?" Kurt.

"Yes."

"Detective Tutein is here to see you. Can you come out?"

Crap. What in holy hell could he possibly want? He'd all but refused me police assistance and tossed me from his office. Plus threatened me about Annalise.

"Yes, I can, but give me just a second." I peeled off yesterday's clothing and slipped Nick's softball t-shirt over my head. I pulled up a fresh pair of jeans, slipped on sandals, and exited my sanctuary.

Kurt met me in the hall. "I invited him in for coffee, but he wanted to stay outside."

"Kurt, Nick really didn't trust this guy, and I don't either. I'm going to meet with him, but keep an eye on us, could you?"

"Do you want me out there with you?" Kurt stood up straighter, to his full six feet two inches.

I pushed my hair behind my ears. "No, I don't think he'll talk to me unless I'm alone. Feel free to come outside, though, if things don't look right."

"I'll be watching from the kitchen window," he promised.

"Good. I'm sure the dogs will stand guard, too." I slipped out the door.

Tutein had parked his car on the apron of our driveway nearest the kitchen door. He sat behind the wheel. I raised my arm in acknowledgment of his presence. He motioned me with his hand to come, pointing at his passenger seat. I hesitated. He gestured again, scowling. Great.

I deposited myself in his car, thinking, "At least I have my phone."

He put the car in reverse and backed rapidly down the drive.

"Excuse me. Where are we going?" I asked.

He didn't answer.

"Let me out, please. Unless I am under arrest, let me out of this car, now," I said, almost shouting, my throat tight, cutting off my air like a tourniquet.

He slammed on the brakes and threw the car into park just outside the gate to Annalise.

"I thought you want my help, Mrs. Kovacs."

"I do, but you're scaring me."

"I'm a police officer. You have nothing to be afraid of, do you?"

Loaded frickin' question. I wrestled with an answer. He spoke again in a mock-courteous tone and Continental accent. "Please accompany me on a drive, Katie. I'd like to talk to you."

His voice raised the hair on my arms. Why was he calling me Katie? It felt wrong, but I didn't have a lot of options.

"All right," I said. "I'm just going to let my father-in-law know where I am."

"Of course," he said.

I texted Julie and Kurt simultaneously. "I have gone for a drive with Detective Tutein. I will return in half an hour. Everything is fine."

The car raced down the narrow rainforest road. Tutein drove with his left wrist draped over the wheel, a study in nonchalance that belied the rapid weaving he achieved with his forearm. I wanted to grab his steering wheel with both hands, but I stayed mute and still.

Tutein veered left and catapulted down an even narrower, bumpier dirt lane without flinching. I gripped the armrest. Thirty seconds later, he stopped the car and a dust cloud settled around us.

We were alone. Only a mile or two from Annalise, but still very, very alone. I rested my hand on my iPhone again, comforted by its solid presence beside my right thigh.

Tutein pushed his seat back and put his arms behind his head, like no police officer I'd ever known.

"Katie, pretty Katie, what kind of trouble you got yourself into?"

Apparently, a whole heap of it. Why had I come out here with this man? I started guiding myself through plans for fight or flight. I flipped my iPhone over without moving my body and typed a text to Kurt and Julie using my peripheral vision. "Help me 5 min west dn dirt rd." I hit send.

Tutein saw me. "You sending up smoke signals? I think you find you have no service, but if you do, no problem. We won't be here long enough for it to make a difference."

I briefly considered attacking him, but I was pretty sure he wouldn't hurt me. My in-laws knew I was here with him. And I needed his help. I needed whatever information I could drag out of him.

"What's going on, Tutein?" I asked, forcing confidence I didn't feel into my voice.

"Detective Tutein to you, Katie. And I just want to have a talk. You have some problems. No more husband, for starters. Did you know Officer Ferber report to me? She tell me that Nick ran off in his airplane. No disappearance. Just a philandering man leaving his wife."

My temper flared. "Left me? I don't think so. That premature judgment had better not stand in the way of a full investigation. He is gone. His plane is gone. He's missing. I want him found."

His predatory sexuality turned to icy command. "*Better not?* Or you do what, exactly?" He paused, and I could hear his keys clinking against the steering column from when he had brushed them with his big hand. "Don't threaten me, or you might end up like your parents. You want something from me? Then you better learn to play nice."

Tutein can make threats, Katie can't. Check. I swallowed. I nodded.

"Look over there," he said, pointing into the bush. "See anyone you recognize?"

My eyes darted hopefully to the dense greenery and trees in front of us—*Nick?*—and I saw the crazy old man who had appeared out of nowhere on my doorstep talking about dead people. He walked toward the police cruiser, opened the back door, and got in.

"Good afternoon, good afternoon," he said. Damn island manners, even in this situation. What a farce.

"Good afternoon," Tutein replied. "You met the lovely Mrs. Katie, right, Tim?"

Tim. That was his name.

"Yah, I meet she at the house where dead people dem buried."

"And what did I tell you about her and the dead people under her house?" Tutein asked him.

"That we tired of continentals dem disrespecting us and taking what ours. That you gonna make sure she do the right thing by me. That if not, you take me to the gov'ment to tell me story. That I wait for you."

"That's right," Tutein said. He turned around and faced the man. "And, in the meantime, I take care of you. You go stay with my cousin." And he turned to me. "You know my cousin, don't you, Katie?"

Everybody was somebody else's cousin on this island. "Who is your cousin?"

"He told me he was a friend of yours. No, wait, he told me he was *not* a friend of yours. My bad. My cousin's name is Pumpy."

I remembered Pumpy quite well. Nearly two years ago, he'd been the tile contractor working on Annalise. He had stolen from me. Worse, he had conspired with Junior, the general contractor, a man who had nearly gotten a worker killed—and would have, if Annalise hadn't saved him. I'd fired them both and my dogs had to chase Junior off. And Annalise had . . . well, she had possibly chopped off his head with a machete when Junior showed up uninvited. Whether she had or not—and I wouldn't put it past her—Junior was a missing person. And Pumpy was his friend and partner. Junior had and Pumpy did despise me. The feelings were mutual.

"I know Pumpy," I said.

Tutein smirked. "So, what am I to do? You want my help in finding your husband. You want me to keep your little secret. You want, you want, you want, but what you gonna give me to help me make these big decisions about whether to help you?"

He kept his eyes on me as he told Tim, "You can go now. I come back for you."

Tutein reached out and tucked a strand of my hair behind my ear. I shuddered. He grinned at me, showing his ivory teeth.

"Yah, meh son," Tim said, and slipped out of the car. I broke Tutein's gaze and watched the old man's bowed back until he blended into the trees and vanished.

I seethed. I raged. I imagined Tutein as fish food. I loathed the man. But I hadn't the foggiest idea of how to wiggle out of his trap without committing a felony against a cop. I gripped my useless phone and kept quiet.

"I think you must return home and consider how best to help me make these difficult choices, Katie. As a sign of good faith, I give you one piece of information, though. Information about your husband." His smirk spread into a gloat.

Seconds ticked by.

I looked away, out the passenger window into the peaceful green dusk. I would not ask him for it.

After an endless minute, Tutein lowered his voice and leaned close enough that his breath hit my cheek in hot puffs. "I hear your husband fly to Mexico." He pulled a few inches away, lifted his hand, and stroked the backs of his fingers down my left cheek, then straightened in his seat.

Bile rose in my throat. Mexico? Puerto Rico or St. Thomas for a day trip I could fathom, and had almost come to accept. But Mexico? Not without telling me. Never without telling me.

"You're wrong. And I'm going to find him, and prove it," I said, feeling spittle shoot from my lips.

Tutein laughed softly, put the car in gear, and pointed it back toward Annalise.

Chapter Ten

Kurt scrubbed his hand from the front of his scalp across the top of his head. Now I knew where Nick picked up the gesture. He had spent the afternoon trying to track Nick through the St. Marcos airport and the FAA. No luck at all there.

After I'd found him in the kitchen and told him my story, he leaned onto his elbows on the breakfast bar and said, "Why would Tutein think Nick flew to Mexico? That's a helluva long trip for a private plane. Nick wouldn't make that trip." He sat up straight on his bar stool and scrubbed his head again.

I leaned back against the island in front of him and held Liv tightly against my chest, trying to pacify myself with her warmth and sweet smell. My blue spiral notebook with my to-do list and notes was on the island behind me. "I don't know. But I know Tutein isn't going to help us." I considered the detective's smarmy suggestion that I "help" him make his decisions and thought about his skin touching mine. No way. "We're sitting on a time bomb with him and the Annalise accusations, too. He could show up with DPNR and haul me away in handcuffs at any moment. We're on our own, Kurt, and we have to move fast."

Julie was preparing dinner with her hands shaking and tears slipping down her cheeks every so often, listening while we talked. They had lost Nick's younger sister Teresa only one and a half years ago. This had to be killing them.

Taylor and Oso ran in and out of the room playing chase. Kurt leaned down and picked Jess up out of her bouncy seat and held her to him in much the same way I was holding Liv. All present and accounted for, except Nick.

"I agree," Kurt said. "Without the police, do you think we should hire someone private to help us?"

"Who? Nick is the one to hire for situations like these. And only someone local could move fast enough to make a difference." I considered my next words carefully. "You know I worked with Nick at Stingray. I also did hundreds of investigations during my ten years as an attorney. We can do this, Kurt."

"Yup, I think we could. I think we have to. Could your contact at Petro-Mex help?"

"I already left a voicemail for him. His name's Ramirez."

Julie set plates in front of us. Sandwiches and chips. Such a wonderful mother, mother-in-law, grandmother . . .

Mother?

The image of a mother entered my mind . . . another mother, a different kitchen. I had seen a mother in a kitchen somewhere.

Elena's mother, Elena's kitchen.

"Kurt, I have an idea. I can't just sit here and wait for Ramirez to call me back. Let's drive down to the compound and make a surprise visit to the widow Monroe. She held back on Nick and me when we interviewed her, but I think I can get her to talk to me without the goon from Petro-Mex standing over her shoulder."

"Good idea," Kurt said, standing up.

"Leave everything here to me," Julie said. "Just go find Nick." Her eyes looked as red as mine felt.

Quickly, Kurt and I deposited babies in bouncies and high chairs, grabbed our sandwiches, and went through the garage toward the truck, which I had parked right outside. On our way out, a machete clattered to our feet from its hook on the garage wall. Kurt and I looked at each other.

"Annalise is full of good ideas, too," I said, and scooped it up.

"I can do better than that," Kurt replied.

He disappeared into the house. I ran after him to grab my notebook. When I returned to the truck to wait for him, I added "Talk to Elena" to the list. Kurt reappeared in the passenger seat of the truck and held up the item he had retrieved: a flare gun.

"Excellent." I mashed the gas pedal to the floor, and we were off.

While I drove, Kurt updated me on the rest of his conversation with the FAA. They had asked him whether he absolutely knew that it was Nick who took the plane. "I had to admit to them I didn't know. Someone coulda stolen it. Or moved it. And no one at the airport had any idea where the plane went or who had taken it," he said. Ultimately, he had convinced the FAA to notify the Coast Guard. The Coasties would look around St. Marcos for signs of a downed plane. "Unfortunately, our plane doesn't have an electronic locator. If it did, they could track its position by the signal. Searching the area is really the best they can do, with so little to go on."

I couldn't disagree.

Twenty minutes later, we sat outside the compound's high fences, Kurt rubbing his hair again, me bouncing my knee. The guard lumbered back to my window from the phone mounted on the side of the security building.

"She no home," the guard said.

"Can you try her again? Maybe she just isn't answering," I replied.

"I try her three times already. When she no answer, I call her other number. Mrs. Monroe answer that. She gone."

"What do you mean, gone? Where?" I asked, my face growing hot.

"I can't tell you that. But I supposed to call Mr. Jiménez if anyone asks about her, so I call him, too, and he on his way. Please wait right here. He coming to talk to you."

He gave me a friendly salute and walked back to the building.

Jiménez? He was the HR guy that showed up uninvited to Elena's and didn't want Nick to have Eddy's computer. This didn't sound good. I filled Kurt in.

Another guard poked his head into our car. "Everything all right here, miss?" he asked. He was older than the other one, with pockmarked skin and a droopy eyelid. I eyed him like Quasimodo. He eyed me like a juicy rib eye. Subtly, I changed gears.

"Oh, hello, sir, yes, we are great. How are you?"

"Fine, fine, thank you," he preened.

I pointed at the other guard. "We were just waiting for him to come back and tell us where Elena Monroe has gone. Do you know Elena?"

"Yes, ma'am. She beautiful. I see her today before she leave for Mexico."

Be careful what you ask for, Katie. Mexico? Mexico?? I remembered Tutein's words: "You should be asking why Eddy Monroe killed himself in front of your house." My face went from hot to icy and I rocked forward and backward in my seat. I willed myself to freeze, to act normal. Kurt closed his hand over mine.

I inhaled deeply and fished again. "Well, we sure are going to miss her around here," I said, my voice barely shaking.

"Yes, me, too," he said wistfully. "She say she not coming back to the island."

"Did her mother go with her?"

"I don't know," the guard answered.

"Can you give me her mobile number so I can call her myself?"

"No, ma'am, I not allowed to give out phone numbers. I sorry."

"Please?"

"I wish I could, but man dem fire me. I can't. Good night, miss." He started backing away.

"OK. Well, thank you. Good night, sir."

He lifted his hand in a gesture of farewell and walked toward the next car in line.

I looked back toward the entrance building and saw Jiménez storming towards us with the guard trailing behind him. Time to leave.

I pulled the truck forward and made a tire-squealing U-turn, then drove for half a mile. Kurt didn't break the silence. When my phone rang, I parked on the side of the road to answer, trying to shake the image of Elena's hand in my husband's at the end of our interview a few days ago. I had faith in Nick, but that didn't mean I liked all this talk about Mexico.

"Hello?" I said. My voice sounded muffled, like I was speaking through a cloth.

"I'm calling for Katie Kovacs." The voice—male, Mexican—sounded familiar.

"Speaking."

"Hola, this is José Ramirez."

"Oh, thank you for calling me back, Mr. Ramirez. I know it's late. Past your working hours," I said, opening my eyes wide and nodding for Kurt's benefit. "Did you get my message that Nick is missing?"

"I did. Dios mío! I am so sorry to hear that. I hope that he is all right."

"Me, too."

"How can I help you?" he asked.

"The police told me that Nick flew his private plane to Mexico yesterday. I am not sure if this is true or not, but I wanted to ask if you knew anything about where he went, or could think of a reason why he would go to Mexico?" I showed my crossed fingers to Kurt and realized I was holding my breath. I forced myself to exhale.

"Hmmmmmm." He paused. "No, Nick didn't say anything to me about going anywhere. Reasons he might go to Mexico, you ask? Let me think." He paused again, longer this time. "I'm sorry, I can't think of any."

I didn't know whether this news was good or bad. "What about Elena, Eddy's wife? I was at the refinery gate a few minutes ago. I tried to visit her, and the guard said she went to Mexico. Did you know this?"

Ramirez spoke so sharply that the phone crackled. "What? No, I did not know that. As the spouse of a Petro-Mex employee, she could return to Mexico at our expense, but I feel certain she did not contact anyone here at the refinery to do so. I am handling all matters related to her and Mr. Monroe personally, and I heard nothing about this. That is most odd, most distressing. I will contact her as soon as we hang up."

My thoughts turned back to Jiménez as I listened to Ramirez. Why was Jiménez intercepting questions about Elena if everything about the Monroes was to go through Ramirez? This didn't feel right—at all.

I had an idea.

"Since I'm not sure of anything at this point, could I ask that Petro-Mex check their security records to see if Nick came onto the property in the last two days, too?"

"Of course," he said. "If I learn anything, I will let you know. Please, if you discover anything else about Nick, will you do the same for me?"

"I will," I said. "Oh! And can I get Elena's mobile number from you?"

"Certainly, but it is in my office. I will call you with it tomorrow."

We said our goodbyes and hung up.

Odd, everything was odd, odd, odd. And painful. I studied the floorboard in the fading light, as if the dirty rubber mats would reveal a hidden message. And they did: a scrap of paper near my feet caught my eye. I leaned over to pick it up and bumped my head on the steering wheel. It was a receipt for parking at the St. Marcos International Airport.

A sign? If not a sign, it was at least a call to action.

"Let's stop by the airport on the way home, Kurt. You've been asking about Nick, but maybe someone there knows how and when Elena left for Mexico."

He nodded, ever the good Mainer. Kurt never wasted a word. We drove the ten minutes to the airport, parked, and walked to the terminal without speaking. I approached the ticket agent at the first open counter, Cape Air, and gave him my best smile. *Trust me.*

"Good day, sir."

"Good evening," he replied.

"I'm sorry to bother you, but I need to ask you a question. A friend of mine flew out of St. Marcos yesterday, and she asked me to pick up something she left at the ticket counter. I forgot which airline she told me she flew. She's short, Mexican, and looks like," I fumbled for words, "well, she looks like Eva Longoria, but curvier."

The agent pursed his lips and said, "I don't remember her. But you see that skycap fella over there? He know everybody and everyt'ing what goes on 'round here."

"Thank you so much," I said.

Kurt and I hastened over to the skycap, whose open face radiated good cheer and a jovial "tip me" helpfulness. He hustled travelers right and left.

"Oh, let me help you with those bags, ma'am, right up here and then step this way," he was saying to a fiftyish white woman who was struggling with two large suitcases and several carry-ons. "What airline you taking today?"

She dropped her bags and answered him in a New York dowager accent. "American Airlines, and please hurry. I'm running late."

We fell in behind them as he ferried her bags then collected her tip with a deep bow. When he turned around, he almost bumped into us. I held out a ten-dollar bill and said, "We're looking for some help, sir."

He pocketed the bill and bestowed an ear-to-ear smile on me. "Certainly, ma'am. How can I assist you today?"

"Yesterday, a woman came through the airport, a very sexy young Mexican woman. I wanted to see if you remembered someone like her." I hated asking this question and knowing I might get an answer I really wouldn't like.

"Very sexy? Oh yeah, I remember a very sexy Mexican girl. She short, right? With her mama? Mama looked like Charo?" He did a cuchi-cuchi wiggle, which normally would have made me smile. Instead, I nodded, queasy. "Yah, mon, I see them. Good-looking women dem. Impossible for a man not to notice them, unless he an anti-man." Anti-man was the local term for homosexual.

I replied, "Oh, great. Did you see what airline they flew out on?"

"Sure, but it not an airline. Some man pick them up in a Jeep and drive them over there." He pointed toward the private hangar where Nick and Kurt kept their plane. "It real early in the morning. I just gotten in and no customers yet, so I watch them." He nodded and smiled in a satisfied way, like someone remembering a really good scene from a movie.

Shit. "Are you sure it was a Jeep? Could it have been a Montero?"

"Montero, Jeep, whatever. It maroon or red. Old. And the man, he a dark-headed white guy. About your age," he said to me.

I turned to ask Kurt if he had any questions, but the skycap said, "You late, though."

"What do you mean?" I asked.

"Other men here asking these same questions yesterday, right after the Mexican cutie leave," he said.

My knees felt weak. "How many men? What did they look like? Who were they?"

"I don't know who they were. They black local guys, two of them. That all I know." The older man bowed at the waist and wheeled his hand truck back to the curb to solicit more business.

As we turned to go, I saw someone standing at the curb watching us. Mr. Jiménez, the angry human resources manager. What in the world was he doing following us? As I stared back at him, he turned and walked to a car waiting for him at the curb.

"Wait!" I yelled after him.

He looked up at me, shook his head no, and got in the car. It drove off into the night.

Shit.

"That the Jiménez fellow we ran away from at the refinery?" Kurt asked.

"Yes," I said.

"Strange," he said. Yeah, understatement. "What do you make of the skycap's information?" Kurt asked.

I bit my lip, holding back tears. Now I would almost rather believe that Derek or Bobby was the reason Nick was missing. Even though it looked bad, I was certain Nick could explain when we found him. Still, it hurt. I could feel my heirloom gold band icy and hard around my finger. Had my mother's faith in my father ever been tested like this? What about my grandmother? And if so, how had they survived this pain, this fear? I motioned toward the car and Kurt and I began to walk.

"Sounds like Nick had passengers with him and they were headed to Mexico," I said. "And that someone was following them."

Chapter Eleven

I sat at Nick's computer in our office less than an hour later, my blue notebook on the desk to my right. As the machine booted up, I noted the time: 9:55 p.m. Nick had left our house forty hours ago. By now, he could have made it nearly around the world, if he so desired. I wondered what it was he had desired, though. I couldn't tell from the few clues I had, and I was fighting to remain positive that the main thing he wanted was me.

I knew he believed in me, and I would believe in him. Period. If he'd gone to Mexico with Elena and her mother, there had to be a good reason, a reason related to the Petro-Mex case. And I would figure that reason out, by God.

I typed in his password and accessed his email. I had read everything stored in his account during my initial panic the previous night, but I wanted to look again. What had I missed?

I saw a new message in his inbox, its header marked in bold. The name of the sender read "A. Friend." How clever. I took a sip of my cinnamon spice tea for courage and opened A. Friend's missive.

"We arrived safely but are still scared. I think you were followed. Thank you for delivering the package to Punta Cana. Good luck."

What the hell? "We arrived safely"? *We?* Could "we" refer to Elena and her mother? And "they," whoever they were, were still scared—of what? Who would have followed Nick—the guys that talked to the skycap?

And "Thank you for delivering the package"? Between ferrying passengers and packages, Nick sounded more like a FedEx deliveryman than a P.I. Where the hell was Punta Cana? I couldn't even remember if I'd heard of it before.

I opened Google Maps in a new tab and clumsily typed in a search for "Punta Caba." I corrected my spelling and tried again: Punta Cana.

Punta Cana was a city on the east coast of the Dominican Republic, one of two countries on the island just west of Puerto Rico. Haiti covered the western half of Hispaniola and the Dominican Republic was to the east, closest to Puerto Rico and St. Marcos.

I forced myself to slow down and go through the logic, step by step. To think like Nick would if he were investigating this for a client. To think like I would, when I wasn't in this much emotional distress. Today someone had sent an email to Nick thanking him for delivering a package to Punta Cana in the Dominican Republic, and that person was scared and thought someone had followed Nick. If this person was correct, Nick had gone to the Dominican Republic yesterday. I knew that didn't rule out flying to Mexico afterwards, but even if he'd just stopped over in Punta Cana, it gave Kurt and me a lead to follow. It gave us our first glimmer of hope. With printouts of the email and the Google map in hand, I dashed down the stairs to the main floor.

"Kurt? Kurt?" I called softly as I neared the bottom step, hoping he hadn't gone to bed yet. I couldn't yell with the three young ones asleep in the house.

Kurt's head and shoulders rounded the corner and I nearly crashed headlong into him. Julie and Ruth, Taylor's old nanny, nearly ran into his back. Julie had called for reinforcement while we were gone earlier. Three grandbabies and one tired, worried grandmother needed an extra set of hands, and who better than Ms. Ruth?

Kurt grabbed my upper arms to stop my forward motion.

I raised the papers in my hand and shook them in the air. "I have a lead. Nick went to the Dominican Republic. To Punta Cana."

Everyone spoke at once. When we regained order, I explained the email from A. Friend to Nick. By silent accord, we walked into the dining room and sat around the glass-topped table that not so long ago had been piled high with a dead pig and a dozen bags of ice.

"You going to Punta Cana? You better book tickets and hotel. Morning soon come," Ms. Ruth said.

"You're right," I said. I didn't think my stress level could rise any higher, but it was climbing like a candy thermometer in Karo syrup. I added her suggestions to my to-do list in the notebook.

"For me, too," Kurt said. "I'm coming with you."

I nodded. "Absolutely, and thank you."

"Did you answer the email?" Julie asked.

"No." What a miss on my part. I felt a nauseating surge of adrenaline. Another add for the list. "I will, though. As soon as we're done talking."

"Maybe you can build some trust and get a real conversation going," Julie said.

That gave me another idea. "I think I can set up Nick's email account to send and receive on my phone. That way I can read his email as soon as it arrives and keep up the dialogue with whoever A. Friend is when we go to Punta Cana."

"Can we read the texts on Nick's phone?" Kurt asked. "On the internet, I mean."

To hear my father-in-law talking about texts would have entertained me on a normal day, but today it barely registered as novel. "I have no idea. But we should try." Another thing to do. My neck tingled, announcing the certain appearance of red stress splotches.

"Whatever we do, we can't assume he isn't on St. Marcos and quit looking for him here," Kurt said. "He could have gone missing after he got back from Punta Cana. Or maybe this email is a hoax, and he never left the island." His voice was nearly an octave higher than usual.

I looked around the table. Kurt was ripping at his cuticles. Julie was biting her lip. Ruth was rocking back and forth, ever so slightly. They looked as close to a nervous breakdown as I felt.

And then Julie worked her magic. She'd always been able to round off sharp edges and soften hard knots. Her words were slow, and her voice was almost deep. "Let's work together on this. I know I can't sleep anyway, and it will make me feel better to do something. I'll book the travel. Kurt, can you get on the AT&T website and research the texting issue?"

"I can." Kurt might eschew the personal use of cell phones, but he was very computer savvy and had logged thousands of internet hours on call as a ship pilot.

Ruth chimed in. "I make some tea and a little bite to eat for we."

My redlined pulse slowed to a survivable level. "I'll work on the email issues with A. Friend and set up Nick's email on my phone. And I'll ask Rashidi to mount an exhaustive land search here, door to door and shore to shore, while we search in DR. And oh God, I almost forgot this one: I'll make sure our cell phones have service in DR."

Heads nodded. Ruth disappeared into the kitchen, Julie and Kurt headed downstairs to their computers, and I went back up to the office. I tackled the phone/email issue first. I knew it would be doable, but it wasn't a task I could complete without finding and following step-by-step instructions. Fifteen minutes later, I had succeeded in messing up the process three times. Before I could try again, Ms. Ruth appeared with tea and chocolate chip cookies.

"Bless you," I told her.

"Ah, child, bless you," she said, and placed her hand lightly, briefly, on my shoulder. I tried to recall a single time she had touched me in the year she had worked for us, besides shaking my hand when she met me, but I could remember none.

"I've missed you, Ruth," I said as she left the room.

She turned her head and smiled at me, then kept walking to the kitchen.

I threw myself back into the email issue, and within three minutes, I had done it. When I'd satisfied myself that I could receive and send email from Nick's account on my iPhone, I opened A. Friend's message again and hit Reply.

Dear A. Friend: This is Nick's wife, Katie. I am checking Nick's email from our house because he never made it home from Punta Cana. He is missing. Please help me find him. Email, text, or call with whatever you know. Anything. Please. Thank you, Katie Kovacs.

I added my cell phone number and email address at the bottom and hit send. Then I prayed.

Next, I got online with AT&T and scanned the countries included in their international call, texting, and data plans. Thank God—they covered the DR.

Finally, even though it was late, I called Rashidi, who promised to put together a team of trusted friends and relatives and scour the island for any sign of Nick and the plane. Then I told him about Tutein.

"Katie, we gonna have to take care of he when this over," Rashidi said, his voice deep and clipped.

"Yes, he is a problem. But one thing at a time right now," I replied.

Rashidi asked, "What you want me to do? Remember, I specialize in 'who you know.'"

This, I could vouch for. Who Rashidi knew had resulted in most of the permits and laborers I'd needed for Annalise in my first year—much of it pre-Nick—on St. Marcos. Whenever I had trouble at Annalise, it was Rashidi to the rescue. He'd even camped on her floors armed with his machete after she was burglarized when Ava deserted her.

"We have to figure out the truth of what, if anything, lies below Annalise," I said.

"Irie," Rashidi said. "I have two old grade school partners that will help. Rob works for the museum as curator, and his wife Laura the librarian at U.V.I."

"I also want to know what happens to someone who breaks this law? I'm really just worried about my responsibility from the Day of the Dead forward. I don't think I can be held responsible for what the first owner did—I didn't have any knowledge of it—so even if the government hassles me about it, I'm not concerned. Let's just pray he wasn't a desecrator and robber of graves in addition to his other illegal pastimes, though. You don't remember any talk of old bones, do you?"

"Nah, meh son. I didn't hear a thing," he replied.

"OK. So, Rash, I need to know the penalties. Are they monetary? If there's a cemetery, do I have to move it? Could they do anything to Annalise? I know you told me they can do anything they want to me, according to your lady friend in the government, but I can't imagine this could result in any long-term jail time."

"Yah, mon, I take care of it. But I gonna focus on Nick. I get Rob and Laura to help on finding out if there anything below Annalise. Now, you may not like this, but I need more help. I bring Ava in, too."

He was right; I didn't like it. Singing together was one thing, but I hadn't been able to count on her before when I needed her. I didn't argue, though. "Do what you have to, Rash. I trust you." I thanked him, and we hung up.

I walked downstairs to check on the others' progress. Julie reported in detail on the itinerary she had arranged, as was her way.

"The earliest I can get you to Punta Cana is 1:35 in the afternoon, and to do that, you and Kurt have to catch a 6:45 a.m. flight to San Juan, then you connect there to Punta Cana."

"That sounds great." The sooner we started our journey, the better I would feel.

She continued. "You're staying at the Puntacana Resort, about a mile and a half from the airport. The rooms are only ninety-five dollars per night. I had heard the DR was inexpensive, but, wow."

A resort on the beach for that price? Nick and I should go there sometime, I thought. If we find him. When we find him. We will find him.

"You're awesome. Thank you."

"Do you want a car?" she asked.

"I don't think so. Our business is at the airport. And the hotel is close."

"I agree," Kurt said. "Now, let me tell you what I found out."

Kurt had had mixed luck. He confirmed that the content of Nick's messages was not readable online. But he learned that AT&T's system showed up-to-the-minute message logging by phone number for both sends and receives. He had handwritten a list of the numbers, which included mine and three others. I hated that the last one Nick had sent to me had been at noon the previous day, and that I had forgotten about it. However, that did shorten the length of his disappearance by seven hours, from the time he left my side at five a.m. to the noontime text.

And Annalise had sent me a message at one p.m. yesterday. I shivered. That suggested the window was shorter by yet another hour. *Oh, Annalise. If only you could speak.*

The big hand on the old wood-framed clock above the great room's mantel was nearing midnight. Kurt and Julie trekked back downstairs to their apartment. Ruth had tucked in half an hour ago in the guest bedroom on the main floor. I scurried around shutting off lights, locking doors, and packing for the trip. I doubled back to the office twice, once for my passport—where I noticed for the first time that Nick's was gone—and one time for my laptop charger. I stopped in to kiss Taylor and the girls before I retreated to my own room. Nick's and my room.

I settled into our bed, cell phone and list of numbers in hand, still wearing Nick's black t-shirt that I'd thrown on before Tutein hauled me off into the bush to threaten me. Had that really only been today? It seemed like weeks ago now.

My eyes wanted to close, but first I typed the same text message to each number on Kurt's short list from AT&T:

"Hey, this is Nick. I got a new cell phone. Just checking in."

If that didn't yield results, I'd switch tactics in the morning. I prayed to God to keep Nick safe, and I closed my eyes.

A hand touched my shoulder, then pushed it. "Katie?" Nick said. "Katie, wake up. It's me."

I fought waking, but my eyes opened after he shook me a few more times. "What time is it?" I asked.

"It's three a.m. I know it's late, but I need to tell you something."

"Where have you been?" I asked.

"Don't you remember, silly? I went shopping for presents to make you smile."

"Oh, yeah. You told me that."

My eyes closed. His hand shook my shoulder again.

"Katie, wake up, listen to me, because I can only talk for a moment. I need you to know I am all right. Don't stop looking for me. Take the picture with you. I'm counting on you."

"Wait! What? Nick?" I jumped up and the cotton sheets slid to the floor as my feet hit it. "Nick?"

Nick was not there. Of course he wasn't. *You're dreaming*, I thought as I climbed back into bed, tears falling. *It was just a dream.*

I heard a crash and jerked awake. Annalise's agitation was sparking in the air around me and I realized she had hurled something to the ground. I got out of bed again and flipped on the light switch. The sound had come from Nick's closet. I opened the door and found his tackle box sitting upright on the floor, five feet down from its shelf above Nick's hanging clothes rack.

"What do you mean, Annalise? A tackle box?"

I squatted down beside it and placed both my hands on its lid. I closed my eyes and Nick's voice filled not just my head, but my whole body. *"I'm all right. Don't stop looking for me. Take the picture with you. I am counting on you."*

I opened the box and pulled out each item, one by one. Hooks, leaders, rubbery squid. Odds and ends I couldn't name. And a water-damaged picture of Nick and his father on a fishing boat called the *Little Mona Lisa*.

"What is this? Annalise, Nick? What am I supposed to get from this? Annalise? Help me, please help me."

Stillness. Complete quiet.

After several long minutes sitting on the floor in front of Nick's closet waiting for an answer or an idea, I gave up. I tucked the picture into my travel bag and returned to bed to sleep for another hour and a half with Nick's voice and Annalise's antics in my head.

By five a.m., Kurt and I had grabbed the coffee cups Ruth held out for us, and I had steered the nose of the Silverado toward the airport. We sipped our coffee in silence.

Nick, I'm coming to find you.

Chapter Twelve

Spanish. Everyone in the DR airport spoke it, and my pidgin Tex-Mex version didn't sound a thing like the guttural pronunciations that were pummeling my ears and setting off tiny explosions in my brain. My head throbbed so badly by the time we made it from customs out to the taxis that I wanted to clamp one hand on either side of it and squeeze it into stillness.

The day was hard, but Kurt made an ideal traveling companion. He stayed quiet, did the heavy lifting, and kept the assertive Puerto Rican and Dominican men away. He was responsible for most of our weight, though; he had maritime maps for half the world in his hard-sided suitcase that was so old it didn't even have wheels. Thriftiness, another trait of a good Mainer. My in-laws had lived in Annalise's downstairs apartment for over six months, and the close proximity meant continual, if congenial, interaction. I sincerely liked them, and Lord knows I appreciated them. I knew very little about my reserved father-in-law, though. He hardly spoke a word.

Towering over the Dominicans around us, Kurt hailed a taxi. The driver spoke in poor English and Kurt answered in perfect Spanish that even sounded somewhat Dominican. He ended the haggling by holding up five fingers, then shaking his head no when the taxi driver asked for more. Masterful.

"Where'd you learn to do that?" I asked as the taxi jolted out of the airport.

"What?" Kurt said.

"Speak Dominican Spanish, or any Spanish at all, for that matter."

"I piloted ships in and out of the Corpus Christi Bay from all over the Caribbean and Central and South America for thirty-five years. And I lived in South Texas. Couldn't help but learn it."

I spent the rest of the short drive staring out the window at the hotels and beaches that seemed two-dimensional without Nick there with me. If I opened one of the front doors, I felt like I would step through a façade into nothingness.

When we arrived at the Puntacana Resort, Kurt paid the driver to wait while we checked in and deposited our bags. There was no time to waste, and I barely registered my surroundings in the rush. The resort was just like every other hotel in the Caribbean, anyway: lush greenery, tinkling steelpans, the hum of conversations over frozen rum drinks. Our rooms? Roofs and beds. Maybe I'd notice more later, but not now. We raced back to the airport.

This time, as we approached the airport by road instead of air, I could see the palm fronds that covered the terminals, making them look like giant thatched-roof huts. When we were ushered through customs and the public terminal by American Airlines and airport personnel an hour ago, I hadn't noticed anything about the aesthetics. Tan on forgettable tan over hard floors. But from the outside I could see it was bigger than I'd realized. The ticket and bag-checking areas were classic Caribbean open-air patios, and even the interior of the terminal wasn't fully enclosed by walls. I could see the beach in the distance.

We stopped at the curb and Kurt negotiated with our driver, who handed him a business card. Kurt read it, and then introduced us formally, which felt peculiar and right at the same time.

"Katie, this is Victor. Victor, Katie."

"Mucho gusto," I said.

"Mucho gusto, señora," Victor said.

I slowed myself down enough to really see him for the first time. Victor looked about my age, although I found it hard to guess men's ages. Especially dark-complexioned men, who to my eye aged better than light-skinned men, who in turn aged better than women of any skin tone. Lucky bastards.

"Victor will drive us anywhere we need to go. I paid him for the day. He will park at our hotel and come for us when we call." He handed me Victor's card and I programmed the number into my mobile.

Victor dropped us off at Terminal Three. We had entered through Terminal One, which housed the international commercial flights and teemed with people. Terminal Three was for private planes, and was enveloped in an atmosphere of serenity. The breeze was cooler, the light softer, and the pace slower. Terminal Three whispered "money—dirty, sexy money here."

Kurt and I started our questions with a gristly old guy manning an information booth. He had an air of courtly pride, but no information. Next we talked to three different uniformed Dominicans in the customer service area. They made our St. Marcos citizenry seem churlish.

Within fifteen minutes—an astonishingly short period of time that still felt endless to me—a young woman ushered us into an office with a tarnished brass plaque on the door that read "G. Marrero." She sat us in two chairs in front of a metal desk and left the room. We waited there, thinking that it was strange to be left alone, considering this age of terrorism. But we weren't in Kansas anymore, for sure. We looked around at the framed certificates and diplomas on the walls, and spotted a bachelor's degree in aerospace engineering from the University of Miami. Miami—as in Miami on the southeast tip of the United States. That meant that G. Marrero should speak English. Please, Lord . . .

As the minutes passed, I grew antsy. I pulled the blue notebook from my purse and updated my notes and to-do list again, but I'd already updated it on the plane, so there wasn't much to add. After half an hour, I was frantic. Since Nick's disappearance, I'd been holding hysteria at bay (although not one hundred percent successfully) with action: action with the purpose of finding my husband. Sitting, waiting, doing nothing while at the mercy of this G. Marrero's schedule was too action-less for me.

I tried to picture Nick and an image of his body strapped into a mangled airplane flashed up. *No, not that one.* I forced a replacement.

Nick standing before me in the backyard of Annalise, promising to forsake all others so long as we both should live, looking like he meant it.

Come on. Hurry, I willed G. Marrero.

"Buenos tardes," someone—presumably with the last name of Marrero—said.

Kurt and I stood, and Gabriel Marrero introduced himself to us as the manager of the terminal and apologized for our long wait.

I jumped in. "Could you help us find out whether our Piper Malibu landed here two days ago?"

Gabriel's English sounded like all consonants. "I am sure we could. Give me all the details."

"Tail number RJ7041," I said. Gabriel jotted notes as I spoke. I tried to read the upside down script, without success. Spanish. "Frankly, we don't know much," I continued, "and the circumstances are suspicious. Could we find out whether it ever landed here, and if it had cleared takeoff with the air traffic control tower, too? Our best guess for departure would be after the noon hour, but before three p.m." I paused, and then added, "If the answer to either of these is a yes, we will have more questions, of course."

Gabriel nodded. He hadn't interrupted my explanation a single time. Now he read the details back for confirmation. The man was quick, and he had taken it in perfectly.

"Most troubling. I am so sorry for your situation," he said. He leaned forward now, tapping his pen rhythmically on his notepad. Ba-da-dum ba-da-dum ba-da-dum. "The things you ask are no problem, and I would be honored to help you. It will be much easier if I talk to our people myself, since most of them don't speak English. So if you will permit me to go do that, I would ask you to wait here. Give me half an hour," he said. "Maybe less."

"Thank you," I said. I appreciated his help, his English, and his wonderful, comforting manners, that Caribbean Latino formality.

"De nada, you're welcome," he said. He left and the sound of his steps receded quickly.

We were alone again in the office. The press of time descended on me.

"I keep trying to think of something, anything we can do to move forward during all this waiting. It's killing me. Nick is out there somewhere. He needs us to hurry," I said.

Kurt nodded, making eye contact with me and holding it. He hadn't shaved that morning and his stubble was coming in gray. It lightened his gypsy face. With their Hungarian ancestry, Nick and his father could really pass for Latino. Tall Latino.

I continued. "Maybe we should check in with the FAA."

"Yup, I think we should do that while we are here today. Not yet, though. Let's see if Nick was even here, first."

Frustrated, I broke eye contact. He was right.

I dumped the contents of my purse on an open area of the desk in front of us.

Kurt grunted. I looked up. He raised an eyebrow.

"I have to do *something*. I'll clean out my purse." It was the perfectly sensible thing to do.

I separated the contents of my handbag into piles: trash, put back in wallet, and return to purse. I walked over to the trashcan and dropped my handful. One of the pieces stared back at me—not trash. It was the list of phone numbers Nick had sent texts to right before he vanished.

I fished it out and read it again, and something niggled my brain. Could any of these be numbers I recognized, people I knew? No. Had someone altered a number? No. Still, one of the numbers seemed to glare at me. I compared the numbers to the ones I'd texted from my own phone late last night.

"Shit!" I said.

"What?" Kurt asked.

"I texted these numbers, but I typed one in wrong. I'm doing it again right now." I double-checked the digits this time, punching harder than necessary, and sent the message. More time lost.

Gabriel strode back into his office, interrupting my self-flagellation.

"Hola, Señor Kovacs, Señora Kovacs," he said. He pulled his chair around to our side of the desk and straddled it, leaning so far forward he almost tipped into us. The man was excited. "My news es bueno."

Now I leaned toward him.

Gabriel said, "Sí, sí, Mr. Kovacs landed your plane at this very airport and entered this very terminal," he consulted his watch and his lips moved silently, "fifty-two hours ago. I talked to the man who directed them when they parked the plane. Not just Mr. Kovacs, but another man and two extremely beautiful women." This last part he conveyed with his hands sculpting the air into an hourglass.

The hourglass was no surprise, but another man? What other man? What the hell had Nick done, anyway, flown a party barge over to the DR? What had happened to "just interviewing a few witnesses, Katie?" *Oh, Nick!*

"The tower confirmed a plane with those tail numbers landed here, but said that they came from San Juan, Puerto Rico," he added.

Kurt and I exchanged a wide-eyed look. So Nick had not flown straight from St. Marcos? But what did that mean?

"Go on," I said.

Gabriel continued, gesturing first at Kurt and then at me as he spoke. "Your son's—your husband's—plane made last contact with the tower at 12:52 p.m., clearing for takeoff."

"Where did he go?" I asked.

"Lo siento," Gabriel said. "I'm sorry. I don't know. Mr. Kovacs didn't file a flight plan."

"Doesn't he have to tell someone where he's going?" I asked.

"No, not unless he's flying using instruments, you know, like in bad weather. Otherwise, a pilot can fly wherever he wants, just like a person driving a car," Gabriel explained.

Kurt added, "He didn't even radio the tower when he took off in St. Marcos, Katie. In fact, they were pretty angry with him about it."

This shocked me, although it jived with trying to "fly under the radar."

"So how do we find out where he went? How do we know? Where is he?" I turned to my father-in-law and grabbed him by his upper arms. "Where is he?" I demanded in a wail. And I broke into sobs.

Gabriel leaped to his feet. He retrieved a cloth handkerchief from his desk drawer and proffered it to me. In the midst of falling apart, my natural instincts kicked in. *Bacteria. Germs. Other People's Bodily Fluids.* I let go of Kurt and accepted the kerchief gingerly. Gabriel meant well, so I did my Academy Award nominee best of pretending to dab my eyes with it.

"Gracias," I said. I handed it back to him and counted the seconds until I could reasonably pull out my hand sanitizer. God, I was a complete and total freak. Still, I was very grateful, and I liked the man. His kind gesture had helped me exert self-control by redirecting my attention to that square of fabric. I thought of men who were kind to women, and again that hateful image of Elena's hand in Nick's flashed into my head.

Please let Nick be OK, and please Lord let him not be in Mexico with that woman.

"Kurt, we'll just need to find everyone we can that saw him. He has to have told *someone* where he was going," I said. Just not me.

Kurt held his jaw and rubbed it with his thumb. "Well, maybe so. And ask them other questions, too, I guess."

"Absolutely. Like, what did they do while they were here? Did they eat? Did they talk to anyone? Did they shop? Did they take a taxi? Rent a car? Did Nick have anyone service the plane? He could have had someone work on it or fuel it up. Did he talk to anyone in the pilots' lounge? Who was with him when he left?" I spit the words out as fast as I could think of them.

"Yup," Kurt said. "We've got a lot of talking to do."

"I can help," Gabriel said, his dark eyes shining from the drama of our unusual situation, but his demeanor earnest. "I will talk to the mechanics and everyone that works with the planes and the pilots."

I said, "Kurt, you and I can ask around in the terminal."

"Yup," he said.

"Good. Thank you," I said to them both. "Let's get moving. Please."

We all stood, and Gabriel shook our hands.

"Wait," he said. "I almost forgot to tell you one last piece of information. I am not sure if it is important or not."

"Yes?" I replied, hoping for a gold nugget.

"When I asked about Americanos, my assistant said that someone asked her about an Americano just an hour ago."

"Someone else is looking for Nick?" I asked.

Kurt said, "It was probably us."

"No, I don't think so. She said this person was looking for a woman. One like you." Gabriel looked at me like a riddle he couldn't figure out. "A tall red-headed American woman."

"But why . . . how would . . . no one even knows we're here, except my mother-in-law!" I couldn't put words around my thoughts. Jiménez? "It's probably a coincidence."

Kurt put his hand on my upper arm protectively. "Description?" he asked.

"Oh, she didn't have one," Gabriel answered. "She said that it was a telephone call. A very strange call. She wondered how they got her number."

"Did they say why they were looking for the woman?" I asked.

"She said they told her they had been separated from their friend, and wanted to know if she had seen her. My assistant told them she could announce the woman's name over the loudspeakers—how do you say it?"

"Page her," I supplied.

"Yes, page her. She said the man said no thank you, and hung up."

"That's not much," I said.

"I'm sorry, but it is all that she knew," Gabriel replied.

Who? Who would ask about someone like me? Jiménez was my chief suspect, but there were those men asking the skycap about Elena in St. Marcos.

"Katie, I think we should get moving," Kurt said.

Dazed, I checked my iPhone. It was 3:30. Crap. We needed to move fast.

The picture of Nick in the mangled plane flashed in my mind again.

Really fast.

Chapter Thirteen

The most likely stop in the terminal for Nick and the other three travelers was for food, so we headed there first. I felt like a neon sign on the Vegas strip as we made our way to the cafeteria, the private terminal's only dining establishment.

Patrons queued for food before a glass case of cold food and drinks. I peeked in. I hadn't eaten anything since five a.m., but the arroz con leche looked a little sketchy and I realized I was not hungry. There were fried fish and chicken with rice and peas, and baskets of coconut biscuits, or coconetes, according to a tiny hand-lettered sign. It was a lot like the fare from the catering trucks I'd always called roach coaches.

Kurt and I had decided that I would do the talking, since a six-foot-two-inch gruff-voiced American man might be intimidating. We surveyed the cafeteria. Three employees in pressed khaki shorts and navy shirts worked behind the counter and another bussed the red Formica tables just beyond it. Others bumped in and out of swinging doors with trays of food and plates. In my limited Spanish, I questioned every employee in the snack bar in turn. "Did you see a very sexy young woman and her mother two days ago? Maybe two men with them?"

One after another, they answered me in the same nervous way: No. No. No. No.

And then a yes.

Or a sí, rather.

A man, of course; a very young man who had cleared the table next to where our foursome lunched. He said he saw them, and what's more, he claimed he heard their conversation. He made no apology for eavesdropping.

"Una sexy mamí, sí," he explained.

Yes, I know.

My years of soaking up the Spanish around me in Texas (and learning as little of it as I could in Spanish class) were coming back to me, and I realized I could understand most of what he was saying. His account was startling.

According to him, the two women and the younger man got up from the table first. They thanked the older man and bid him adios.

"And then they walked out of the restaurant?" In my rush, I had switched to English, so Kurt translated.

Out of the airport, it turned out. And the older man stayed behind, drinking café. Saying nothing.

So which one was Nick? The old one or the young one? I pulled up a picture of my husband on my iPhone and showed it to the young man. I had taken it on Monday at Ike's Bay, less than a week ago, a crying baby in a carrier on his front and a screaming young boy in a pack on his back.

"Sí, drinking café," he said, and pointed at one of the tables in the dining area.

The older one.

A bird chirped. I looked from the snack bar into the main room of the terminal. A bright yellow sugarbird was circling the beams of the ceiling, searching for a way out. As I watched, it ducked lower, tilted its wing and body, and darted into the sunshine. Lucky bird.

"Drinking coffee. Anything else?" Kurt asked.

"He had a bag. From there." The young man pointed at the gift shop across the terminal. "He look in his bag and drink coffee. He use his phone."

Was this good news? Nick had stayed behind. Elena and her entourage had left. Elena had told the Petro-Mex security guard she was in Mexico when he spoke to her last night, but Nick had not gone with her. At least not from the cafeteria. Maybe not at all?

I had believed in Nick all along. But certainty would be very nice. I wanted to know—and have everyone else know—that my husband did not traipse across the Caribbean and Mexico after a femme fatale that every man remembered with a gleam in his eye and a grin on his face.

Kurt's taut voice broke into my reverie. "Katie, if he didn't go with them to Mexico, or wherever they went, that raises the chances that he didn't make it to wherever he intended to go."

This broke through to me. He was right.

"However, all we know for sure at this point is that he didn't leave the cafeteria with them," he continued.

"They left the terminal," I pointed out.

"They might have come back," he said.

"That's not what I heard," I said.

"You're hearing what you want to hear, then," Kurt said, without any change in the tone of his voice.

My frustration overcame my good judgment. "What are you saying, Kurt? That you think Nick ran off with this woman to Mexico?"

"Not that I think so, but that it's possible until we rule it out."

I hadn't expected this answer. I didn't like this answer. "You think it's possible Nick left me?"

"A house full of babies is a lot of responsibility," he said in a voice that sounded like he had a lot more to say.

"The babies or me?"

"Well, he ran off to surf a lot, and . . ."

"And?" I said, daring him to finish his thought.

There's a saying that discretion is the better part of valor. Kurt abandoned discretion and braved my wrath.

"And he really wanted you to lose the baby weight," he said.

He turned back to the worker and asked whether he had ever seen the women and their companion again.

My mouth dropped. Red filled my vision. Nick had talked to his dad about me being fat? And his dad thought it was possible that he had left me? I worked my jaw, trying to get it to help me form words, words like *asshole* and *Who do you think you are, Mr. Perfect?*

Meanwhile, the busboy shook his head back and forth.

"Did you see where the older man went when he finished his coffee, and whether he was with anyone or alone?" Kurt asked.

Again, the young man shook his head.

Kurt looked over at me and took stock of my expression. "Pull it together, Katie. Let's see if Gabriel has found out anything more."

"Pull it together?" I hissed. "After I find out you and Nick sit around talking about his terrible life and my giant fat ass?"

"That is not what I said. Let's go," he said.

I bit down so hard I wondered which would break first, my jaw or my teeth. A quick iPhone check showed me it was now 4:30 p.m. Only three hours until nightfall. I did need to pull it together. We did need to get moving. We needed to alert the FAA of the new developments. We had to get someone out there searching in the right place for Nick. Or at least around the Dominican Republic, whether that was the right place or not. I didn't have the luxury of a temper tantrum. I filed my anger at Nick and Kurt away for later.

But I took one last shot. "It may not be what you talked about, but it's sure what you meant a minute ago. Message received loud and clear, Kurt."

He didn't answer.

I overcompensated with effusive thanks to the young busboy and we started back to Gabriel's office with a wall of emotion between us. Halfway there we saw Gabriel's back as he entered his office, and without a word passing between us, we broke into a run. I skidded to a stop at the door in my sandals.

Gabriel sat at his desk with papers in his hand. At our abrupt entrance, he looked up, his eyes round and eyebrows in high arcs.

"Well?" I asked, out of breath.

"Nothing," Gabriel said. "I found out nothing."

"What do you mean?" I asked.

"I couldn't find anyone that knew where your husband intended to go when he left here."

I said, "We were told that the three people he came here with left in a taxi. That means, possibly, he flew out alone. And that would mean, again, possibly, he was flying back to St. Marcos."

Gabriel nodded. "If you say so. I only know that he left here at 12:52."

"Did anyone *say* whether he was alone when he left?" I demanded. I didn't like hearing my voice this shrill, but I also didn't like how thin Gabriel's questioning sounded, and I was raw from my interchange with Kurt. What had happened to all the questions I'd suggested he ask? Did the man not understand that yes-no questions yielded next to nothing? That you had to start there, but circle around and approach the issue from every angle?

He looked back down at his desk and his shoulders hunched up. "No one said," he responded.

Kurt shot me a look that said, "Enough."

"All right. We've made some progress in the last hour, even if we still have a ways to go," Kurt said. "Thank you, Gabriel."

"One other thing," Gabriel said, addressing Kurt instead of me now. "I checked our Dominican systems for a record of a plane crash since Mr. Kovacs left Punta Cana. There is none. And I have my assistant calling the other airports in the DR looking for your plane by its tail numbers, in case he put down somewhere in our country."

"Excellent idea. Much appreciated," Kurt said, even more gracious than before. Making up for his shrewish, fat daughter-in-law.

I tried to follow his lead and aimed for firm rather than strident. Sometimes my temperament got in the way of my common sense. *He's helping us, and he doesn't have to, Katie. Don't run him off.* I needed to accept Gabriel's generosity rather than resent his inexperience, but I was just fuming. At everyone. Nick. His dad. This courtly nincompoop who hadn't accomplished anything yet except to confirm that Nick's plane had taken off and landed. I couldn't believe that only a little while ago I'd been thinking how much I liked him. I didn't like him. I wanted to bop him on the head.

I raised my voice—a lot. I smacked the side of my hand in the other palm to emphasize each point. "Here it is, guys. Nick's been missing for two days. We've gone to our local police. They were less than no help. We called the FAA, who called the Coast Guard. But they couldn't do jack either, because we had no idea where Nick had gone. But he came here and he left here. And I know—I *know*—that if he could have contacted us, he would have. That means there's a very high probability that his plane went down somewhere. We need people searching for him. Now."

Gabriel was stiff. "There is no reason to shout, Mrs. Kovacs."

"There is a reason to shout! My husband is missing!"

"I don't agree with your tone, but I agree with your point. Gabriel, can we contact the FAA together now?" Kurt said.

Gabriel flipped a vintage Rolodex with cards gone yellow with age. I closed my eyes. Here, with the soft Caribbean air on my flushed skin, without the white noise of air conditioners, I could imagine Gabriel under a bamboo ceiling fan dialing a clunky black rotary phone. My pulse quickened. I opened my eyes to see him pressing the buttons on his cell phone.

Someone must have answered on the other end, because Gabriel explained who he was and passed the phone to Kurt, saying, "You're on."

Kurt told our story. It sounded improbable and so full of holes you could, well, fly a plane through it, but Kurt stressed the reasons we believed Nick had gone down between the Dominican Republic and St. Marcos, and soft-pedaled the Mexico angle and the world of other possibilities. He listened for a minute, said thank you, and exchanged contact information with someone. The call was far too brief for my liking.

"What did they say?" I asked after he hung up.

"They knew who we were from my earlier call. They agreed to search between here and St. Marcos," he said. "He—Burt Taylor was his name—said they would coordinate it with the Coast Guard tonight, but that nothing can be done until daylight tomorrow."

Twelve more hours. At least twelve more hours. A long, long time. It was a big ocean out there. The FAA and Coast Guard had the resources we did not; we had no choice but to wait for their help with the search. But there was much we could do in the meantime. That I could do.

Hold on, Nick.

Hold on.

Chapter Fourteen

By the time we'd finished with Gabriel and the FAA, the day shift at the airport had ended. Kurt had called ahead to Victor for our ride. We walked out with dusk falling around us. Sweat rolled down my inner thighs under my knee-length orange skirt that was uncomfortably snug in the waist. More sweat clung to the hair at the base of my neck. I had melted like a crayon, like the mango tango from Taylor's giant Crayola box. My anger had melted, too, and was being replaced by a deep sadness.

Victor pulled his white 1999 Oldsmobile Cutlass to the curb. He kept it in immaculate condition, especially considering the battle islanders fight with rust and sand. He jumped out to open the door. Kurt must have paid him well.

"Buenas noches, señor y señora."

Kurt and I mumbled buenas noches back to him, and Kurt lowered himself into the front seat while I settled into the back. We hadn't said a word to each other since we left Gabriel's office. Victor talked to Kurt quickly and I gave up trying to understand after only a few seconds. Kurt engaged in an animated conversation with Victor, whose hands spent more time in the air than on the steering wheel.

I let my head drop back against the tan ribbed upholstery and tried not to think of all the unwashed heads that had done so before mine. Oil. Dandruff. Dead skin. Lice. Bed bugs. I was so tired I didn't even flinch.

But my head jerked up when I heard Kurt say Nick's name. Victor slowly repeated it twice.

"Kurt, what's up? What are you guys saying about Nick?" I asked.

"Victor met Elena and her party," he replied.

"What?" I leaned forward across the front seat between them.

"Yes, hold on, though. We're not done talking. Let me find out everything he knows."

We pulled up at the passenger drop-off at the Puntacana Resort. Victor put the car in park and kept his mouth running.

I was hanging on every word now, although I didn't understand half of it. I bit a fingernail. How fitting that I would lose my husband and find myself looking for him in a strange land in which I, too, was lost. A flash of something burst inside me. Anger.

If Nick had just told me where he was going, what he was up to—

But I shut it down; now was not the time to indulge my emotions. I had already lost control once today. Victor knew something, and I wanted to know it, too.

A hotel doorman leaned down to Victor's open window. The best I could tell, he asked Victor to drop us off and move along. Victor waved him away with the back of his hand. "Sí, pronto"—yes, soon—and rolled up his window.

The conversation resumed for another few minutes, and then the car grew quiet. Kurt nodded as he squeezed his lips with his thumb and forefinger.

He turned to face me. "OK, Elena and her mama and the younger guy rode with Victor. He's sure of it. The time of day fits, he picked them up at the right terminal, and they match the description."

"That's great!" I said.

"Victor said they were worried about someone following them, and they kept saying maybe the mafioso was on to them. He took them to catch a bus to Santo Domingo. They didn't say anything about Nick or where they were going, but they did say that everyone would think they went back to Mexico."

All those words—ten minutes of talking—and Kurt could sum it up in so few. We had confirmation that Nick had not rejoined Elena's group. No one had gone to Mexico. The universe of possible locations to search for Nick shrank by a fraction. Had he pointed his plane back towards home, to St. Marcos, to me?

"Did he get the name of the man? Can he describe him?" I asked. I heard my voice crack. I licked my lips and swallowed.

Kurt and Victor talked briefly. Kurt said, "No name. But Victor said he looked Mexican, too, but tall, sort of tall, with a mustache and a big gold medallion around his neck." Victor said something else to Kurt. "Correction: He said he looked Mexican or Dominican or Puerto Rican; in other words, he looked Latino."

The doorman reappeared and politely rapped his knuckles on Victor's window. Victor held up one finger and nodded without making eye contact with him.

"You mentioned the mafioso. What mafioso?" I asked.

"He didn't know."

"I would guess Mexican cartel heavies," I said, thinking back on my conversation with Nick about the Chihuahua cartel and the whispers about terrorists and mafia in our Petro-Mex meeting. I shared it with Kurt now, and then asked, "Could Monroe's death have something to do with one of the cartels?"

"Monroe wasn't Mexican, was he?"

"No, he was American, and plain vanilla Caucasian. Petro-Mex gave us his file, and I want to say he was from some little town in Louisiana. In his picture, his hair was strawberry blond."

"I asked him if they talked about St. Marcos or a dead man. He said they didn't," Kurt said.

Victor cut in. "Perdóname, señor, pero yo recuerdo algo." I could figure out that one: Pardon me, sir, but I remember something. He continued, and Kurt's eyebrows rose into peaks.

Kurt translated. "This is interesting. Victor said Elena and the man were lovers. Kissing, stroking." Victor said something else, and Kurt continued, "Calling each other by lovers' names. The mother was not very involved in the conversation. She sat in the front with Victor."

I felt my jaw drop. "You're kidding me! Mrs. Monroe was sucking face with some mystery guy, and running off to the DR with him one week after Mr. Monroe died? And Nick was their pilot? My Nick, who was supposed to be investigating Monroe's death?" My Nick, who was *not* sucking face with Mrs. Monroe, no matter what his father thought?

"What in the world is going on?" I yelled.

Kurt and Victor shrank back.

I took a breath. *Down, girl.*

Kurt asked me, "How long ago did the Monroes marry?"

"Only six months ago." I bumped my palm against my forehead. "Oh man, I completely forgot to tell you something. When I was in Tutein's office, he said that Petro-Mex gave Elena to Monroe as a retention bonus. He called her the 'mail-order mamí.'"

Kurt didn't blink at this information. "So, no love match?"

"Doesn't sound like it."

My excitement tapered off quickly. Nick had still lied to me about something, more than one something, and hadn't told me where he was going. I couldn't exactly anoint him a saint.

The harried doorman leaned over the hood of the Cutlass and smacked it sharply with his palm, once, then twice. Victor shouted what sounded like Dominican curse words back at him.

Kurt continued. "Does the guy sound familiar to you, Katie?"

I squinted my mind's eye back and it pulled up an image of the man who had pulled Nick aside at the Ag Fair. "Yes. Yes, he does. When we met with Elena, she took Nick's card, which identified him as a pilot, not just an investigator. She remarked specifically on that. Three hours later at the Ag Fair, a guy who could match the description Victor gave you pulled Nick aside and talked to him for about ten minutes. Young, Latino, and on the tall side. Mustache. Top button undone like 'I'm too sexy for my shirt.' I remember a flash of gold on his chest, too. I asked Nick about him later and he lied."

"Nick lied to you? About what?" Kurt sounded as disconcerted as I'd ever heard him sound. *You and me both, Kurt. Do you still want to lecture me about your unhappy son and his fat wife?*

"Yes, he lied. He left me with the girls while he took Taylor to the bathroom. When he came back, he told me that he had walked Taylor straight to the potty. But it wasn't true. I watched him. He took a ten-minute detour out of sight with that guy before he returned and went to the bathroom."

"That's odd." Kurt was staring out the window, his lips tight and brow furrowed.

"Very. I was pretty mad at him about it," I admitted. *Am. Am pretty mad at him.*

Kurt said, "I'm sorry, Katie."

"Yup," I said, borrowing a play from his book.

Victor had been watching us like we were tennis players in a lengthy volley. His eyes glowed like Gabriel's had when he was helping us. We were much more exciting than the average fare, vacationers talking about food, alcohol, golf, sun and sex. Certainly not talking about Elena and Nick. Or had they?

"Kurt, did anyone else ask him about Elena's group, or about Nick? And can you make sure he knows what Nick looks like?"

Kurt showed Victor the picture of Nick and him with the airplane as he relayed my question. Victor replied in the negative and Kurt stated the obvious. "No one asked about them."

Horns blared behind us. Victor turned around and shook his open palm at the other drivers. I suspected the doorman had put them up to it.

What else should we ask Victor? My head swam with all the little knowns and unknowns floating through it. I fished for their relevance, but caught nothing.

Kurt tipped Victor an amount equal to a week's earnings and arranged for him to pick us up the next morning. To the doorman's relief, Victor finally pulled away.

We entered the hotel through yet another open-air entrance, this one into a vast lobby with massive ferns on each side of a central corridor and tongue-in-groove ceilings that reminded me of Annalise. Kurt stopped in the reception area amid a stream of golfers on their way toward the smoky bar.

My heart rate slowed down. Here, the tourists spoke English. I could read the signs directing us to the restaurants and the pool. Nick was missing, I was in the Dominican Republic, but I felt less foreign. I relaxed a little. And then Kurt said, "Katie, I don't want to scare you, but I think we need to be very careful."

OK, maybe not so relaxed anymore.

"What makes you say that?"

"This whole time, I've thought Nick had a simple plane wreck or was in a car crash. That he had amnesia or was unconscious. Or at worst, that he ran off somewhere."

"I—" I started to jump on him about his earlier comments, and then just stopped. I wasn't going to get into it with Kurt again.

"But now I'm concerned about foul play. And if someone went after Nick and we're here nosing around asking questions, well, we could end up in the same predicament. Hell, Katie, I'm convinced now that the man who called the airport today was looking for you."

Had someone killed my husband?

The familiar cadence of American English around me changed from a comforting hum to a distracting arrhythmia. Snatches of conversations assaulted my eardrums. I winced. Were there people here watching Kurt and me?

I let my brain process my thoughts, but it was my heart that spoke.

Nick told you he was all right.

And so he had. In my dreams, he'd told me to search until I found him. That was real enough for me. Maybe someone had hurt him, but I had to believe him, and to keep myself safe so I could find him.

"You're right," I said, my voice lower than before. "How about we change our rooms to a suite. And then we can eat and strategize."

"Yup. I will feel better if I'm there to protect you," he said.

Protect me? With what? Kurt had only his bare hands. Big hands, strong hands, but that was it. That flare gun he carried yesterday would have eased my terrors right now. Or the machete. But Annalise wasn't here to toss one into our hands. I didn't even have the pepper spray I kept in my car back on St. Marcos. The best idea I could come up with was stealing our steak knives at dinner, and if that was all we had, we might as well just carry ballpoint pens. We could use them to stab our attackers' eyes out. Or write, "Stop, you cad!" on a paper napkin and wave it at them.

"OK. How about I get us a table at one of the restaurants while you work on the rooms?" I asked.

"No, let's stick together."

I eyed the growing crowd.

Yes, I liked his idea better.

Chapter Fifteen

After a forty-five-minute wait at the bar, during which we worked out our strategy, we dined at La Yola, a restaurant shaped like a fishing boat. It was right on the water, with a glass floor to the sea life below. Somehow, the 360-degree view calmed me, even though I wasn't expecting the Chihuahuas' mafioso to come up at me through the floor. We didn't see anyone watching us, anyway.

The restaurant smelled like dead fish, which matched how I felt. Kurt ordered pork roast but visions of Wilbur revolted me. I opted for the penne pasta with fresh vegetables. When it arrived, the food looked decent enough, but everything tasted like sawdust. Kurt pushed his pork around on his plate. We stared at our food in uncomfortable silence.

After dinner we headed back to our new accommodations, which the hotel called a casita rather than a suite. Same difference. We had paid the exorbitant in-room wifi charge at check-in, and after I'd showered and changed I booted up my laptop at the small dining table and perched on a chair with a red velour seat. It matched the sofa upholstered in cream with giant red hibiscus. Red everywhere, like flags in front of the bull: me. I longed for a mellow blue and a soothing green.

While the startup sequence ran, I checked my phone. The old iPhone hadn't rung all day. No message indicators, either. Surely that couldn't be right . . . I pressed and held the home and start buttons for a reboot.

The two screens came to life almost simultaneously. I logged into email on the laptop like a fisherman pulling up a lobster trap. And I had a catch.

I spoke loud enough for Kurt to hear from the bathroom, where the sound of the shower had ceased a minute earlier. "Kurt, I have an email from A. Friend, and I should have the same message on my iPhone but don't. Apparently, my iPhone isn't transmitting data. It looks like it came in hours ago, about three o'clock."

Kurt walked in, freshly dressed, hair wet. "What does it say?"

"Mrs. Kovacs: Very sorry to hear about Nick. He didn't say where he was going. We assumed he was just going back to St. Marcos. A. Friend." I made an "arggggggggg" sound and thumped my forehead against the table. "Not very helpful, A. Friend."

"Well, it confirmed Nick was coming home," Kurt said as he walked back toward the bathroom.

"Not really. It was only a guess," I called after him. "I wish that A. Friend had said who they are and what's going on. And what package Nick delivered," I said, recalling the original message. I looked down at the iPhone, which now had message indicators for texts and email. Lost time again. *I'm sorry, Nick.*

I scrolled through the texts. There were none from any of the numbers Kurt had copied from Nick's phone for me. One from Julie caught my eye, though. "Your brother called. I told him what's going on. He said he'll land in Punta Cana tomorrow at 1:35 p.m."

Collin. My big brother by eleven months. Collin worked anti-drug operations with the New Mexico state police and was truly a badass, even if I was his proud little sister. He had always bossed me around some, but when our parents died two years before, he had taken on the father role to me in a way that made my throat tight.

I called his mobile and got his voicemail. "Collin, I hear you need a ride from the airport in Punta Cana tomorrow. Coincidentally, I will be at the airport just at that time. You didn't have to come, but I'm so glad you are. We are really scared. I love you."

I took in the casita. Hell, we had room for him here if we spent another night. One room held a queen bed and the other had two twins.

I walked over to see what progress Kurt had made while I was on the phone. He had positioned himself at the coffee table in the sitting area with a laminated map of the northwestern Caribbean spread out in front of him. Beside it were a pen and yellow pad for notes, and he held a big dry wax pen for marking the maps.

"What are you doing?" I asked.

"I'm going to plot search areas," he said.

"Won't the Coast Guard do that?"

"I don't trust them. I trust myself."

"Oh. How do you know where to look? He could be anywhere between here and St. Marcos, couldn't he?" Hopefully between here and St. Marcos.

"Yes, but I'm going to start broad tonight. I'll familiarize myself with the direction the water moves and the bodies of land in the area. Tomorrow I'll look for more information to pinpoint the search area."

I trusted him, come to think of it, much more than he trusted the Coast Guard.

I needed his help. He needed mine. We didn't need friction between us.

"Kurt, I'm sorry I got mad at you earlier. I have to be able to handle the truth, and you didn't say anything I wasn't already worried about."

He grunted. "It was stupid of me to say any of it. I know my son loves you and the kids. Every man gets a little antsy now and then, especially with a house full of babies. Doesn't mean anything."

I wondered if he was right. Well, I couldn't dwell on it now. Onward.

"My brother is coming," I told him. "I just got the message from Julie."

Kurt had met my brother several times and they got along well.

"Good. He's just the right person to have with us," Kurt said.

"I think so, too. Hey, I'm going to see if I can get Julie and the kids on Skype. I'll let you know when it's time to say hello, if you'd like."

"Yup," he said, and he dropped his attention back to his maps.

Notwithstanding hurting my feelings earlier—a lot—Kurt was the right person to have, too. His maritime expertise and aeronautical knowledge were godsends. Kurt had pursued an airplane pilot license almost as a joke. "Everybody thinks I fly a plane when I tell them I'm a pilot, so I might as well." He had twenty-five years of experience in the air to go with his thirty-five on the water.

Nick had first soloed and earned his pilot's license while he was still in high school, but he had quit flying until his father moved to St. Marcos. He had earned his instrument rating just a month ago, which allowed him to fly in bad weather and poor visibility by relying just on his instruments. Really, though, while he was a naturally gifted pilot whose instructor said had a feel for the air, he hadn't logged many more cockpit hours above the requirements. Maybe not enough hours.

But he had visited me in my dreams and told me he was all right.

Have faith, Katie, you have to have more faith.

I texted Julie for twenty minutes to no avail, trying to get her to join me via video on Skype. Finally, I gave up and just sent her an email update and a message to read to Taylor. I missed my three little munchkins. What I wouldn't give to curl up with my warm husband and warm babies around me right now.

I ran back through the rest of my texts and emails quickly. Rashidi reported that he and his searchers had turned up nothing. I let him know that Nick had shown up in and left Punta Cana, presumably back to St. Marcos. I hesitated to suggest he call off the search, but I wanted him to know the likelihood of finding Nick on St. Marcos had decreased. Theoretically, it was possible that he had made it back and someone else had taken the plane after his return. Possible, yet unlikely.

Ava had sent me an update on their graveyard sleuthing. My God, I'd forgotten about the Annalise problems. Rashidi had put her in charge and she was working with the friends he'd told me about, Rob the curator and Laura the librarian. No breakthroughs yet.

The rest were messages of support from well-wishers. I pulled out the spiral notebook and updated my lists, then put my head down on my forearm and closed my eyes. I would answer the messages later, much later, when I could tell everyone our worries were over, and that Nick had returned home with me.

A little while later, I pried my eyelids open and lifted my cheek off the puddle of drool on my arm. "Kurt, I'm going to try to sleep," I said.

"Yup," he responded. "Think I'll do the same. 'Night."

Kurt walked to the couch and starting pushing it across the room.

"What are you doing?" I asked.

"If bad guys show up, I'd like to have some advance warning."

I pitched in and we made a barrier of sofa, chairs, and end tables against the door.

I went through the motions of getting ready for bed. Then I did something I hadn't done in so long I couldn't remember the last time. I knelt beside the bed with my hands clasped as my parents had taught me to pray.

"Dear God, please keep Nick safe. Please help us find him as fast as possible. I know I don't tell you often enough, but I am so grateful for my husband and kids and all of our blessings. I can't promise I'll always do better, but I can promise I am appreciative. Amen. Oh—and please, when this is all over, please help my husband understand that he has to be more careful, truthful, and communicative."

Before I got in bed, I created a booby trap against my bedroom door with the desk, lamp, and chair. Much better.

I was almost afraid to close my eyes. Nearly every time I'd fallen asleep since he had disappeared, Nick had visited my dreams. I longed to see him, and I feared waking up if I didn't. Somewhere along the way, the decision was taken from me, and I lost myself to slumber. But the dream that came was very different, and yet wholly familiar.

After I met Nick but before we got together, I dreamed about him a lot. The result? Sexy, realistic nighttime experiences that I called spontaneous combustion. Teenage boys call them wet dreams. I awoke flushed, sweating, and moaning. *God, don't let Kurt hear me.* As fantastic as I felt, it was short-lived. I woke up remembering that Nick was missing.

My body was torturing my heart, and they both cried out for Nick.

Chapter Sixteen

My phone alarm rang at 6:30 a.m. I listened for the sound of my father-in-law stirring, but it was quiet. I pushed snooze and fell back asleep.

"I didn't want to interrupt you last night, honey, because you seemed like you were having a good time, but I need to talk to you. Can you wake up for me?" It was Nick, sitting at the foot of my bed in my suite at the Puntacana Resort.

"I'm up, I'm up, I'm up," I said. I reached for him, but he was too far away to touch.

"I can talk to Annalise from here," he said.

"Talk in words, like real talk?"

"Yes. I'll tell you all about it when you find me. But you need to hurry, Katie. And you can't rely on anyone else. My little Wild Irish Kate."

The phone alarm rang again and I sat up, the dream so fresh I could still taste the words in my mouth. I remembered what he said, but I had no idea what he meant. Between Annalise and Nick, it would help if I could get one straightforward message. Here I was again, confounded and panicked. And very, very sad.

One hour later, Victor met us outside the hotel, and ten minutes after that he deposited us at the entrance to Terminal Three. We bid him adios as he went off to park and await our call. I smoothed my green-checked capri pants down and tucked in my white sleeveless blouse again. My pants felt looser today; nothing like a stress and terror diet. I adjusted my straw-brimmed hat, which I'd purchased for an exorbitant sum straight out of the hands of a woman in the hotel lobby that morning and tucked every last strand of my red hair into.

Today, as part of our safety strategy, Kurt and I intended to blend in, just in case someone was looking for me. Or us. His version of blending was donning a fisherman's cap, an untucked tropical shirt over baggy Tommy Bahama khaki shorts, and a pair of new deck shoes. Atrocious white tube socks with three red stripes around the tops were my touch. In a normal environment we would have attracted attention, but in this crowd, our outfits camouflaged us perfectly.

We had arranged yesterday to meet Gabriel at eight a.m. We walked at tortoise-like tourist speed to Gabriel's office, but it was locked up tight. He might be helpful and friendly, but he was still a native of the islands, and lived and worked on island time.

"Dammit!" I said.

"I could use a coffee. Want one?" Kurt asked me.

"No, I want to wait here for Gabriel."

He scanned the terminal. "We really need to stay together. Just because we don't see anyone that looks scary doesn't mean you aren't at risk."

He was probably right, and my tight capris weren't really suited to high karate kicks if self-defense became necessary. After one more look around the terminal for the tardy Mr. Marrero, I walked with Kurt to the cafeteria and we picked up heavenly-smelling Arabica coffees. The young man we'd spoken to the day before waved to us discreetly from where he was clearing a table in the dining area. I waved back. Kurt didn't notice him and walked to a nearby newsstand. So much for staying together.

The young man looked around, right and left, left and right, then darted over to me. He wore dark sunglasses and a circa-1990 walkman that had round ear-sized headphones with spongy covers. I expected to hear Dominican music blaring from them, but instead I caught a snatch of "Hotel California" before he turned it off. I hoped it wasn't prophetic.

"Hey lady, your husband, the man who eat here?" he asked me in English so guttural I would almost have understood his Spanish better.

"Yes, what about him?" I asked.

"Tú hablas español?" He asked me if I spoke Spanish.

"Un poco," I said.

"OK, I tell you. Your husband, he no talk, but the other man did."

"What other man?"

"The man that walk behind him and his amigos?" he said in the form of a question, begging me to understand.

Walk behind? I formed a mental image of men walking behind Nick. Aha! "Men following him?"

He looked relieved that I understood. "Sí. A man following your husband. I see him and he watching them in the gift shop. Like on TV." He leaned toward me and said, "I want to be a detective, like Magnum, P.I." Vintage American TV was a staple on Caribbean stations. I didn't comment, so he went on. "Then he follow them here and talk on his phone." He frowned. "Same man following me last night. I no tell you about them, so I happy to see you today."

"Why did he follow you?" Fear tingled its way up my arms from my fingers, all the way to my face, where it settled in my lips, leaving them numb.

"He ask if I know who he is. I say no. I not stupid." He smiled with the confidence of youth. "He ask if I tell the Americanos about him. I say, 'Tell who? Tell what?' He say good, but if I do, he kill me. He and his partner beat me up so I know he's true." He thumped his chest primally and took off his sunglasses to show me his two black eyes.

Shit! What if those men were watching us now? We had to finish this conversation, fast. This kid was doing exactly what the men had warned him not to do—talking to me. I could not let myself worry about what might happen to this boy later. Or at least, I would try not to.

I kept my English simple. "When he was here in the cafeteria, did you hear him say anything?" I tried it in Spanish for good measure, hoping I said it right. "Él habla?"

"Sí. He talk on the phone, in English, but like from the islands. He tell his boss man that the plane no fly to Mexico now, and he back very soon. He laugh. Ha ha."

Everything in the terminal moved in slow motion as I considered this. If he was right, the man had followed Nick and his passengers, and he had told his boss that Nick, Elena, the man, and her mother would not fly to Mexico, and laughed. It sounded like the man thought the group was going to try to go to Mexico.

"Did he say why Nick could not fly to Mexico?"

"He say, 'Sylis fix the plane. We careful. No one see us.'"

Sylis? Did Sylis and this man cause Nick not to make it home—or know why he hadn't made it? I yelled for my father-in-law. I needed Spanish-speaking reinforcement, fast. "Kurt, can you come over here?"

Kurt put up the newspaper and made his way over.

But at about that same time, the cafeteria manager realized his employee was not working. Personally, I didn't think that was such a big deal in the islands, but el jefe came after the busboy with a rag, flicking it at his thighs and shouting, "Trabaja ahora. Ahora!" You get to work, NOW.

The young man raised his palms, shook his head back and forth and mouthed, "I'm sorry," in Spanish.

"What did the man look like?" I yelled.

"Negro," he mouthed, disappearing into the cafeteria's back room.

I felt my knees buckle.

"What's up?" Kurt asked as he stepped forward just in time to catch me.

I held on to him and rallied as best I could. I almost couldn't get the words out between my panicked gasps. "The busboy from yesterday that saw Elena and Nick? Well, he told me just now that a man followed them to the cafeteria and told some 'boss man' that a guy named Sylis fixed Nick's plane so it wouldn't make it to Mexico."

"Did he describe him? Or say how they fixed the plane?"

"Negro—which means black, right?—is all he said. He didn't say how they fixed the plane, and I'm not sure how much more he knew. Kurt, he had two black eyes—the guy found him last night and told him he would kill him if he talked to us. The man already knew he talked to us yesterday!"

Kurt stroked his thumb across his lips over and over. I hoped he was thinking and not having an aneurysm, like I seemed to be. "We need to talk to that kid some more, Katie."

"Yes, we do," I said. Movement near Gabriel's office caught my eye. "Look, there's Gabriel, finally." I pointed far across the terminal floor. "We'll have to come back to the kid later. We need to get on the phone with the FAA, ASAP."

Kurt nodded. We tried to tourist-walk again, but I found it really hard to walk like a turtle when my heart was racing like a rabbit. We rushed into Gabriel's office just seconds behind him. Gabriel smiled when he saw us, the kind of smile that covers your whole face. His white teeth gleamed against his dark skin and hair. Apparently, he had forgiven or forgotten my outburst yesterday.

"Kovacs, please come in. I trust your evening was a pleasant one? May I get you an espresso?" Gabriel put down his briefcase and turned on a small espresso machine, betraying absolutely no sense of urgency. I wanted to scream.

"No, thank you," Kurt and I said at exactly the same time.

I continued. "We are fine, but we have learned several new things that we think will be helpful. We really need to get in touch with the FAA for a status report immediately. And with the Coast Guard so we can stay abreast of their search."

"Please, tell me your news so we can make the phone call," Gabriel said. He pressed brew on his machine and turned toward us.

I gave him the short version of the information gleaned from Victor and the busboy, omitting the black eyes and death threats.

"Your news about the men following Mr. Kovacs is interesting. Very, very interesting." Gabriel dialed his phone and said, "I will talk to the FAA. I have some ideas about—" Gabriel changed paths mid-sentence. "Oh, hello, yes, this is Gabriel Marrero, Punta Cana International Airport, manager of Terminal Three. I am with the family who has reported its plane missing, registration number RJ7041." He put his hand over the mouthpiece as if to speak to us, then put it back and said, "So the Coast Guard is searching the waters off the west side of St. Marcos? Do you have a contact name for me with the Coast Guard, and a phone number?" He spoke perfectly clear English with a thick Dominican accent. "I understand they know how to reach us, but we would like to make contact with them ourselves." He scribbled something on a sticky note and hung up the phone.

"Well?" I asked.

"They said the Coast Guard is searching near St. Marcos this morning and will work their way towards Puerto Rico. But they were quite reluctant to give me a name and number for the Coast Guard, other than their central number for Puerto Rico. They finally gave me a number for the operations desk." He dialed again. "So we will give it a shot, no? Hello?" He repeated his introduction and requested to speak to someone with an update. "I appreciate that someone will call us if they find him. But we would like to be able to share information, if and when we come across it, directly with the Coast Guard searchers. I see. Well, we will call this number then. Can I confirm you have the right contact information to reach us? Thank you."

He hung up the phone, glowering this time. "Not helpful at all. Don't call us, we'll call you."

Kurt said, "I have a good contact, very high up, within the Coast Guard. If we need to use him later, we can. For now, I don't know where else to tell them to search. I assume they will make their way east along the flight path from San Juan to St. Marcos, taking into account elapsed time, weather conditions, and the movement of the water."

"One would assume," Gabriel said. "Hopefully we will hear from them soon. While we wait, I had a thought that maybe you would like to talk to some of our employees who work in the area where your plane was tied down while Nick was here? Maybe someone saw one of these two men that the busboy saw, down near Nick's plane?"

I realized I had gripped a handful of capris in each hand while Gabriel was on the phone. I let go now and exhaled through my mouth. I willed all the tiny muscles in my face to relax. I rolled my neck and it made several popping sounds. I heard Nick's voice again: "Don't rely on anyone else."

Kurt said, "Yup. We would."

I added, "Thank you for letting us talk to them directly, Gabriel. Sounds like a great idea. Let's get moving, the faster the better. We have to find Nick."

The men stared at me. Only for a few seconds, but long enough to let me know that my optimism about finding Nick alive was mine alone.

"Let's go, gentlemen." I led the way.

Chapter Seventeen

The smell of jet fuel polluted the air outside the terminal. We weaved in and out of doorways, across the tarmac, and finally into the open bay of a cavernous hangar. I couldn't hear a word Gabriel said over the planes' engines as we walked, but I got the impression he was narrating our tour. He pointed to a door in the deep end of the hangar that turned out to open onto a small windowless office. Metal desktop, too many chairs, utilitarian. No less stinky, but quieter.

"I bring people to talk to you now, no?" Gabriel asked.

I thought carefully through all I had learned from watching Nick conduct investigations. "How do we know whether these people worked the right day and shift to cross paths with Nick or the plane? And how do we talk to the ones who were on shift then, but aren't now?"

Kurt nodded and I felt a shiver of pride. Gabriel raised an index finger and tapped the length of it against his nose. "I can compare schedules for you. We will call anyone we need to talk to who's not working today."

"Good. We're ready as soon as you can round the first person up," I said.

"One more thing," Gabriel said. "I need to be present for these interviews. Since I'm arranging them, and these are our employees, well, I am sure you understand."

I understand they won't want to talk in front of the terminal manager.

I would have done the same thing as an employment lawyer in my old life, but I still didn't like it. "If you must, but speed is critical," I said. "As is obtaining accurate information, and all of it. My husband's life is at stake."

"Good. I'll ask Nancy to help with the schedules," Gabriel said. "She can start calling people in immediately." He left the office.

"Have them bring any records or logs of their work so we can check for our registration number," I called after him.

He turned and flashed me an OK sign.

For the next twenty minutes, Kurt and I talked out our theories and planned our questions, which I jotted in the notebook. Then the employees began to arrive. The three of us—Gabriel, Kurt, and I—talked to every employee that Gabriel and his assistant thought had possible access to the planes tied down around Terminal Three. Kurt took the lead with the Spanish speakers and I led for those that spoke English. For the next two hours we spoke to mechanics, men that drove the gas truck, shuttle drivers, baggage handlers, and skycaps, with barely a minute of downtime between subjects. Sometimes they stood in a line outside the door. None had seen any black island men lurking about. No one had seen anything out of the ordinary.

A few did remember our plane—the fuel truck operator remembered filling it up, and showed us our registration number and some Spanish script I couldn't decipher in his log book—but none of them had seen anyone working on it. No one knew how many people had boarded it for departure or where it went.

Meanwhile, our phones remained stubbornly silent with no word from the Coast Guard or FAA. My iPhone notifications remained at zero, which really bothered me. I hoped my messages could get through. Nothing was going our way.

My frustration level crept up as I poked at my phone between interviews. I looked up and saw a woman walk by pushing a cart laden with a large trashcan, a mop, dustpan, and broom.

"What about her?" I asked Gabriel.

"The janitor? She doesn't work on the planes," he said.

"So? Does she have access to the hangar?" I asked.

"Yes," he admitted.

"Well, anyone could have seen something. It doesn't hurt to talk to her."

He shrugged. "As you wish."

Gabriel disappeared for five minutes and returned with the woman. She was middle-aged and thick through the waist, which gave her short body a squarish shape. She did not look up or greet us when she came in.

Gabriel bade her sit down. The language switched over to Spanish, so Kurt handled the questions. I was surprised by how much more I understood today than I had the day before. The accent confused my ear less, and the meanings of words in context were more evident to me. I'd be fluent by tomorrow at this rate. My high school Spanish teacher would be proud.

Kurt learned that the janitor had worked from eight a.m. to five p.m. three days before and lunched at one o'clock, right after Nick took off. She worked alone during the day shifts to keep the hangar tidy; the custodians reserved deep cleaning for the nighttime, when they could work without disrupting business.

In Spanish, Kurt asked, "So you pick up trash, clean spills, empty garbage? What else?"

She agreed and added that she kept bathrooms stocked and clean.

Kurt nodded. Gabriel and I took notes.

Next, Kurt described our plane and Nick. Had she seen them? She said yes, she had seen the plane, but not Nick. She liked the little plane with the blue stripes. She remembered the Stingray logo, a magnifying glass over a fish's dead eye.

I shifted forward in my seat. She was the first person to mention the logo. An observant woman.

Kurt noticed, too, and spoke with more energy. "So if you didn't see anyone that looked like Nick, did you see anyone else around the plane?"

She had. She saw the gas truck service it. This jived with the account from the truck driver. But before that, she'd seen another man working on it, one she didn't recognize. He was a black man, and he had on the coveralls all the other workers wore, so she guessed he was new.

All the mechanics had sworn they had not touched the plane. Their manager had brought the service log for that day, and no one had recorded any work on RJ7041.

Gabriel broke in, his voice higher than before. "Are you sure? A man wearing our coveralls serviced the plane? In what way?"

She would not look at Gabriel, and her voice shook. Surprisingly, she started to speak some English. "Sí. He pour something in the tanks."

Now she had us all quivering. Gabriel continued to take the lead, but switched to English, too. I bit my lip to keep from interrupting him. "Could you see what it was? Could you see the containers?"

"No. I was too far away." She dropped her face. "Lo siento."

Collective deflation.

So close. I sighed heavily. "It's OK," I said. "You've done well. Bueno. Did you see anything else? Anything not normal, anything different, strange?"

"I found something in the trash later, señora," she said, speaking directly to me for the first time. "Maybe important, maybe not, but a little strange," she added.

Just like that, we all quickened again. "Yes?" I urged her.

"Maybe is nothing. But empty rum bottles in the trash. Many big bottles. Cruzan Rum."

Deflation again. We knew most of the charter jets offered bar service. Gabriel explained to us now, "The passengers of many of these private jets like to party on their way to vacation. That's why we have a contractor with a crew to clean out the planes. Sometimes they are quite filthy. Vomit. Drugs, even. Disgusting, really."

Apparently the woman spoke English pretty well, because she shook her head no and spoke to me again. "Not like that. Sometimes party planes come. None come that day. I see the trash, and I know what they throw away. This trash?" She switched back to Spanish. "No mixers, no paper napkins, no olives, no toothpicks. This was different." Her voice didn't waver now.

Kurt rattled off a quick translation for me. Then he shuffled and straightened his papers. He gathered his pens. He cleared his throat. He gave all the signs of a man ending an interview.

I was confused. Why was he disengaging? Was her information significant or not? Kurt showed nothing on his stern face, another feature he shared with Nick, whose outward demeanor reminded some people of Heathcliff from *Wuthering Heights*. I knew he and his father had playful streaks and warm hearts. But you wouldn't know it from looking at them, and you sure didn't want to play poker against them. Kurt had his poker face in place now.

Abruptly, Kurt stood up, bowed slightly at the waist, shook the woman's hand and thanked her. Gabriel excused her. She scurried out, but cast me a backward glance and a decisive nod.

How very, very strange all around.

"Anyone else?" I asked Gabriel.

He called in his young assistant, whose long dark curls I immediately envied. "Nancy, any others?"

"No, sir, you have talked to everyone who worked that shift," she said.

"The janitor wasn't on the list, though. Anyone else like the janitor?" I said.

Nancy understood my question. "There are others that work inside the terminal, but if you add the custodian, you have talked to everyone who works outside and around the hangar and was on shift when your husband was here."

Kurt stood up. "Thank you both. This was great. Now, you must excuse us. Katie and I have a phone call. Gabriel, I am sure we will return this afternoon, but if you hear from the FAA or Coast Guard, please let us know, OK?"

"Of course, of course," Gabriel said.

Kurt's long legs ate up the floor in two strides before I had even gathered my things and stood up. "Katie?" he said, beckoning from the door.

"Yes, of course," I said, echoing Gabriel.

We followed Nancy and her pearls and long curly hair as she clicked her way back to the terminal. Kurt pushed through the door without a word and I called out, "Thanks!" over my shoulder as I hurried to keep up. What the hell? His sudden departure and wordy but false summary of our day were out of character.

My father-in-law had some explaining to do.

Chapter Eighteen

I loped after Kurt, who was all but sprinting to Victor's car. When had he called Victor?

"What's going on?" I asked him when we had buckled in.

"We need to get back to the laptops. I want to check on something. Too soon to say."

Like father, like son. "OK," I said. It wasn't OK, but I didn't have a choice. That much I knew from living with the Kovacs men.

My iPhone buzzed. Incoming text. I pulled it onscreen and read, "But Nick is missing. Prove you are Nick. Who did you meet in PC?"

Holy creepers! A message from one of the numbers Nick had texted. I typed as fast as I could, and then retyped it all because it was unintelligible garbage. "I would not betray that confidence over text." I hit send.

Thirty seconds later, the light flashed again.

"I think this is his wife, and that we've already communicated."

Yes, I do believe we have. "You are A. Friend," I typed. Send.

"Yes, I am."

"I need help," I sent.

"I cannot help you, but I wish you well."

"What is your name?" I asked.

I watched for the flashing red light, but none came.

We arrived at the Puntacana Resort. If Kurt had sprinted before, he broke a world record for the hundred-yard dash now. I had no prayer of keeping up. I struggled out of the car, pants sticking to thighs as usual, and negotiated a pickup time with Victor in my now-passable Spanish. We needed to pick up my brother at 1:35, so we agreed to leave for the airport at 1:15.

I hustled after Kurt, checking my message light again as I trotted. Nothing. I caught Kurt at the door to our casita and followed him in, out of breath. *Need more exercise.*

Kurt grabbed his laptop and got to work. I ordered us lunch from room service while my laptop booted up and my iPhone refused to give me any messages. I resent the message to A. Friend. I also texted Julie, who immediately answered and suggested a quick Skype while my kids were all strapped into high chairs for lunch.

In less than a minute, we were connected. Julie had positioned her laptop camera so my three beautiful children filled the screen. My heart stopped.

"Hi, guys, it's Mom," I said.

"Hi, Mommy!" Taylor replied. He looked adorable, even with smears of ketchup marring his perfect face. "Liv and Jess, say hi to Mommy." He turned and looked at his sisters. "They can't talk yet, Mommy, but they would say hi if they could."

I laughed. Julie's face appeared behind Taylor. "Hi, Julie. Kurt is here with me in body, but his mind is elsewhere. He's researching something online."

"No problem. I want all hands on deck to find Nick. Tell Kurt I love him," Julie said.

"I will."

"Bye, Mommy," Taylor said, and slithered out of his high chair. He had learned how to unbuckle his own strap recently, but he still liked to sit in the chair to compete with the twins at eye level for attention. Well, I'd had him for fifteen seconds. I couldn't expect much more from the little steam engine.

"Bye, sweetie pie," I said. A knock sounded. Room service. "Hold on, Julie, I have to grab our food."

I realized too late that I shouldn't be opening the door to strangers with two men looking for me. But I got lucky; it was only the porter. He swiped my Visa and I locked the door. I deposited Kurt's lunch in front of him. He hadn't registered the knock or my response to it, nor did he acknowledge the plate now.

I returned to my laptop and motioned for Julie to continue while I ate.

"We've had an interesting morning," she said. "I know you guys will need to hurry to the airport to get Collin, so I'll make this fast."

"We're doing good on time. What's up?"

"We had visitors today. Detective Tutein showed up with some of his minions and a representative from DPNR. Katie, they had a warrant for your arrest for disturbing human remains and failing to report their discovery."

I nearly choked on my fish taco. "That fast? Oh my God!"

"I know. They scared Ruth and me, although she chuptzed them. You would have loved that, at least. She's resting right now, or I'm sure she'd tell you this story herself."

"Go, Ruth."

"Yes, that's what I said. Sort of. And then there was the magnificent Annalise."

"What did she do?" I asked.

"You know that hive of bees on the library window upstairs, above the door to the kitchen? She dropped it. It nearly landed on them, too. They ran to their car screaming like little children."

I hooted. "That's my girl."

"Before then, though, when they were still hassling us, I told them you had left St. Marcos on a trip, and that I didn't know when you'd return. Tutein said to tell you he would be the first person you saw when you got off the plane. The DPNR rep then told me that he would come back with an injunction ordering us out of the house and requiring us to excavate the property at our expense."

"They're playing hardball." This ranked as a small problem compared to a lost husband, but it was still huge. And poor Annalise. What a violation this would be.

Julie rubbed the back of her neck with one hand. "Yes, they are. I asked him when, and he said soon. But I have no idea what that means."

"I guess it means if they come back, you guys may have to visit Aunt Ava. Well, we need a local attorney to help us fight this."

"Rashidi is helping me find one. He's on his way here to stay with us, anyway. His guys are still out searching the island, but they haven't turned anything up."

"Good, I'm glad he will stay with you. Thank you, Julie. I'm so sorry this is happening."

"Just find Nick."

"We're trying. I emailed you the developments last night."

"I got it. Sorry I didn't see your texts. I left you a voicemail. The girls were fussy and took all my attention."

At that moment, Kurt jumped to his feet and shook my water glass with his yell. "Damn right!"

"What is it?" I asked, turning to him.

"What is it?" Julie asked me.

Kurt scrubbed his hand through his gray hair, which was standing up like a platoon of soldiers at attention. His glazed eyes focused on the screen, and he dropped back onto the couch, saying, "I knew I had read something about what alcohol can do to an engine. And I found it."

"What's he talking about?" Julie asked. She had moved so close to the screen that her nose looked like the nose of our airplane, but without the blue paint.

I tied it together the best I could, considering that Kurt had cut me out of the pertinents until just now. "A janitor at the airport thinks she saw a man pour something into Nick's fuel tanks. She also found Cruzan Rum bottles in the trash. Kurt appears to have researched alcohol and engines."

"That could be important information, right?"

I nodded. I thought about the locals looking for Elena at the St. Marcos airport. The two black men that had roughed up the busboy for talking to us, the same two that said they had fixed Nick's plane. The ones that might be looking for me.

Kurt typed again, fast for him, but not so very fast. His thick fingers got in his way. He cursed under his breath. My heart swelled. *Thank you God for Kurt.*

"Well?" Julie asked.

"I think we've lost him to his research again. But he believes he found information on the effect of alcohol on engines. Stay tuned. This is our big find of the day, by the way. We interviewed every employee at the hangar. We didn't get zip from anyone else, including the FAA or Coast Guard. No word there, other than the search is starting nearest St. Marcos."

"How is the alcohol significant?"

"Well, if it went into Nick's gas tanks, it could be the reason he's not home now," I said. I saw the time. Shit, it was later than I thought. "Kurt, we have to leave," I said. "Julie, I love you guys."

"We love you both, too. Oh, and Katie, one last thing. Ava called right before lunch. She and her friends found something, a slave graveyard near Annalise. They're coming out this afternoon to search."

"That's excellent news, but it sounds like if they aren't blazingly fast, your government visitors will beat them out there. I hope not. All right, bye, Julie." I blew kisses to the girls, but they were more interested in their Cheerios than in me.

We ended the connection.

"Kurt, we have to go," I repeated.

"Huh? Go? OK," he said. He heaved a long sigh. "I think I'll leave this machine going to speed things up when we get home."

I wrapped Kurt's food in a napkin and placed it in his hand. His eyebrows went up and he grabbed it. "Thanks," he said. He wolfed it down as we made our way back through the hotel to the car. I fought down my impatience while he chewed. *Time to clue me in, Gramps.*

Finally—*finally*—Kurt swallowed his last mega-bite. I said, "What do you think's going on?"

"Dunno for sure, but if those bottles of rum were poured into Nick's tanks, they could shut down the engines. The alcohol would overheat the engine, and the sugar would caramelize on the pistons. If that's what happened, I need to find someone or something to tell me how long that would take."

He was acting like this was good news, but to me it just meant that Nick's plane had crashed, which was bad news. "But why is this important, Kurt? Why are you so excited about it?"

"Because if we know what happened to his plane in Punta Cana, we can zero in on where he went down. If he went down."

"And then we can find him!" I shouted.

"Yes. Then we can find him."

Chapter Nineteen

Now I was jazzed. Kurt and I rushed to the baggage claim area in the terminal we had flown into only yesterday. We had clues. I bounced up and down on my toes. *Hurry, Collin.* I texted him our whereabouts.

"Got it. ETA two minutes," he sent back.

"Why didn't you tell Gabriel about your rum theory? And why did you tell him we had a phone call when we didn't?"

Kurt rubbed his eyes. Red veins carved lines through them. "I'm suspicious of everyone now, Katie. Gabriel didn't identify the janitor as a witness, you did. She was ignoring him and talking straight to you. And if I hadn't realized the significance of the rum, he might have convinced you it was nothing."

"Do you think . . ." I couldn't get the rest of the words out. Gabriel's insipid questioning the day before, his cheerfulness, his lack of appreciation for the rapid passing of time all cycloned in my brain. Suspicious? Maybe. But I didn't think so. He hadn't set off my radar.

"No, he's probably fine. I'm sure I just got paranoid."

Before I could say anything more, I looked up and saw my brother. He walked toward us, wearing his threadbare Hooters t-shirt and his Levi's 501 button-fly jeans, all "Danger Zone" playing with Tom Cruise striding to his plane in *Top Gun.* That was Collin. I ran to him and threw my arms around his solid frame, bumping his big duffel bag out of the way to get to him.

"Thank you, Collin, thank you for coming," I said. My eyes started leaking.

"I got here as fast as I could, sis. I'm sorry, so so sorry. Let's go find Nick," my brother said without letting go. We measured only two inches' difference in height, but he outweighed me by a comforting fifty pounds of muscle. He released me and stuck his hand out to Kurt. They shook.

"Sir, sorry about your son. I hope I can be of some help," Collin said.

Kurt nodded. "Thank you. I'm glad to have you here."

Collin looked me up and down. "I don't mean to offend, sis, but that outfit looks like something Grandma would have worn on a cruise, God rest her soul."

"Bite me, Collin. This is my 'blend as a tourist' outfit. Kurt and I are a little worried that there are bad guys after us."

"What bad guys?" he asked, his cop's eyes pinning me to the spot in which I stood.

I spit out the details in rapid fire. "Quick version: we think Nick ran into trouble when he was investigating a death on St. Marcos for the Petro-Mex refinery. It looks like some men were following him here. And a man was overheard bragging that his partner fixed Nick's plane. At least one of them was black and talked like he was from the islands. Now Nick and his plane are gone. A man has been asking about me, too. Oh, and there's hints that these guys may be the hired hands for a Mexican cartel, maybe one called the Chihuahuas. Those bad guys."

Kurt jumped in. "Talked like he was from the islands? Where did that come from, Katie?"

Oh, shit. I hadn't told Kurt that part? My brain was fried. "I'm sorry, Kurt. From the busboy."

Collin was shaking his head back and forth. "Holy Mother of God, Katie Connell Kovacs. The Chihuahua cartel is serious bad guys. My first partner in Anti-Drug in New Mexico was killed by them. A really nice guy, with a wife and an infant daughter. How in the world are they related to this?"

"Collin, hold that thought. I promise we'll get right back to that question. Did you check a bag?" I asked.

"Nope. I'm traveling lean. Flexibility is the key to air power," he said.

"What?" I asked.

"Just something my lady friend says. She's an Army reservist. H-60 Black Hawk helos," he said.

This was astonishing, to say the least. Collin with a lady friend? In the Army? A Black Hawk pilot? I didn't know they let women fly attack helicopters, or that many wanted to. Except for Meg Ryan in *Courage Under Fire*, but that was the movies. And why would a tough woman date my outwardly chauvinistic brother? No fool am I, though. I kept my mouth shut about this last question.

Collin's announcement didn't faze Kurt, but then again, not much did.

I said, "We have a question for an experienced pilot. Maybe she could help us?"

"Lay it on me, and I'll call her," Collin said.

"Who's her?" I asked.

"Tamara," he said. He chucked me on the chin with his fist. "I think you'll meet this one, sis."

I couldn't remember if I had ever met one of Collin's girlfriends. Curiouser and curiouser, as they say.

We were still standing in the bustling baggage claim area. I herded us over to some empty seats by a bank of what used to be pay phones, only the phones had been ripped out of the booths. Much quieter. We sat down and Kurt explained the rum and engines to Collin, who hit speed dial as Kurt spilled the last of his theory.

We hung on every word as Collin spoke into his phone. "Babe, I made it to the DR, and I need a favor, ASAP." Pause. "I love you, too. OK, I'm going to feed you facts, then ask you a question about them. Ready? Piper Malibu flying westward from Punta Cana, DR, to St. Marcos, U.S.V.I., three days ago at one o'clock p.m. Suspected intrusion of several bottles of rum into fuel tanks prior to takeoff. Don't know speed traveling or altitude, but can you make a guess?" Pause. "Good. We want to know what happened to the plane. Physically, what would the rum do, and geographically, if it went down, can you give us a compass point?" Pause. Longer this time. "When could you have the info?" Pause. "You're the best. I love you. Bye."

Collin snapped his phone shut. "No problem. One hour. She'll call me. Now, what do we do in the meantime?"

I grabbed his hand. "Really? That easy?"

He squeezed my hand and lifted it to his breastbone. "That easy. She has specialized knowledge, and we're lucky today. And we're going to stay lucky. I feel it."

My heart lifted. More hope. "Well, we have several things left to do here. I'd like to talk to that busboy, and we should circle back with Gabriel."

Kurt said, "Yup, I agree."

My iPhone buzzed. I held my hand up in the stop gesture while I read the message from A. Friend: "Nick would understand. We are in jeopardy. Please do not contact us again. Best of luck to you."

Whoa. Not the helpful kind of friend.

I showed the screen to Kurt, who raised his eyebrows and shrugged. He had no words. For once, I had no words either.

Kurt called for Victor and I filled Collin in on the mysterious A. Friend as we made our way out of the commercial terminal. Victor ferried us back to Terminal Three, which now felt like a second home to me, if I had died and gone to hell. When we found Nick, I did not ever want to come back here, even if it was a gorgeous and inexpensive place to visit. To get back inside, we pushed our way through a sizable crowd gathered around an ambulance, the biggest crowd I'd seen at the private terminal yet.

The lunch rush had ended at the cafeteria, and only a few people were sitting in the dining area. When I asked the girl behind the cash register for the manager, she told me in a trembling voice that the manager was unavailable. I asked for our busboy friend. At this, she started to sob.

"He left, he gone. He not coming back," she sobbed.

"Where did he go?" I asked.

"He walk out—" sob, "he walk out—" She pointed at the ambulance at the curb. "And he just fall down, and he dead. He dead," she repeated, and then started crying too hard to speak any more.

Collin whirled around and loped out to the rubbernecking crowd. I stood in cement shoes and lost sight of him. Collin spoke Spanish like a native-born Mexican. He said it was a job necessity, working anti-drug in New Mexico. While it was not quite the same as Dominican Spanish, he would have no problems communicating here. Starting now.

Kurt spoke to the girl, his voice gentle.

She choked out, "Gracias, señor," and ran to the swinging door that led to the kitchen.

Kurt put his arm around me. My shoulders were rigid. He pulled me to him anyway. I concentrated on drawing air in and out of the tiny space left in my lungs under the tremendous lead weight on my chest.

After what seemed like hours, Collin returned. "She had the dead part right. Someone shivved him. With a screwdriver. Poor kid."

Kurt patted my arm with the hand he had around me. I'd talked to the boy. He was murdered because he talked to me.

Collin asked, "Any chance this is a heartbreaking coincidence, people?"

I couldn't answer.

"None," Kurt said.

"We've got to get moving, then. We don't want to be next. Anything else we need to do before we bolt?"

They both turned to me, deferred to me. "No," I managed to force out.

Kurt elaborated. "We were going to talk to the terminal manager, a man that has helped us. But we have what we need. Let's go."

Kurt pulled me along. I was falling down with each step but never hit the floor. The struggle to stay upright and keep walking brought me back to some sense of equilibrium.

So, again, we made the short trip from the airport to the hotel, and the long walk from the lobby to our casita, this time with me in quasi-zombie mode. As we walked, Collin asked us more about the possible link to the Chihuahua cartel. I forced the words out to explain their connection to Petro-Mex, and the clues that kept emerging about some mafioso-type involvement.

"I've read about the Chihuahuas' feud with Petro-Mex, and I deal with them and other cartels every day. I just never imagined they would reach out this far. If you are Ramón Riojas and run the Chihuahuas, this makes sense, though, if you think it through. You said that refinery is one of the biggest in the world and supplies gasoline straight to mainland U.S.?"

I nodded. Barely.

"If the cartel could interrupt the refinery's operations for even one day, it would raise U.S. gas prices. And the U.S. government would not exactly thank Petro-Mex for bringing their problems across the border."

I gulped for enough air to get out my next thought. "What I don't understand is if this is related to the Chihuahuas or some other cartel, why would they use two St. Marcos locals, and not two cartel thugs from Mexico?"

"Oh, they use local talent all the time. I wouldn't expect anything different," Collin answered. "How is this tied to Nick's investigation around the guy who died in your driveway, though?"

"We have no idea," I said.

We entered the casita and Kurt threw himself on the sofa in front of his laptop. I planted myself in front of mine at the table and Collin set down his bag and joined me.

"How can I help you, sis?"

My phone rang. Julie. I held up a finger and Collin nodded.

"Julie?"

Static. The call dropped. *Crap.* I dialed her number. No answer. I left a voicemail. Damn the phone service in the rainforest. Damn the cartel. Damn the guys who killed the busboy. I needed a hug. From Nick.

"That kid died because he talked to me, Collin."

He shook his head. "He died because of bad people doing bad things."

Collin's phone rang.

"Tamara! Yo, talk to me, gorgeous. Wait, I can barely hear you. Let me walk outside." He left the room and shut the door behind him.

My father-in-law was studying the laminated map on the table and the screen in front of him. I was the odd man out with nothing to do. Well, I needed to re-focus on mission-critical work and quit wallowing in this. A young man was dead, but my guilt wasn't going to bring him back.

I scrolled through my email. One from José Ramirez asking me to update him, letting me know they'd found no trace of Nick visiting the refinery before he disappeared, and asking if I'd listened to his voicemail. Later. I scrolled through Nick's email. Nothing from A. Friend. I checked my texts. Again, nothing. No voicemail, either.

Not normal. I hadn't logged one single voicemail since we'd arrived in Punta Cana, and I normally received three to four a day. Granted, Nick always left some of those messages, but I still got one or more from a caller other than Nick every day. And when I'd talked to her earlier, Julie had said she left me a voicemail, and now Ramirez had as well.

I called it, just to be sure. "You have five new messages and one saved message." *Mother Fuuu . . .* I hated the F word. I hated these missing voicemail even more. I hated everything about this situation, starting with a husband who had lied to me and ending with a dead busboy.

First message. Ava. Checking on me. Updating me on the slave graveyard research.

Second message. Julie. Sorry she missed the texts. Thanks for my email. She missed us. She was scared.

Third message. José Ramirez. "I reached Mrs. Monroe on her mobile number. She said that, yes, she has returned to Mexico, and does not plan to come back to St. Marcos. She said that her husband's suicide broke her heart, and she asked me to please consider her feelings and cease the investigation. I have very mixed feelings on this, Ms. Kovacs, but I have been instructed to tell Stingray to stop investigating on our behalf. Please send me your billing up until this time. I suspect I would also be told not to give you Mrs. Monroe's number, so I did not ask permission." He spoke the digits into the phone.

Jesus. Why had the voicemail notification not worked? I scratched the number down on a yellow pad on the coffee table and pulled up the texts on my phone as I continued to listen to my messages. Sure enough, Elena's number matched one that had texted Nick, one I had texted myself, but from which I had gotten no response.

Fourth message. Emily, my best friend from my old life in Dallas. "Katie, I just heard about Nick. I am praying for you guys. I love you."

Fifth message. Detective Tutein. "You think you can get out of trouble by running away and leaving your mother-in-law to take your heat? The judge is gonna rule within a week on the injunction evicting your family from your house. I know the judge well. His wife is the sister of my sister's husband. Any cooperation with me goes a long way in his court. I am a reasonable man, and I think I see ways for you to make all your troubles go away before then. Nice family, by the way. I especially like those kids of yours. I look forward to seeing you soon, lovely Katie."

Bile rose in my throat and my stomach threatened upheaval. *That bastard.* How brazen was a cop that left a voicemail like that, knowing he would get away with it? He wasn't going to, not if I could help it, but right now my one and only worry had to be finding Nick. I should be getting help from local law enforcement, and instead, I got this. It sounded an awful lot like a threat against my children, and here I was, stuck in the Dominican Republic.

And Nick. I couldn't stop to think about Nick, what shape he might be in now, whether he was even alive.

He told you he was all right. You just have to hurry.

Funny, he was communicating more clearly with me now than he had before he disappeared, which would really make me mad if I let myself think about it.

Collin burst in. "Hold the press, team. I've got information."

This got Kurt's attention.

"Here's what Tamara and her buddies came up with. You probably already know or you wouldn't have asked for this information, but rum is a double whammy on a piston-driven engine. The alcohol overheats the cylinders, and the sugar caramelizes on the pistons. The question is how much rum, and how long would the plane fly before the engine shut down, given the varying amounts of rum possible."

I broke in. "The witness said there were several of the big Cruzan bottles."

"That's what Tamara thought. She said if someone knew enough to use the rum, surely they'd know the right amount, which would be about a gallon in each tank, call it four liters per tank."

"Makes sense," I said. "Our witness said the bottles filled a trash bin. Can you imagine someone standing there, pouring eight liters into the tanks? He must have had a hand trolley or cart of some kind. Not that it matters. Keep going."

"Yeah, the asshole had some balls. So, assuming he had time to get three or four liters per tank poured in, and assuming Nick set his air speed at a hundred and sixty knots, he could probably make it thirty to thirty-five miles before he lost the engines. Tamara and her buddies expect he'd be at an altitude of 8,500 feet when it happened."

His words pierced my heart. I knew Nick had to have crashed, I had known it in my core for days, and I knew the current goal was to find his crash site. But hearing this made it real and more painful. My hands started shaking and I clasped them together. So much. So much all at once.

Collin kept going. "So let's assume a couple of positive things. First, that Nick keeps his ditch kit in the co-pilot seat, like any good pilot would do over water. So he's going to have an inflatable life raft and a survival kit."

"Yes, he does," I said. "He always does. When I fly with him, we put it between my feet. He never flies without it."

"Excellent. Next, we're going to assume he coasts to a picture perfect dead-stick landing on the water. Here's another positive: Piper Malibus have retractable landing gear. Nick will have the landing gear up, so when he hits the water, the plane should stay upright. And he's got a minute, up to three, to ditch. That's no problem whatsoever for a guy like him. He gets out with his ditch kit, pops the inflatable on the raft, hops in, and paddles away before the plane sinks. I can see it happening. And last but not least in the good news department, the seas were calm at one to three feet forty-eight hours ago."

This was encouraging. I could see it, too. This is how it would have gone down. Tamara was an expert. And Nick had told me he was fine. But what if he hit his head on the dash when the plane hit the water? It could have knocked him out. Or what if we were wrong and there was no rum in the plane? What if he had a stroke or a heart attack and just crashed the plane? What if the bad guys had planted a bomb, and it went off?

STOP IT.

I had held off an anxiety attack so far. I had to stay positive. Nick was counting on me.

"OK," I said, and both men looked at me like I had pierced their eardrums. I ratcheted back. "Show me on the map. Where is he?"

Kurt pulled his map around for Collin and me to see and took out his wax pen and a ruler. He positioned the pen on Punta Cana and drew a straight line from there to St. Marcos along the ruler. Then he measured the distance against the scale on the map. He drew an X at the thirty-mile mark. He drew another X at the thirty-five-mile mark. Then he took out his compass, slipped the wax pen into it, and set it to draw a circle around the center point between the two X's with a ten-mile radius.

"Some people would be more precise, but this is the quick and dirty," he said. "Let's say he landed somewhere in here."

"That's almost exactly where Tamara said to look," Collin said. "Which way does the sea move out there?"

Kurt tapped his pen on an area to the east of the center point of his circle. "Primarily westward. Although this passage here—the Mona passage between Puerto Rico and the Dominican Republic—is a tough one. Lots of variation in current, lots of sand bars. But it moves mostly to the west."

We studied the map together.

"How long could he stay afloat, just drifting?" I asked.

"Indefinitely," Kurt said. "But he only has enough water in the survival kit for a few days. After that, he needs rain."

I looked out the window. Nothing but blue skies out there.

Kurt saw my glance. "Don't forget, though, Katie, there are squalls nearly every afternoon. He's getting some water."

Collin spoke. "Look here, guys. I know the water is moving to the west, but look at these islands. One of them is pretty big and it's close to our projected splash zone. What do you know about Mona and Monito?"

Mona Lisa, I thought.

Now why had those words come into my head? Mona Lisa? I had never heard of those islands.

Kurt said, "I dunno. Guess we could get online and find out." He started typing his keys.

Thoughts ricocheted around my head. *Rubber raft. Tackle box with a picture of Mona Lisa. My Wild Irish Kate.*

What was I supposed to be seeing?

The opening beats of "Eye of the Tiger" thumped in my head in time to my heartbeat, and I knew.

Holy shit.

Nick had been telling me this all along. He had tried to tell me, and I didn't get it, but now it was clear, so clear that it was undeniable. But how could I explain it to Kurt and Collin—this insanity, these dreams, these messages from Nick to me?

"I'm not crazy," I blurted out.

So they both looked at me like I was.

"I'm not crazy," I repeated. "I've had these dreams, since Nick disappeared. They didn't make sense. But I need to tell you about them. Because now they do. I know where he is, and we need to charter a boat and go get him."

Chapter Twenty

I babbled incoherently about the dreams, *Mona Lisa*, the raft, *Wild Irish Kate*, about how Nick had told me he was fine, not to give up, but to hurry because he was counting on me to come for him—me and only me—and not to rely on anyone else. When I was finished, my eyes dropped from theirs and I sat without breathing.

Please believe me.

Silence.

Then Kurt spoke in his matter-of-fact way, as if I had presented them with a spreadsheet of scientific formulas leading us to this conclusion, instead of the nonsense I had just spewed. "Can we get to Mona from here?"

He and Collin trained their eyes on the map.

"It looks like it's about halfway," Collin said. "We can't get there from here tonight by boat. We'd have to leave in daylight. So, I guess the question is how do we get there the fastest: boat, plane, or some combination?"

I huffed a breath out. I swallowed. They didn't think I was crazy.

Kurt said, "It has to be faster from here." He pointed to Rincón, the westernmost town in Puerto Rico closest to Mona. "If we could be here, on a boat at daybreak, we'd have a following sea. I'd guess it'd be a four-hour trip out there with a good boat and decent weather, maybe less."

I sat down at my laptop and pulled up Expedia and typed in a travel search. "We can't fly to Rincón, but we could fly from Punta Cana to Mayagüez at eight tonight, and from there it's probably a thirty-minute taxi ride over to Rincón."

We all looked at the clock: 5:30 p.m. Very doable.

"We need to call the FAA and the Coast Guard. I can do that," Kurt said.

"I can get on the phone with Julie and see if she can help with a hotel and boat charter," I said.

"I'll book the tickets," Collin said.

"All I have left to do is click to purchase," I said.

"Cool. Then I'll paint my toenails. Can I borrow some nail polish?" Collin replied.

I rolled my eyes at him.

Collin mock-sighed. "OK, I'll call Tamara instead and run our conclusions by her for a final logic check. I'm going to fill her in about the Chihuahuas, too."

When we were all done, we would still have an hour to pack and grab food at the airport before hopping on the plane.

"Let's do it," I said.

We scattered to our tasks. I tried Julie and got voicemail, so I texted her: "Julie, we can't reach you on the phone. We need help. Skype?" *Come on.* She answered immediately. *Yes.*

"Skype open. Ready."

I connected. "No time for details, Julie, but we've made progress and need your help. Drop-everything kind of help."

"Ruth is here with the kids. I can do whatever you need." I heard something in her voice. Maybe my excitement was infectious? No. My stomach knotted. No time for more trouble. I pushed on.

"We need a charter boat for tomorrow morning at the crack of dawn in Rincón, Puerto Rico, to take us out to Mona Island. And a hotel in Rincón."

"Hotel in Rincón, boat from Rincón to Mona, earliest possible departure."

"Yes."

"I'm on it."

A thought, a crazy thought, came to my mind. "Julie, wait." I scrolled through the contacts in my phone. Found him. "Humor me. Call this number first and see if this guy is available to be in Rincón for a charter." I read off the digits. "Don't waste a lot of time, just one phone call, leave a voicemail, but then go straight to searching for another. But if he's available under the same time frame, I want him."

"What's his name?"

"Bill." The captain of the *Wild Irish Kate.* "He's a childhood surfer friend of Nick's. He captains a boat out of San Juan named the *Wild Irish Kate* for a rich American who likes to play in the Caribbean. Nick chartered him once a few years ago."

"Got it. And I think I remember him. Let me know what's going on when you can."

"I will, I promise."

Julie took a deep breath. "I don't want to worry you, Katie, but there is one thing that happened this afternoon that you need to know."

My tummy seized up. I'd been right. Trouble. "Tell me."

"Taylor was outside playing right after we talked to you earlier. Ruth and I were watching him, and he was in the driveway. And then he was gone, in the blink of an eye. The only reason we knew to look so fast was that Annalise set off every alarm in the house. I swear, she about pierced our eardrums."

"Is Taylor all right?" There was panic in my voice.

"He's fine. But what happened is strange and scary. The crazy old guy that told you there were skeletons under Annalise had picked him up and was walking down the driveway with him. We saw and ran after him. He was very calm and friendly when he saw us. He handed Taylor back to me, and he said, 'Sure easy to lose a boy.' And he just walked off. When we got back to the house, we saw that all of the dogs were asleep. I think they'd been drugged, Katie. So everything is OK now, but we don't know what to make of it."

Tutein. That asshole Tutein.

"I think I do. Tutein left me a voicemail telling me what beautiful children I have, and he said I still have a chance to make all the problems with Annalise go away before the court makes its ruling on the injunction. I think he's sending us a message."

"I don't like this message."

"Me either. Please, ask Rashidi to stay with you guys from now on. Don't let anyone go off alone." The seizing in my stomach had turned to roiling nausea. "Oh, Julie, I'm so sorry."

My children. My husband. How could I protect everyone at once? I didn't want to tell the guys, but I knew I had to.

We hung up. I turned to the men. All of us had completed our tasks.

"I need to go first," I said. I updated them quickly and the mood sobered. We moved on to Collin, who said Tamara thought our Mona scenario made sense.

Kurt reported on the FAA and Coast Guard. "I called our contact numbers and gave them our new information. The FAA said they will also call the Coast Guard and ask them to direct some of their search capabilities tomorrow between Puerto Rico and the Dominican Republic. The Coast Guard person gave me the same line they did last time, so I called my friend Ralph and asked for help. He's going to rattle sabers and call me back."

On cue, Kurt's phone rang. "Yup. Uh-huh. Yeah, OK. Thanks." He hung up and nodded. Quintessential Kurt.

Collin lost patience first. "Well?"

"My friend got through. They'll start flyovers in the Mona Passage tomorrow. It's too late today, not enough light. But he also said that tomorrow is day four and the resources will change for a recovery operation rather than a rescue."

"Recovery?" I asked.

"Body recovery," Collin said, putting his hand on my forearm. "But don't worry, Katie. They're just reading from a script. He's out there. We'll find him."

The adrenaline in my body dilated my pupils. I concentrated on expanding and filling my lungs, then emptying them, five times. It helped. Enough to keep me upright, at least.

Kurt and I threw our bags together and we reconvened in the sitting area five minutes later.

I asked, "Time to go?"

"Ready," he said.

"Just one more thing," Collin said. "I made out a black guy watching us at the airport, and by the time we'd gotten to the hotel, he'd picked us up and was on our tail. I wasn't a hundred percent sure at the time, but I am now. When I went out to talk to Tamara, I saw him and another black guy casing our room. Hadn't had a chance to tell you yet, but now's the time."

"Oh my God!" I said, too loudly.

Kurt said, "If they're out there, why don't they just try to kill us like they did that boy today?"

Nice thought, Kurt.

"I don't think they would want to attract attention by killing us unless they have to," Collin said. "I'll bet they just want to follow us in case we know something, especially about Nick or his passengers, who they seem to very much want dead."

"Shit! What are we going to do?" I asked.

Collin said, "We need to scatter like a covey of quail."

"Like that means something to me. Tell me in a way I can understand, big brother."

"There are two of them and three of us. We need to leave one at a time, scatter in three directions—Katie go left, Kurt go right, and I'll go forward— move fast, take confusing routes, walk past Victor's car, find a new taxi. We'll meet there. If that doesn't work, we can visit a Plan B in the taxi."

Kurt did his usual—he nodded. I gulped, then parroted him.

My phone flashed. No time to check messages.

Collin said, "Katie, you go first. Then Kurt. I'll bring up the rear and carry all three bags. Ready, guys?"

Kurt and I answered yes, him with more steam than me.

"Go, Katie," Collin ordered.

With my heart thundering, I handed him my bag and lunged out the door, then righted myself. *Don't look at them.* I didn't turn around, but I saw a black-skinned figure start to move in my side vision. *Shit shit shit.* I checked my watch. I needed to kill five minutes and make it good.

I made a sharp left toward the lobby. When I got there, I turned down a long hall of rooms. My purse slipped off my shoulder and bounced against my legs with each step. I forced my eyes to remain forward, no matter how badly I wanted to glance over my shoulder. I went up a flight of stairs.

As I reached the top of the staircase I tried to adjust my purse—and ended up dropping it. It tumbled out of my hands and everything in it spilled down the top three steps. My heart hammered in my chest and I kept my eyes on the tile floor as I crouched down and started shoveling things into my bag. Top step. Lipstick. Sunglasses. Passport. Second step. Keys. Checkbook. Pens. Third from the top. A pair of earrings. A roll of mints. I put my wallet in last and stood up, then saw my blue spiral notebook halfway down the hall. It must have bounced out of my purse earlier. I looked up and straight into the eyes of a black man walking down the long hallway toward me—and my notebook.

Shit.

Everything we'd learned so far was in that notebook. I couldn't just leave it—it was a map directly to my husband. I sprinted down the steps and back through the hall on a collision course with the man. We reached the notebook at the same time and as he bent over to retrieve it, I grabbed a pen out of my purse, ready to gouge his eyes out. He stood up.

"You dropped this, ma'am," he said in a voice that gave away his origins: Midwest, U.S.A. A tourist.

My fingers released the pen.

"Th-th-thank you, very much."

I took it from him as another black man bolted around the corner behind him. I didn't stick around to meet him. With my hand in my purse gripping my notebook, I wheeled and sprinted back up the stairs and into the short hallway at the top of them, where I ran head-on into one of the exact two people I did not want to meet. My breath was literally knocked out against his chest. His black eyes gleamed with recognition and triumph, and he grabbed me by my upper arm as I tried to spin back in the direction I'd come. His grip was strong. He wasn't overly tall, maybe five foot ten, but he was lean and muscular.

He spoke, and it was an island lilt. "Good afternoon, miss. Would you come with me, please?" His mock courtesy and tight smile over gleaming teeth were sinister.

Sylis? Or his buddy? Who knew, who cared. My fear slipped away and years of compulsory practice in the dojo took over. He was bigger, he was stronger, but I was smarter and felt sure he underestimated me. I pretended to trip and shot my free arm into a hammer punch to his groin, then followed his sagging body with a side kick under his chin. My teacher had always praised my side kicks as my most effective move. His head snapped back—I heard his teeth meet with a loud clack—and he fell backwards to the floor.

I didn't stick around to see if I'd knocked him out, but I was hoping for the best as I sprinted around a corner to the right, found another set of stairs, and headed down. I walked out onto the pool deck, trying not to look like I was heaving for breath. I circled the pool and entered the lobby from another angle, browsing the boutique windows as my breath slowed down, but not my pulse. I exited the far side of the lobby and walked around to the front of the hotel, where I saw Victor's car.

I chanced another glance around. There were men everywhere. Black men, Latino men, men that could be from St. Marcos, men that could be from Mexico or not. Men that could be interested in me or care less. I walked past

Victor's Cutlass and down to the end of the row of cars for hire. I searched for a sign of Kurt or Collin. Nothing.

"Taxi?" I asked, leaning down to speak to a driver through the open window of his large van. I panted.

"Sí," he said.

I hopped onto the first bench in the back. His radio was playing Kat DeLuna's obnoxious "Whine Up." U.S. pop music, Dominican-style. And I was trapped in his car with it, having a mini-panic attack. Not ideal. My blood pressure started rising.

"Where to, miss?" he asked. "Miss" sounded like "mees" in his accent.

"Wait. Two more men coming."

"I charge you for wait," he said. He sounded happy about it.

"Yes, charge me, that's fine." As long as he kept the taxi in park until Kurt and Collin came; that's all I cared about.

Footsteps. I willed my eyes to stay on the floorboard. The door opened and Kurt dropped onto the seat beside me.

"One of the guys went after you. Did you see him?"

"Yeah," I said. "I saw him all right."

"We go now?" the driver asked.

"No, wait. One more man," I replied.

"I still charge you," he said.

"Yes, that is fine." This time he had definitely sounded happy. "Did anyone follow you?"

"I think so, or at least one guy did. I didn't see him when I reached the cars, though."

"That's good."

"Yup."

Suddenly the car door on the other side of me opened. There had been no footsteps. Collin settled himself in, tossing our three bags across our laps. I should have packed lighter.

"I go now?" the driver asked.

"Yes, the airport, please," I said.

"Cape Air," Collin said.

Collin didn't say a word to us. His eyes roamed the people and cars around us but his head never moved. Kurt and I stayed silent. The driver pulled his taxi van away from the curb and eased around the other parked cars. Collin's eyes hardened and I followed his gaze. One Afro-Caribe man stood at the entrance to the lobby, craning his neck and searching all the cars.

"Is that one of them?" I whispered.

"Yes. Get down," Collin said. "I don't see the other guy, and he could be watching us from a different direction."

I flattened my upper body. "Why not you guys, too?" I asked. "I don't think you'll see the other one."

"I'm the new guy. They're not as likely to recognize me. They're looking for two men and a woman, or for a man and a woman. Definitely not for two men. Maybe they'll recognize Kurt, maybe not, but let's give this a try."

The van cruised past the men and Kurt kept his face averted. Collin played it cool, pretending to scroll through messages on his phone, but actually watching them from behind his sunglasses.

"Why don't you think we'll see the other one?" Collin asked.

"Because thanks to Dad, I think I knocked him out with a side kick."

"No shit?" Collin asked.

I noticed that something felt breezy around my crotch. I looked down, then reached tentatively for the seam of my capris. Yep, split.

"No shit," I said. "Which is why I'll need to change these pants into something a little less revealing."

Kurt spoke. "You kicked one of the guys and knocked him unconscious?"

I started to answer, but Collin got there first. "Katie was the Karate Kid when she was younger. State champion at the age of twelve. She was something else."

Kurt nodded, surprised. "Huh," he said. Respectful.

I changed the subject slightly. "Do you think the guy saw us?" I asked.

"I don't think so. But even if he didn't, this won't fool him for long, if he's any good. As soon as he realizes we aren't in our room, he'll head to the airport. Guaranteed."

"And his buddy won't be out forever," I added.

The van turned onto the main road. I counted slowly to twenty and then sat up. The driver had acted as if my behavior was totally normal.

I whispered close to Collin's ear. "Our driver is acting funny."

"Yeah," he said. "He's sensing a profitable opportunity, I think."

"Could he go back and rat us out?"

"I'd bet you anything he would."

"We could pay him enough to ensure he sticks around the airport."

"I like your thinking," he said.

Collin negotiated a deal with the driver to wait for us, making up a story about one of us needing to return to the hotel. While they talked, I checked my phone. Ah, the message from earlier. A text from Julie. Or rather, several texts.

"I reached Nick's friend Bill, and we made an executive decision. He is in San Juan. He wants to help, and he swore he could have you to Mona faster than anyone out of Rincón could. He wants to pick you up from the airport there and take you straight to his boat. You can sleep on the boat instead of in a hotel. I said yes and booked you tickets." She gave the flight information and e-ticket confirmation numbers.

I felt a twinge of dread that faded fast. I used to get seasick, but since I'd had the twins, it had gone away. Thank God. I texted back. "Sounds good. Thank you."

"Change of plans, guys," I said.

Kurt made a sound like "hruh." I took that to mean, "Please tell me about the change in plans, Katie."

"Julie booked us tickets to San Juan. We're catching a fast boat out of there tonight with Nick's high school friend who captains the *Wild Irish Kate*." I had already told them about *Kate* earlier.

"Are you sure? Will that get us there fastest?" Collin asked.

"Julie said she quizzed him, and he convinced her that it was our best option. I trust him." And this is what Nick said to do. Sort of.

"Sounds like as good a plan as any," Collin said.

Kurt looked squinty-eyed, but he finally nodded. *There you go, Kurt.*

"I'll call and cancel our Mayagüez tickets," I said.

"Hold off," Collin replied. "Let's leave it out there as a red herring."

"What?"

"A false clue. In case they're monitoring credit cards to figure out where we've gone."

Ah. How had I lived to thirty-seven years of age and not had "red herring" in my vocabulary?

"Maybe we should all get as much cash as our debit cards will allow while we're still where the bad guys expect us to be, so we can stay off the credit cards for the rest of the trip?"

"Wow, sis, that's a halfway decent idea."

"I'm smarter than I look. I was also thinking that tiny towns in Puerto Rico may not be the best place to use credit cards, anyway."

"Cash makes for fast transactions, too," Collin said.

The van pulled to the curb outside our terminal, except it wasn't our terminal anymore.

"American Airlines, please," I said.

"I thought he say Cape Air?" the driver asked, pointing at Collin with his head.

"Our mistake. American Airlines," Collin said.

The van's tires squealed.

Wild Irish Kate, here we come.

Chapter Twenty-one

The wheels of our plane touched down with a thump at San Juan's Edward Munoz International Airport at 9:15 p.m., right on time. It had been a turbulent approach. My hands hurt. I looked at my palms and saw red stripes. Apparently, I'd had a death clutch on the armrests.

Fifteen minutes and one shuttle ride later, we entered the San Juan airport, carry-ons in hand. The message buzz sounded from my iPhone.

"Bill will meet you at baggage claim," Julie texted.

I replied. "Thanks." I had never seen Bill before, and I hoped Julie had given him a description of us. Exhaustion weighed me down. I felt the heaviness under my eyes that meant big black circles. I was sure they would match the dark spots that had multiplied all over my white blouse, which was now paired with blue jean shorts with an intact crotch seam. I swiped my lank hair back from my forehead and my hand came away greasy. I hoped the boat would have a shower.

After nearly three years in and out of here from St. Marcos, I knew the San Juan airport as well as I knew my children's faces. Kurt and Collin surfed my wake as I powered ahead, Kurt on autopilot but Collin on full alert. Collin had assured us that we'd shaken our followers in Punta Cana, and no one on the plane had looked anything like them or shown any interest in us. But Collin said not to get our hopes up that we were free of them yet.

"They'll have nearly an hour while we're in the air. It wouldn't take much for them to figure out we flew to San Juan. Hell, if they play the odds they'll know we have to fly through here to connect to anywhere else. With just a phone call they can arrange for hired help to greet us in Puerto Rico, even on speculation," he said.

How lovely. I wondered if they'd make that call for hired help from Mexico or St. Marcos. I remembered Jiménez's behavior toward our investigation. I was still suspicious he was involved with the cartel.

I was glad Collin warned us, though. He had made a huge difference already. I led them through the revolving glass doors into baggage claim. It was wall-to-wall as usual, humans crowded up to the carousels and all the way out to the plate glass windows facing ground transportation.

I saw Bill immediately. Not because I recognized him from any past description from Nick, but because the sandy-haired Caucasian man held up a poster that said "KATIE KOVACS" in black magic marker. Collin and Kurt saw him, too.

"Uh oh," I said. If we stopped, we'd give our identity away to anyone looking for us.

"Keep walking," Collin said.

We strode past him and he didn't so much as glance in our direction. What I saw next nearly stopped me short.

A Puerto Rican man held up a sign that read "Katie Kovacs."

Collin muttered under his breath just loud enough for us to hear. "Definitely keep walking now."

We reached the far end of baggage claim and stopped to discuss.

"Well, looks like we have two greeting committees. One friendly, one unfriendly. Do you know which is which, Katie?" Collin asked.

I bobbed my head up and down. "Bill is Caucasian, not Puerto Rican. The first guy, for sure."

Kurt said, "I didn't recognize him. I knew Bill when he was a kid. He and Nick surfed together, and he was a dark-headed boy. I can't say as I agree with you, Katie. It could be either guy. That second fellow might not be Puerto Rican."

Collin said, "Oh, this is great."

"I've got Bill's number. I'll just call him," I said.

"Tell him to meet us by the curb," Collin peered out the windows, "by the taxi stand, in one minute."

I dialed. It rang and rang. "No answer, not even voicemail. I'll text him." I typed our message quickly and hit send. Still, neither man looked down or reached for a phone.

"Shit," Collin said.

"I have an idea," I said. "How about one of us walks up to the person next to each of them and asks them if they have seen Bill. Loudly. Whichever one is Bill should react."

"Sounds good. Only problem is, I'll bet our follower has seen Bill and his sign. All he has to do now is follow Bill. I'll go," Collin said.

He started to walk off, then stopped. "You guys go wait by the taxi stand. Stand apart. Don't look at each other."

He barreled his way through the crowd and stopped by the darker of the two men.

"You go first," I said to Kurt.

And off he went, no words necessary.

Collin appeared to carry out his plan, but the more Puerto-Rican-looking of our two Bill prospects did not react. Collin wheeled around and headed toward the lighter-complected man.

Time for me to leave. I turned away and walked to the taxi stand. I leaned against the wall, twenty feet away from Kurt. A text came in on my iPhone.

Collin. "I have our Bill. He left phone in car. Stay put."

I forwarded Collin's text to Kurt. This was nerve-wracking. I checked Nick's and my email as a way to kill time and keep myself grounded. Nothing there to hold my attention. Five minutes passed. I felt eyes on me. *Don't look up.* I wished I had my hat to cover my hair, but even though I wore it to the airport in the DR, I'd stuffed it into my suitcase when we checked in for our flight. How hard would I be to identify in the San Juan airport? "Bring me the tall, pale, late-thirties woman with long red hair and a serious set of saddle bags under her eyes." Ha, no problem.

A junker Impala pulled up to the curb in front of me. Collin's voice called from the passenger side, "Get in."

I got in. The Impala lurched forward. Collin repeated his command, and Kurt sat beside me in the backseat. Again, the Impala lurched forward.

"Guys, this is Bill Thomas. Bill, this is Katie and Kurt," Collin said. I could barely hear him over Whitesnake advising us to take it down slow and easy. I wondered if Bill was playing it on eight-track.

"Welcome to San Juan," Bill said. He careened around a slower vehicle. "Let's go get Nick."

I tried not to gape. My quick glimpse of Bill in baggage claim had not done him justice. At nearly forty years of age, he had wavy shoulder-length hair, scraggly and sun-bleached. He was Jeff Spicoli from *Fast Times at Ridgemont High*, the twenty-year reunion version. I had trouble picturing my husband hanging out with Bill, but reminded myself it was years ago. The surfers' bond and all that.

"Hi, Bill," I said.

"Hi, yourself. So you're Nick's hot wife. Wow. Now I know why he hitched a ride with me through a hurricane to get to you."

I didn't know what to say to that, so I chose silence, which Kurt filled, thank goodness.

Kurt said, "I'm Nick's father. We've met."

"Yes sir, we have, and don't hold it against me. I've grown up a lot since then. Not completely, but a lot."

He almost clipped the bumper of a car as he pulled in front of it, and the driver blared his horn. It was lost on Bill.

"We have to assume the bad guys are on to us. But I have a plan."

Bill momentarily took his eyes from the road to watch Collin. His hand started tapping on the steering wheel, beating out a crazy rhythm and occasionally crashing an imaginary cymbal to his right. The bad guys wouldn't need to worry about us if Bill killed us off in San Juan traffic. *Eyes on road, both hands on wheel.*

Collin continued. "Bill said it will take us about five hours to cruise around the coast and stage ourselves nearest Mona. He wants to make our final approach in daylight, because the waters are a little treacherous out there, due to the reefs and all. It's ten p.m. now. So let's go check into a hotel on the beach near the marina. Make it look to any followers like we've tucked in for the night. Bill knows just the place."

"Yeah, there's a Holiday Inn Express about a half mile from the San Juan Bay Marina, which is where the *Kate* is," Bill said.

"We'll get a ground floor room with beach access, slip out the beach side at about midnight, and walk to the marina. If we're followed and anyone is watching in the lobby, they'll never see us."

Kurt said, "What if they're out back?"

Collin said, "Then we get the joy of changing the plan. Because flexibility is the key to air power."

I jumped into the conversation. "I like it. To make it look authentic, we should get two rooms." And I could shower and change in one. Thank God.

Bill gave us directions from the hotel to the *Wild Irish Kate*. "I'm going to sleep until you guys get there, so just come on the boat and in through the back door. Yell for me. I'll wake up. She's fueled and ready to go."

He brought the Impala to a quick stop that whipped my head forward and then back. "Well, look at that, I got you here safe and sound," he said.

God help us, this was the man we were trusting to get us to Nick.

Hang on, Nick. We're getting closer.

At least, I hoped we were.

Chapter Twenty-two

Collin insisted on paying for the rooms.

"Don't worry, sis, you can pay me back later. In fact, I'll even take a personal check."

I punched his arm. My brother's humor and confidence were a lifesaver. If you focused on my helpers—Kurt and Collin—and not my missing husband or the problems back at Annalise, I was pretty darn lucky.

When we got to our musty beachside rooms, Collin and Kurt napped in theirs while I showered in mine. I worried about thugs breaking in the entire time and wished I'd barricaded the door, but blessedly no thugs showed up and the hot water made up for the dank smell. After I got out, I saw a request from Julie to Skype.

We established a connection. I heard the beautiful strains of "What I Did for Love" playing softly in the background before the video showed an image. Julie had taught music all her life until she moved to St. Marcos. I identified the big, emotional Broadway numbers with her.

"Hey," I said.

Julie was not alone. Rashidi's friendly face glowed in my LCD screen beside her. "Hey," they both said.

Julie spoke quickly. "We want to hear everything you have time to tell us, but we also have to let you know what happened here today."

That sounded bad, and her face looked worse. "More than crazy Tim carrying off Taylor? What's up?" I asked. "The kids? Tutein?"

"Sort of Tutein. Not really. Good news on that front, though. Rashidi was out with Ava, Laura, and Rob earlier. They found your slave graveyard."

Rashidi said, "We gonna fix things, Katie. There's a grave dug up within the last few days, but hard to say. Very suspicious. Anyway, don't worry, we got it in hand."

I sure hoped he was right. "You guys are awesome. Even thinking about this right now is more than I can handle. Thank you so much."

He ducked his head, letting an avalanche of beads and dreadlocks fall forward, and he smiled.

Julie spoke again. "We had a little more excitement here, as well. While Rashidi was out at the graveyard, Ruth and I were here with the kids, feeding them dinner. This was maybe two hours ago, after I talked to you. It had just gotten dark. We both felt this vibration, then the dishes started shaking, and the pictures were rattling on their hooks against the walls, and books were falling off shelves. I thought we were having an earthquake."

Earthquakes were not uncommon on St. Marcos, so this was a reasonable explanation, unless you lived up at Annalise. I knew what was coming next.

"Of course it wasn't an earthquake, it was Annalise. We grabbed the kids. The dogs outside started barking like mad, and Oso went crazy, running around all of us like he was herding sheep. And then I heard a screaming noise from outside."

My hand flew to my throat.

"The noise was a voice, and it became clear it was a man. He was carrying on like a banshee. We looked out the kitchen windows. We saw two local men with their hands in the air, and we saw Dan-Dan with a machete, swinging it around their heads. Dan-Dan was the one screaming."

"Oh my God, Julie! Are you guys OK?"

"Oh honey, we're fine, thanks to Dan-Dan and the dogs. Ruth and I called out to Dan-Dan to see if he needed help, and he told us that these two men were no match for the likes of him, or as he said, 'These anti-mans ain't no match for me a'tall'." She made a passable attempt at a local accent. "The dogs knew Dan-Dan was their ally, and they circled around the other two men. Want to guess who they were?"

"My money is on Pumpy and loony Tim. Again."

"And your money wins," she said.

"What did you do?" I asked.

"Ruth and I decided it would do no good to call the police. So we told Dan-Dan to take care of them. Last we saw, he had marched them off into the night with all the dogs except Oso with him. Rashidi got here about ten minutes after it happened, and he didn't see any sign of them."

"Unreal," I said. And it was. I pictured Pumpy and the old wacko tied up next to a bonfire way back in the bush with Dan-Dan dancing around them in full war paint. I liked it.

"Taylor worships Dan-Dan even more now. He has out that wooden pig he gave him, and he's playing Dan-Dan the hero games."

"As well he should," I said. My sweet boy.

Rashidi added, "Annalise was ready to help, but Dan-Dan took care of things before they got close enough to feel her wrath."

Pumpy had seen Annalise's wrath before, but now he was showing up again anyway. The man was not a fast learner.

"Way to go, Annalise," I said, raising my voice. I laughed at myself inside; it wasn't like Annalise was hard of hearing.

Rashidi spoke again. "So Katie, we gotta take care of this thing with DPNR. It can't wait for you and Nick to get back. We meeting with Attorney Vince Robinson tomorrow. He coming out here so Julie can be in the meeting, too."

I loved his absolute faith in Nick's well-being and return, and I fought back a tear. "Yeah, I agree. Thank you, guys."

"No problem. Now update us on Nick," Julie said. "And why you left the DR."

As bad as it was for me to be missing Nick and scared to death, it was worse for Julie. Nick was her son, and she'd lost her daughter not so long ago. Plus, I had the satisfaction of action, of searching. I was in the know on every bit of information we could find. Julie was stuck at home, powerless and outside the loop. Not to mention facing down Tutein alone. Yet she remained composed, at least on the surface.

So I filled them in, sparing no detail, including my crazy dreams and our harrowing time with the men following us. And with Bill's driving.

Rashidi said, "You, Nick, and Annalise just made for each other. And from what I hear, you got a message from him this morning, so that mean he still fine, then."

Julie's mouth was so tight from holding back tears that she had the wrinkles of a lifelong smoker, even though she was a true Sandra Dee and had never touched a single one. "He's going to be all right, Katie. I know he is."

"He is, Julie," I said. My mouth felt pretty tight, too. "He is." I slowed down and a yawn overtook me. "I know the kids must be long since asleep?"

"Yes. I'm sorry, honey," Julie said.

"Please kiss them all over their faces for me and tell them I love them. And see if Ruth will let you hug her."

"Absolutely," Julie replied. "Giving that a try should be quite entertaining."

Rashidi said, "Ava say she love you. She working hard on this. She got Rob and Laura whipped into a frenzy. Not a minute go by we not praying for you, thinking of you and Nick. And Ava say to tell you she not gonna let you down this time, not ever again."

I had maintained rigid control until this point. How had Ava snuck up on my blindside? My tears pooled and I wiped my eyes.

"Well, I'll pray for all of you, too. Please keep my babies safe. I'm afraid I have to go roust the men now. Time for us to catch a ride on the *Wild Irish Kate*."

I straightened up and popped my neck to each side, readying myself for the return to action. We said our goodbyes. I stared at the screen as the speaker made the call-ending noise that always made me think of Sylvester the Cat collapsing in a heap after Tweety Bird pelted him over the head. I sat up straighter. I would not collapse.

I stared past the hunter green drapes that were pulled back to reveal the black night and ocean through the glass door. We were about to get on a boat with a stranger and race at top speed through unfamiliar waters in the dead of night. I tested myself for fear and found none. None except the fear that we were too late or looking in the wrong place.

But I couldn't think those thoughts. I had to believe. I had to be the one. Nick was counting on me. I drew in a deep breath and closed my eyes, picturing Nick's face. I opened them, grabbed my bag, and headed next door.

Here I come, baby.

Chapter Twenty-three

The *Wild Irish Kate* rocked back and forth at her mooring, a spirited racehorse in the starting gate ready for the Kentucky Derby. My God, she was huge. She was a luxurious sixty-foot Hatteras motor yacht, and she looked practically brand new. I felt like I was stepping into a cracked-out episode of *Lifestyles of the Rich and Famous*.

Kurt rubbed his hand along her side as we climbed aboard. Collin let out an appreciative wolf whistle. The girl had sex appeal, for sure.

We entered the back door to the cabin and found Bill awake. And mixing a cocktail in the galley, on Corian countertops, no less. The salon between him and us was filled with white leather furniture on almond-colored Berber carpet. I checked for dirt on my shoes and hands before entering.

"Greetings, passengers. Welcome to *Kate*," he said, raising his glass in salute. I'd forgotten Nick had said Bill spent his life trying to fill his hollow leg. "We're at sea in five minutes. I need a first mate to help me navigate out of the marina, and then you're all free to find a sleeping berth or anything else you want. Food, drink, shower, movies. *Kate* has it all."

How had Spicoli landed a sweet gig like this? Had the owner actually met him? I would have hired someone more like Felix from *The Odd Couple*. I also would have thrown slipcovers over the furniture and plastic sheeting over the carpet. But Nick trusted Bill, and if I could trust my dreams, Nick had all but told me to use Bill and *Kate* for his rescue.

Kurt signed up for the first mate job, quite a step down for the former chief pilot. I suspected he did it for his own safety. He was eyeing Bill's sloshing glass as if he could vaporize it with his glare.

Kurt finished quickly with the lines and we pushed off. As we slipped through the water between cruise ships, multi-masted sailboats, giant sport fishers, and motor yachts like the *Kate*, Collin and I stood on the foredeck with the wind in our faces. Nothing in the world felt as good on my skin as the velvety Caribbean air. Nothing except Nick's skin on mine.

The lights of Old San Juan cut the darkness around us and made it seem like dawn, but there was no mistaking this party town. At fifteen minutes past midnight, San Juan Bay Marina and Old San Juan were rocking. Shakira's promise that her hips don't lie warped slightly as it poured out of a brightly lit party boat. Partiers shrieked with laughter. The smell of alcohol, overripe dinners, and sour vomit undercut the scent of salt water and fish. Decadence. I only ever had this sense of the world dying slowly at the witching hour, as I remembered my own brittle attempts to drink away my pain and mortality.

I needed to shake this gloom before it drained the resources I needed for what lay ahead. Between worrying about this rescue-not-recovery mission and about Tutein threatening my kids, I was redlined. I turned to Collin for a change of subject.

"So who is this Tamara, and what is she to you?"

"She's with the federal Drug Enforcement Agency. I met her when we did some joint ops with them in Santa Fe," Collin said.

"That's half an answer," I said.

"You're going to make me say it."

"I am." I patted his shoulder. "You can do it, Col."

Collin re-tucked in his already tucked-in shirt. "She's my fiancée."

I hadn't expected that, and despite everything, I chortled. "Fiancée? You're getting married? I definitely need more information. She's my freakin' future sister-in-law." I twisted his earlobe gently, a trick our father had used to get our attention when we were kids. "Topless dancers in mobile homes across the Southwest are mourning the day already, I'll bet."

It was still light enough that I could see Collin smile. "OK, I deserved that. But those days are over. I'm practically a married man already."

"Good for you."

"She's great. You'll love her. Strong, but not in a dykey way. Hot, of course."

"That's a relief, Collin. I was really worried about whether she was dykey or hot." I snorted. "As if."

"Oh, shut up." He put his arm around my shoulders and pulled me close. "When we get Nick home, I'll see if she can come with me to visit you guys. I want you to meet her soon."

"And I want you to meet my baby girls. We'll all look forward to it," I said for my absent husband and me. If I made plans for us, then he had to be all right.

Kate picked up speed as we left the harbor and headed out to sea. True darkness enveloped us. It was like God had dumped a giant well of black ink over a glass dome, cloaking the island under its bell and leaving us outside it. The stars were shining so brightly they reflected off the blackness.

Collin and I sidled along the railing to the aft deck and climbed the stairs to the flying bridge, where Kurt had joined Bill earlier. Bill was reciting the details of the trip to him now like a grunt answering to a superior officer. A grunt with sun-streaked curls, weathered skin, and a wrinkled Jimmy Buffet Key West Camp shirt. Kurt would grill our captain for the entire five-hour trip unless Bill got brave enough to fight him off.

I interrupted to give Bill a breather. "So, did the owner have any problem with you chartering out to us?"

Bill's blond-tipped brows scrunched together. "The owner? Oh, I didn't ask him."

Three voices exclaimed, "What?" at the same time. My lawyer's mind went straight to which felonies we would be jailed for when the owner found out about our trip. Was this theft, or was there a lesser offense of joyriding in three-million-dollar boats? Maybe even just a trespass if we got really lucky? Holy crap, what if Bill ran her onto a reef tomorrow?

Bill held up his left hand to ward us off while he steered with his right. "He'll never know. He's off on some Mediterranean cruise with his newest twenty-five-year-old wife. He told me to take *Kate* out and keep her running. That's all I'm doing, and you guys are just along for the ride." He smiled, showing a chipped tooth. "No problem, mon."

"So, who do we pay for the charter, you or him?" I asked.

"You don't pay anybody. Nick's my friend. Well, you can pay for gas and groceries, but that's all we need."

On the surface, his offer was quite generous, but at the rate he consumed rum and cranberry juice, "groceries" might cost more than a charter. Except that rum cost less than milk in the islands. So, no problem, mon.

"You guys should sleep. I'll wake you when we stop for gas and supplies in Aguadilla. We'll push off from there after sunrise and then we'll reach Mona in about three hours," Bill said.

"I thought we were going to Rincón?" I asked.

"Aguadilla is the launching place to Mona from this direction. Rincón is the shortest route if you're coming across the island proper or by water from the south," Bill said. "And *Kate's* owner ponied up for the mega engines, so we'll cruise at twenty knots or better all night. With nice flat seas like these, she'll just rock you to sleep like a baby." Bill let go of the helm and laid his cheek against his pressed palms, pantomiming sleep.

Kurt reached over and grabbed the wheel. If he'd been a few seconds slower he would have had to fight Collin and me for it.

Bill didn't notice. "Katie, you wanna splash a fresh drink in here for me before you leave?"

I stuttered my answer. "I, well, I—"

Collin jumped in. "Whatcha drinking, Captain?" He grabbed the cup from Bill's hand.

I mouthed "thank you" to him, and he winked. Ever since Collin had almost single-handedly shipped me off to solo-rehab on St. Marcos a few years ago when I couldn't find my way out of a Bloody Mary haze back in Dallas, I literally hadn't touched a drink. And I didn't want to touch one now. I trusted myself, but I didn't want to push it.

Collin and I clambered back down the stairs. The steps were nearly invisible in the dark and I clung to the handrail. Once I was in the salon, I flipped on the light switch with relief.

I picked up my travel bag and slung it over my shoulder. The last clean clothes I had brought were already on my body. I needed a washing machine soon or I would smell rank. I went in search of one, and to my joy, found a tiny laundry closet. I dumped my clothes in the wash and continued exploring.

The cabin had three bedrooms and two bathrooms—or three staterooms and two heads, in boating lingo—a kitchen/dining area called the galley, and the salon, AKA TV room. Plus the laundry closet. A professional decorator had created a Caribbean masterpiece, colorful but not overdone. I wondered which of the owner's twenty-five-year-old wives was named Kate. Probably the immediately previous one, given how new the yacht appeared. Kate should anticipate a name change in her near future.

I dropped my bag on the floor of a bedroom featuring paintings of palm trees and a shiny leopard-print bedspread. Surprisingly, the decor worked. The room appeared unoccupied, so I draped my body across the bed, thinking I should really take off my shoes before I fell asleep. I was dreaming before I had a chance to do anything about it.

"You're on the *Kate*. I knew you would figure it out."

It was Nick's voice. Far away.

"Nick?" I said. I struggled to swim to the surface from the deep end of sleep. I opened my eyes and could just make out his face. Why was he so blurry? I rubbed my eyes.

"It's me, baby. I'm really tired, so I can only talk to you for a minute or two."

A hazy film still clouded my view of him. He appeared to be lying on his side with his eyes half closed.

I said, "I'm right here. I'm listening. I love you."

"I love you, too. And you've done so good. Annalise and I have given you all the information you need. She was a big help. She said to tell you she'll protect the kids." He lifted his hand as if to stroke my cheek, but I felt nothing. *Oh, Nick, reach a little further.* "I have to sleep now," he said. His face flickered.

I said, "Don't go, love. Stay with me."

"Hurry, Katie. And show Bill the picture. I love you."

And he was gone, nothing but a black screenshot in my mind.

"Nick? Nick? What do you mean? What picture? What am I missing? Don't go!" I reached for where he had been, my hands groping desperately and coming up empty.

"Katie, you're dreaming, wake up," Collin said, gently shaking my shoulder. "It's OK. I'm right here."

I rubbed my eyes. Tears. Again.

"Thank you. Sorry. Was I loud?"

"Not too bad. I was just about to go to sleep in the next bedroom, so I heard you. You almost punched me in the eye when I got close. Were you having another dream with Nick?"

"Yes. He said he's tired. He asked us to hurry. Oh, Collin, what if we don't find him? What if we don't make it in time?" I sat up and put my head on my brother's shoulder and let the tears flow. He rocked me back and forth like our mother used to do. No one else could make it all better like my big brother, the one who, no matter how different we seemed on the outside, was my closest match, down to the mitochondria of our DNA and the minute details of our childhoods.

I don't know how long he held me, but I know my eyes closed again and I slept without dreaming. Bill's voice over the intercom woke me next as he called out our arrival at Aguadilla. I roused myself from sleep, scared, but determined and ready.

Soon, we would aim the bow of *Kate* toward Mona—and Nick.

Chapter Twenty-four

Morning. The sun cut gemstones into crystal blue water that sparkled like a necklace around us. Bill had *Kate* opened up, and she sliced through the water at twenty-one knots, roughly equivalent to twenty-five miles per hour, land speed. Fast and beautiful.

My heart strained toward Mona. Bill said we would see the island long before we reached her. I was sitting on the foredeck alone with my hat tied under my chin and my blue notebook clutched in my right hand. I had updated it and was planning to review it to get myself ready for the day.

I lay back and tucked the notebook under my body. I would read it soon, but right now, I needed to try to sleep again. To forget that I was out of text-cell-Skype range from Julie. Bill had shown us the boat's satellite phone last night, but Julie didn't have its number. I couldn't even pretend no news was good news. I promised myself I would call her later, when we found Nick. Caught in the paralysis of anxiety, I fell into a half-sleep and time passed by like the spray of water on the hull.

Then the engines throttled back and *Kate* slowed dramatically. I stood up and shielded my eyes. Ahead of us, a gorgeous, multicolored maze of coral reefs was taunting *Kate* to find her way through. Most beautiful to my eyes, though, was the hump of earth on the other side of the reefs: Mona, tantalizingly close to us. Off to our right and farther in the distance was a smaller island that seemed taller than Mona. Both islands looked bare and forbidding from this vantage point. My gosh, I hoped Bill had laid off the rum. We all needed to stay sharp. We might spot Nick any time now.

The winds were higher and the seas rougher here than they'd been off San Juan the night before. I picked my way carefully around the side of the cabin, holding onto the railing with one hand and the blue bible in the other. The men had assembled on the flying bridge. Kurt stood over Bill's shoulder at the small table, a large map in front of them. I set my notebook down beside it. Bill was talking him through the reef passage, tracing the path with his finger. Collin had the wheel, although *Kate* was stopped, or as stopped as a sixty-foot boat could be in moving water and a brisk wind.

"I've navigated through here a hundred times to bring people out to scuba dive and see Mona and Monito. It's marked. See the buoys?" Bill said, and he pointed into the water in front of us.

Kurt grunted. He had turned gruff with Bill. I imagined him at work as a pilot: stoic would come out as taciturn, spare as uncommunicative, and gruff as bad-tempered. I now knew that we got the soft and cuddly Kurt at home.

Collin filled me in. "No sign of any followers. I think we left our goon sitting on his thumbs in the lobby of the Holiday Inn Express in Old San Juan."

"I thought we shook our tail at the airport?" I asked.

Collin grinned at me. "That's because while you showered, napped, and did your hair, I was out saving the world. The Puerto Rican gent from baggage claim and one other guy had made themselves comfy in the brown chairs with the fire-retardant upholstery by the front door."

"Why didn't you tell us?" I asked.

"I told Kurt when I came back to the room. I guess I just forgot to mention it to you until now."

Like hell he forgot. I was perturbed, but I tried to get over it. "I can't believe they're so persistent."

"They're paid to be," Collin said.

I cast a pensive glance backward but saw nothing but blue water behind us, all the way to the horizon.

Collin nursed a coffee. It smelled good. My eyes must have sent that message, because he said, "Want one, Katie?"

Kiss up. "Sure. I can get it, though."

"Nah, you just stay there and look pretty as a picture. I need to refill the carafe anyway. Let your big brother take care of you."

Something tweaked my brain and I sat down on the L-shaped settee in a half-trance. Collin trekked down to the galley for my coffee and Kurt continued to interrogate Bill as prickles crept over my body. I got lost in the sensation that I was forgetting something important.

Collin appeared at the top of the stairs with the carafe and a mug of black coffee. I sipped too fast and it burned my mouth, and I remembered, just like that.

"Shit!" I yelled.

"What's the matter?" Collin asked.

I scrambled down the stairs and flew through the cabin into my bedroom for the picture—Nick had asked me to show Bill a picture. And the only picture that made sense to show Bill would be the picture from the tackle box, the one that Annalise had led me to after my second or third Nick dream. Because Nick and Annalise pointed me to it, I had brought it. Now if I could just remember where I put it—

Collin said from behind me, "What the heck has gotten into you?"

I ignored him and threw everything out of my bag and pawed through my things. Nothing. I shook each piece of clothing and checked each pocket. Nothing. I felt carefully inside the bottom of the empty bag. Still nothing. I jammed my hands into the bag's inner zippered pocket. There—I pulled out the water-spotted picture of Nick and Kurt on a fishing boat and sprinted past Collin, who flattened himself against the wall to let me by. I ran back through the boat and up the stairs to the bridge and stuck the picture too close in front of Bill's face.

"Whoa, whatcha got there?" he said as he warded it off and I panted for breath.

I pulled it back three inches. "Sorry." Pant. "I need you to see this picture. Right now." Pant.

"Ohhkaaaaay," he said. "Kurt, could you take the helm?"

Kurt stepped in gladly. I doubted he would give it back without a fight.

Bill looked at the photo. "That's nice, Katie. Kurt and Nick. Fishing. Catching, it looks like. Very nice." He was looking at me with more interest than at the photo, as if I'd thrown a rod in my engine.

"Nick wanted me to show it to you. There has to be something important about it. Does it mean anything to you? Please look at it again."

Bill tilted his head sideways and lifted one corner of his lips. "When did you talk to Nick?" He did not look at the picture. I contemplated my options:

scream at him, sock him in the nose, or aim his face at the picture with my fingers clamped in his hair?

Before I could pick one, Collin, shorter than Bill by at least four inches, leaned around Bill's shoulder to see the picture. "Can I take a look?"

Bill handed it to him. "Sure. Because I don't see anything special. Other than a boat not nearly as nice as *Kate*." He grinned.

Collin stroked his chin whiskers, his lips fully pursed. "Katie, is this the picture of the boat you told Kurt and me about? I thought you called it the *Mona Lisa*."

"I did."

"Did you see that's not actually the name?" He turned the picture toward me.

"What do you mean?" *Oh God, did I screw this up?* I stepped closer so I could see it.

"It's called the *Little Mona Lisa*. Little."

I was close enough to see it now. The boat's name, in a lovely baroque script, was plainly not *Mona Lisa*, but *Little Mona Lisa*.

Bill said, "Hey, that's cool. Like Monito. That big island in front of us is Mona, and the little one to the right is Monito."

Out of the mouths of men with childlike minds.

Collin and I stared at each other. Wagner's *Flight of the Valkyries* started playing in my head.

Kurt spoke first. "Bill, plot me a course over to Monito, will you?"

Bill looked confused. Collin poured another mug of coffee from his carafe and handed it to him. "Change of plans, buddy. Flexibility is the key to air power."

"What?" Bill asked.

"We need you to take us to Monito," Collin said. "Stat."

Bill accepted fate. He grabbed the map and a wax pen and carefully drew a meandering red path through the reefs to Monito. He handed it to Kurt, who took it without a word and began an intent study, grunting and nodding. Also looking up occasionally to ensure he was on course, thank goodness.

Bill turned back to the conundrum of Mona versus Monito. "I thought you believed Nick is on Mona?" Bill asked.

"Yes and no," Collin said. "We identified a large area for his possible splashdown, and then we relied on the magic of Katie to get us the rest of the way there." Collin gestured toward me with his coffee cup. "What do you call your skills, Katie?"

I called it my sixth sense, but I thought of it as an inner ear, the kind that heard unspoken things. But how to explain it? I'd never tried to, outside friends and family. Well, Bill counted as friends, now, for sure. I girded myself for his ridicule and gave it my best.

"My sixth sense. I'm a really good communicator. I receive messages from some unusual places. Like from my husband, even when he's not around, but usually just when something's wrong. It's not like Nick sends me mind-messages to get more eggs when I'm at the grocery store." Bill laughed. "Nick started contacting me in my dreams when he disappeared. He told me he was safe but needed me to come for him. He sent me a visual of a rubber life raft. He reminded me of the *Wild Irish Kate*, which I believe was his way of telling me to call you for help. He told me not to count on anyone else to find him, that only I could do it. And when we had focused on Mona for our search, he told me to show you this picture. Unfortunately, I'm not always one hundred percent accurate, or I'd have gotten that one earlier." I raised my hands, palms upward, then dropped my arms. "So here we are. Monito." I waited for his reaction.

Bill spoke directly to me. "You mean you can read people's minds and shit? Like, you know what I'm thinking right now?"

You're thinking you'd get another rum and cranberry juice if Kurt weren't watching you like a hawk, I thought. "Not like that. I just . . . get messages . . . from things, not everyone or everything. Just those closest to me, when there's trouble. Not you."

Bill stared at Collin and me. He switched his gaze over to Kurt. "Kurt? You believe in all this?"

"Yup. Seen it with my own eyes, even. So, Monito it is," Kurt said.

After five hours' bonding in the middle of the night, Kurt had brainwashed Bill. He may have thought we were all smoking from the same wacky weed, but Bill took the leap on Kurt's say so.

"Well, Kurt, good thing we figured this out now. The cut over to Monito is right there." Bill pointed at the next buoy. "Want to trade places?"

"No, I'm good. I piloted for thirty-five years. I like a sense of control." He didn't look at Bill, but he added, "As long as you're OK with that."

Nicely done, Kurt. I suspected I had just seen the last of Bill in the captain's chair for this trip.

"Be my guest. I'll get the binoculars, and we'll start searching for Nick," Bill said.

He disappeared below for two minutes and returned with a box of petite binoculars.

"My boss bought enough so that if the boat was full he would have a set for every person on board. Must be nice to have that much coin. Rocks for us, today."

We each took a pair. Top of the line, of course, Robin Leach's imaginary voice informed me.

Bill said, as if he were asking us if we knew the sun would come up tomorrow, "You guys know that we can't get *Kate* all the way up to Monito, right?"

No, I didn't know that. I didn't know squat about Monito until two minutes ago. Not good news, but I decided a comment along these lines would not be productive.

"Does the mini Whaler work?" Collin asked, referring to the smaller boat strapped to the back of *Kate.*

"Yep, she does. The reef and rocks are impenetrable in places, though, even for the little Whaler. But we have a two-seater kayak and an inflatable raft, too. Again, my boss bought everything he could think of, plus a few."

Collin grinned, but in a stern all-business way. I'd seen this many times before. It often involved cars squealing around corners on two wheels and guns firing, but luckily we were on an unarmed cruiser. Officer Connell was about to take charge of the mission, just as Captain Kovacs had taken over the helm. How many alpha males does it take to screw in a light bulb? I wasn't sure, but I knew it only took one of me to find my husband.

"Bill, that satellite phone you told me your boss keeps charged under the bar? We have to keep it fully accessible, starting now. Time to check in with the federal powers that be. We need those flyovers your Coast Guard friend promised us, Kurt."

Kurt held out his hand. "I'm all over it." He took the phone. His tone was confident.

When he hung up, he said, "They're already on their way from San Juan. We should see whirlybirds in an hour or so."

An hour was an eternity. I stared back at the sky in the direction from which we'd come and wished the helicopters godspeed.

Chapter Twenty-five

Kate weaved through the rocks, reefs, and sandbars for the next hour. I kept my binoculars to my eyes, working my way back and forth like a slow-motion metronome over the surface of the water. The notes of "Für Elise" echoed in my brain in time to the beat-keeper, a memory from piano lessons long ago. I felt myself bobbing my head to the music in my search-dance. I was definitely near delirium.

My eyes ached from too little sleep and straining in the sun. I was scared even to blink for fear of missing Nick. So far, though, I had seen only three sea turtles and a lonely porpoise. We inched ever nearer to Monito Island, my Little Mona Lisa, scant more than a rock cliff face with green-tufted hair. Gazing at it, I felt so lightheaded that I could swear I saw a Fourth of July sparkler right in front of my nose. How could Nick even get up there? And how would we get him down if he did? Bill's boss carried every small sea craft imaginable, but I doubted he stocked rock climbing and rappelling gear.

"We need to circle the island, right? Didn't we decide that Nick most likely approached from the west?" I asked.

"Yup," Kurt said. "Can you mark the map for me, Bill?"

Bill set down his binoculars on the table and prepped the map for Kurt. While he was at work, the sound of a helicopter filled my ears, a hopeful sound. Thwack thwack thwack, the blades beat the air, pounding, capable. I knew that if anyone could find Nick, it would be the helicopter crew. I did a mental fist pump.

Kate's radio crackled. "Coast Guard *Nikita* for *Wild Irish Kate*. Do you read?"

Kurt had arranged for radio contact between the helo and us through his friend, who apparently had the stroke to make things happen, and then some.

Kurt hit the mike button. "*Wild Irish Kate*, copy that, *Nikita*. What do you see from up there?"

"We see a flat-top island with scrubby bushes, and that's it. Monito proper devoid of humans. Repeat, no sign of subject on Monito."

No. I refused to accept that. They were wrong.

"They're wrong," I said. "They are wrong!"

Kurt didn't look at me, but he clicked to speak. "What about the cliffs and water around the island?"

"Hard to say, but we saw nothing on the first pass. There's not even an iguana on top of the island. Really desolate. We're going to check out Mona and Desecheo, and then we'll come back and do some low hovers around the sides of Monito."

But he's on Monito! Why are they leaving Monito?

"Where's Desecheo?" I asked.

Bill said, "It's a tiny island much closer to Puerto Rico."

"That makes no sense," I said. "It's highly unlikely Nick would have kept paddling against the current that far to the east. Mona, maybe, but not Desecheo. Kurt, tell them. Make them stop!"

"They said they'll come back for the low passes," Collin said. "If we argue with them, we'll lose their cooperative spirit. Let's just get in as close as we can and circle until they come back. Look alive, everyone."

No one could argue with that. But I wanted to. I was furious. I shouted at the sky, coloring the air with curses and beating it with my fist. Damn them. Already the sound of the helo was receding in the distance.

But Collin was right, we couldn't risk alienating the pilots. And hadn't Nick said only I could find him? I hadn't thought he meant literally. Getting to this one tiny island in the whole gigantic world was finding him, as far as I was concerned. But I would, by God, be the one or die trying. I grabbed my binoculars and hat and leaned over the railing, putting my eyes as close to the island as I could get them.

Collin and Bill had retrained their binocs on Monito, too. No one but *Kate* made a sound as we trolled around the island clockwise.

I focused on the vertical surfaces, since the Coast Guard had ruled out the horizontal. The water broke against the foot of the cliffs, and even under them in the places where the sea had cut away the base of the rocks. I wondered if the water could have sucked Nick under the cliffs.

Don't think like that.

Some spots seemed friendlier than that, though, almost gentle. And we were in the Caribbean, not the North Sea, so even the rough spots weren't brutal.

Bill read my mind. Without taking his glasses from his eyes, he said, "It looks worse than it is. I won't lie—I've heard those rocks are wicked sharp, but there are plenty of protected areas."

His words salved my nerves some. And I knew that with the warm sun, Nick wouldn't die of hypothermia. The greater threats were dehydration and sunstroke.

Think positive, Katie.

I made a list of points in Nick's favor: no poisonous snakes, no great white sharks, no hurricanes this week. My emotions rollercoastered, but I anchored myself at that rail and never took the binocs away from my eyes.

When a picture of crazy Tim carrying Taylor away from Annalise snuck into my mind, I heard Nick's voice: *Annalise said to tell you she'll protect the kids.*

Ugh.

Could I trust my dreams? Could I believe what Nick said? We would know soon. I pushed Annalise and the kids out of my head and focused.

I kept sweeping, looking, searching forward, then back again. In one direction, a kaleidoscope of water and rock. In the other, a kaleidoscope of rock and water. Forward again. Back, but not quite as far. Farther forward. Lesser back. And again. And again. Everything looked crushingly the same. Water. Reef. Rock. Waves. Spray.

I didn't know what to look for so I looked for anything that broke the pattern. Nick's arm waving. A piece of wing with blue paint, a magnifying glass over a dead fish's eye. Nick's dark hair. Anything. But for hours now, all I had seen was nothing. I hadn't even taken a break for water and my mouth was parched.

I commented for the hundredth time to Collin, "Everything looks the same. It's so damn hard to see."

"Treat it like one of those optical puzzles. Relax your mind and let your eyes and instinct work together. It makes things pop out of the picture," Collin said.

Yeah, right.

And then, as I swept forward yet again, relaxing my mind as Collin suggested, something I saw tugged at me deep inside.

Turn around, Katie.

I wasn't sure if it was my own voice or if someone else said the words to me. But I listened. I turned around and pointed my binoculars back, way past my normal sweep, backwards in the direction we had come.

Nothing.

No, wait. Something?

What was that? A rock nook and something lumpy on the horizontal plane?

Binoculars still to my face, I gripped the handrail blindly and stumbled toward the stern along the starboard walkway while *Kate* continued around Monito. I reached the back of the boat, straining to get a better view of the variation in pattern I saw at the base of the island. The anomaly called me to the rocks like a Siren.

"Stop," I screamed, straining my throat. I dropped my binoculars for a split second and aimed my words at Bill, who had stationed himself halfway up the stairs to the flying bridge. "Stop, stop, stop!"

"Full stop," Bill relayed up to Kurt, his voice penetrating the sound of *Kate's* engine.

Kate lurched slightly then sagged into the water as Kurt throttled all the way back. I grabbed the handrail and trained my binoculars on the rocks again.

I heard Collin clambering toward the back of the boat.

"What do you see?" he asked.

"I'm not sure. There—see the break in the rock with that piece jutting out toward the water that makes a sort of vertically protected face?" I pointed. "We couldn't see it coming around. You have to be facing this way to see it."

Collin pointed his binocs in the direction I indicated. "Yeah, I got it," Collin said.

"Go up, tight in the back of the crease, about ten feet above the water."

"OK."

"See how the rock slants down to the water from there, like a ramp? Go up the ramp. Until you get to a rock shelf under an overhang. Do you see anything there? I think I see something with soft edges instead of hard corners. It could be a person lying down."

Collin repeated my instructions in a whisper as he searched the rock. "Oh my God. I see it. You're right, Katie. Good job—amazing eyes. Keep watching. I'll get Kurt to move us back as near to it as we can get, then we can take one of the smaller boats in closer to get a better look." Collin ran down the walkway as the boat gently pitched in the waves.

You bet I'll keep watching. Nick, if that's you, honey, we're here. It would help if you would sit up or move around. Wave a white flag on a stick. Blow me a kiss. Something, baby. Anything.

As *Kate* started a slow pivot, I fought the powerful urge to dive over the rail and swim to Monito. Kurt lined us up in the opposite direction and cruised at double our previous speed to the edge of the next section of the reef.

"Bill, can you come up here and help me get closer?" Kurt yelled. He pulled the throttles back until *Kate* idled.

Bill didn't answer; he just ran up the stairs. Seconds later, *Kate* started moving again in a cautious waddle. To me, it looked like Kurt was planting her atop the reefs. Our forward progress seemed minimal, just precious seconds wasted. Then I heard Bill coming back down the stairs. Kurt stopped the engines again.

"Anchor away," Bill called out.

I took advantage of *Kate's* stillness to search the rocks again. I had a much better view now, but I couldn't tell if what I saw was my husband or not. *Kate* started swaying and my stomach heaved, but I clamped my teeth and swallowed down the bile.

Whir. Splash. Whirr-rrr-rr-rrr-rrr. I listened to the anchor as it sank to the ocean floor, looking for a sandy patch to claw.

Bill grunted. "Got it. Anchor secure."

Now my ears picked out Kurt's heavy tread on the stairs. Bill, then Kurt, joined Collin and me at the bow. We all stared at my find.

"What do you think?" I asked, praying one of them would tell me what I wanted to hear. "Is it Nick?"

"I can't tell. It's too big to be a bird or gecko, and it's not just rock," Bill said.

"Yup," Kurt said.

"We have to get a closer look," I said.

My eyes hurt from focusing on the rock shelf. I dropped them to the surface of the water for a quick rest and caught a disturbing new sight.

"Guys, look, there, twenty yards in front of us," I shouted, pointing and waving my arm up and down. "There's something stuck on the reef under the water, right below the surface."

Three sets of binocs lowered to point at the water.

Kurt spoke first. "Something's caught underwater. Something nonorganic." He dropped the binocs.

"Could it be the raft?" I asked.

Collin had already started moving back toward the stern. "I definitely think it's the life raft."

At first, this crushed my spirit. Then I realized that if what I saw on the rocks was Nick, he didn't need the raft. It had already done its job getting him here. In fact, if this was his raft, that raised the odds considerably that what I saw on the rocks could actually be Nick. My mind romped with this information in a joyous circle.

Collin started to take charge. "Let's get the Whaler in."

Bill said, "We can't get the Whaler all the way to the rocks. But we can get it halfway or a little better. I think we should put the kayak in, too."

Collin continued to assert his authority. "All right. Two of us should go in the Whaler, then, and one of us needs to paddle the kayak while one of us stays with *Kate*."

We all headed for the back of the boat. The diesel fumes filled my nose and I fought nausea again. Bill walked over to lower the Whaler and I opened a floor bin to haul out life jackets, paddles, and an inflatable raft. I was desperate for something to do, anything to get my mind off that lump on the rocks.

"Do you want to carry the inflatable in the Whaler?" I asked.

Bill replied, "Yeah, why not. Make sure to bungee-cord it on tight."

Kurt and I began loading the Whaler.

"Collin, can you man the kayak?" I asked. He was the strongest of us all.

"Absolutely." Collin unstrapped the kayak from its storage spot on the rear of the boat. He lowered it into the water by its line and started to climb in after it.

Kurt stopped him. "Wear this, take this," he said. He handed Collin two life jackets.

"Yeah, good idea." Collin put one on and disappeared over the side of the ladder, carrying the other life preserver and the long paddle under his arm.

"Which of you guys are staying with the boat?" I asked.

Kurt and Bill looked at each other. "You're younger and have more experience with small boats in these waters. You go, I'll stay," Kurt said to him.

"Good. Then I'll go with Bill," I said.

"Yup. Just bring back my boy," Kurt said.

I looked through the supplies on the Whaler. Something was missing. I scrambled into the cabin and grabbed two red Gatorades.

"Bill, is there a first aid kit on the Whaler?" I called out.

"I don't think so. Grab the one under the galley sink."

I knocked over half the cleaning supplies in the cabinet before I found the waterproof pouch. I tucked it under one arm and held the Gatorades under the other and ran the few steps back to Bill and the Whaler. Bill had it ready to go, and I tossed my last few items in. He pushed the button to lower it into the water. I donned a life jacket and stuck my arm through the straps of one more, just in case.

Then I looked toward Monito. Collin was already halfway there. *Go, Collin. Bring me back my husband.* I followed Bill down the ladder and into the Whaler.

"Hang on," he said as the low craft wobbled with our weight.

Kurt peered over the side, ready to bring our cables back up when we were free. Bill started the engine, unhooked the lines, and gunned the motor. She was ready.

Bill perched on his knees to get a better view of the reef. The Whaler growled and then roared as he urged it slowly forward. I braced myself as he cut the wheel from side to side, weaving through the obstacle course between us and Monito.

As we neared Collin, Bill eased off the throttle.

"Can you pull me up alongside Collin? I want to hand him a Gatorade. It's likely he'll be the first person to get to Nick."

If it's Nick.

It had to be, because I'd already seen the life raft from my dream, and if the life raft was here, he was here.

"Sure," Bill said, and maneuvered closer.

I held up the Gatorade and stretched my arm over the water. Collin nodded and took it from me. He jammed it inside the front of his life vest.

From this vantage point and without binoculars, I still couldn't tell whether we were approaching a rock or my husband. The adrenaline in my system was making me dizzy, but I braced myself on the gunwale and kept watching.

"I don't know how much closer I can get," Bill shouted to Collin over the noise of our idling motor. "But I'll keep working at it. I'll have to troll now."

Collin gave a thumbs-up and resumed his paddling, each stroke followed rapidly by another that sent the kayak surging toward the rocks. Bill raised the engine until the blades barely broke the water's surface. He set the engine to troll and we puttered forward.

I closed my eyes and whispered. The time had come to ask for help, to jump the emergency-room line.

Our father, who art in Heaven, hallowed be thy name. Thy kingdom come, thy will be done, on Earth as it is in Heaven. Give us this day our daily bread, and forgive our trespasses, as we forgive those who trespass against us. Lead us not into temptation, but deliver us from evil, for thine is the Kingdom, the Power, and the Glory, forever. Amen.

Thy will be done. My throat swelled.

We watched, floating close enough to see Collin clearly, but we were useless to him. He reached the base of the rocks and searched for a handhold for what seemed like hours. When it looked like he had found one, he tossed his paddle onto the rock above him and hauled himself up hand over hand. The line for the kayak was tied around his waist but slack. Finally, he was high enough to plant a foot on the rock. He pushed himself up, moved one hand upwards, planted the other foot, pushed up, moved the other hand up. Again. The kayak lifted off the water. Again. Again. Now the skinny watercraft was vertical, and with one more pull/push, Collin climbed over the edge and was on the rock. He lifted the kayak hand over hand until he could rest it on the rock beside him.

I could never have done what I just watched my brother do. I wondered if even Bill or Kurt could have made that ascent pulling the water-laden boat. I imagined Nick doing it without the boat, after a plane crash and God knows how long floating in a life raft. I swallowed.

And then Collin disappeared from our view. We floated. Neither Bill nor I said a word.

No Collin.

And then he reappeared.

He gave us a giant "O" over his head, like a scuba diver. The symbol for "OK."

"That looks like good news to me," Bill said.

"Yeah?" I answered, but I didn't take my eyes away from Collin until he disappeared again. "You think so?"

Bill reached for my hand and held it with one of his, then patted it with his other. "I do."

And I started crying. My eyes poured out enough tears to fill that little boat. Bill leaned over with a clumsy hug, and I scrubbed the tears away. *Thank you God, thank you, oh thank you.* Bill stood up and made a giant "O" for Kurt to see as well, and the Whaler pitched. He half-fell, half-hopped down and held onto both sides. We both laughed, relief making the rocking boat funnier than it was.

Collin was taking forever. Water lapped at the hull and the sun baked our heads. I sucked in the salt air and could just make out the pungent scent of the rocks stained white by the birds that were watching us from above.

Bill broke the silence. "I wonder why that helicopter never came back? Good thing we didn't count on them."

I looked at Bill and nodded. I had given up on help when they left hours ago. So much for the Coast Guard. Nick told me I had to be the one to find him, and I was. I looked past Bill at *Kate* in the distance and saw something disturbing.

A boat was approaching her, winding through the same reefs she had wound through, but moving faster than she had. A smaller boat, low-slung and sleek.

"Bill," I said.

I didn't have to point or say another word. Bill's face registered what he read on mine, and he turned to see what had set me back. He squinted and put his hand over his eyes.

"Can you tell what it is?" I asked. "I mean, it's a boat, but, you know . . ."

"Not yet. I'm sure it's nothing, though," he said.

I wasn't so sure it was nothing, but we couldn't do anything about it now. Well, I could do one thing. I stood up and waved for Kurt's attention, then used my biggest pointing gestures to direct his attention to the boat. Whether Kurt saw me, I did not know.

Bill grabbed my leg. "Katie, look," he said.

I'd started the boat tilting back and forth again, so I sat down carefully and spun around on my seat. When I turned my head back toward Monito, my heart filled my throat and blood pounded hot in my ears. Collin was standing on the rock shelf supporting a very limp Nick on his arm. But Nick was upright. Nick was alive and standing right in front of me on Monito.

"That tough son of a bitch," Bill said. "He crashes a plane in the middle of the ocean, paddles to an island, climbs a sheer rock face, and survives on nothing but air for days out here." Bill slapped me a high five. There were tears in his eyes.

"How in the world is Collin going to get him down from there?" I asked.

"Piece of cake for a badass like Collin," Bill said.

I thought it looked impossible. While I gaped, Collin put the life vest on Nick and pulled the straps tight. Nick's body jerked like a rag doll with each tug. Still supporting Nick with one arm, Collin lowered the kayak to the water.

And then he pushed my husband off the rocks and into the sea below, jumping in after him.

"What is he doing?" I screamed.

"It's going to be OK," Bill said. He patted my shoulder. "I'd have done the same thing. Nick has on a life vest. Collin's right there with him."

As scared as it made me, Bill was right. Already Collin had shoved Nick across the kayak. We watched as Collin tried several times to get himself in but failed. Each time he slipped off the side, my stomach plunged. Finally, he gave up and swam, pulling the kayak behind him by its line. The bulky swimmer and boat moved an inch at a time toward us with Nick's feet trailing like anchors behind it. Collin was strong, but he was not a trained swimmer.

While Collin struggled, I didn't take my eyes off Nick. Bill did, though.

"Looks like that boat is pulled up to the *Kate*," he said.

I whipped my head toward *Kate*. The black boat was beside her. The distorted sound of Puerto Rican music moved over the surf and wind. Kurt was leaning down, talking to the boat's occupants. My glance registered three of them, and I was relieved to see Collin still towing Nick when I turned back around.

"What's going on?" I asked Bill.

"I can't tell," he said.

Nick and Collin kept moving closer.

"They're pointing something at Kurt," Bill said, and his voice rose.

No, please no. "What is it?" I listened for a gunshot.

"It's," Bill hesitated. "It looks like—oh, Katie, it was a camera. They took a picture. And Kurt just waved to them. They're leaving. Yeah, it looks like they're headed to the cut back to Mona."

I leaned over the side of the Whaler and vomited. I felt better.

And then the kayak bumped the Whaler. Collin grabbed the side of our boat, gasping for air, and Nick raised his hand an inch or two.

His voice was a fraction of its normal volume, but scratchy as always and recognizably him. "Where's my wife?" he said.

"I'm right here, baby, I'm right here," I said. I leaned over the side of the Whaler as far as I dared. I wanted to touch that man more than I wanted to breathe.

"What took you so long?" he said, and I knew without a doubt that he was fine. Weak, but sense of humor intact. My Nick.

Bill and Collin had lined up the kayak with the Whaler. My hands found Nick's face. Warmth flooded my body.

"Someone forgot to tell me where he was going four days ago. A mere oversight, I'm sure," I said. I laughed. The time to discuss that, and many other things, would come later. Now, the joy pulsing from my heart almost blasted the top of my head skyward.

With Collin and Bill's help, Nick crawled into the boat and collapsed against me.

Nick rolled his head back until he could see my face. "There you are. My Katie."

I pressed my lips against his cracked red forehead and whispered into his hairline. "I love you. I love you, Nick. Let's go home."

Thy will be done.

Chapter Twenty-six

Nick took thimble-sized sips of Gatorade as I cut his clothes off him.

"Do I need an audience for this?" he rasped, referring to Collin and Kurt. Bill was back in the captain's perch, rocketing us toward Rincón, Puerto Rico.

"Sorry, brother-in-law, but as much trouble as we've been through to find you, you're stuck with all of us," Collin said.

Kurt nodded, because that's what Kurt did. But he was smiling, ear to ear.

I said, "Shhh, Nick. Save your energy. We're going to take you rock climbing later." This earned me a laugh, which turned into a dry cough. More Gatorade.

"I never want to climb another rock in my life. I don't even want to look at a rock. And I sure never want to use one as a pillow again," he said.

I removed his pocket watch from its clasp on his belt loop. "I think we're going to have to get this fixed again," I said. I popped open the face and salt water trickled out and onto the bed. The pictures of Taylor, the girls, and me were barely recognizable. I started to pry them out.

"Don't," Nick said. He shook his head. "I want to keep them, just like that."

I smiled at him and shut the watch, then put it in my own pocket for safekeeping. I tossed pieces of his stiff clothing into the trashcan. I wanted to put him in the shower but decided in favor of a damp washcloth for now. This filth had to come off in layers. I worked as gently as I could.

"Ow," Nick said. "Sunburn."

I let up. The man deserved a short reprieve. I pulled the zebra-striped sheet over him, then I put my face over his and looked into his eyes. He mustered an exhausted smile. I touched his cheek with my fingertips and kissed his red nose, beautiful but still slightly dirty. His eyes closed.

As Nick faded, I turned to Kurt. "Why didn't the choppers ever come back?"

He shook his head. "They radioed that they found Haitian refugees on Desecheo. They said they'd resume our search when they finished that rescue."

Nick's eyes popped open. He raised his head from the pillow and propped himself on one elbow. "Are you talking about the Coast Guard? Are you in contact with them?"

"Yup," Kurt said.

"Whatever you do, please, don't tell them or anyone you've found me yet."

"What?" Kurt asked.

"What!" I echoed.

"I have so much to tell you. Long story short, the bad guys think I'm dead. We need to keep it that way for now."

Kurt's brows shot up, but after a minute of reflection he said, "Let me see what I can do without making a media announcement. I think it's a serious offense to waste the Coast Guard's resources, son. Just help me understand enough that I can explain the situation to my contact."

Nick nodded and slumped back on his pillow, his eyes closing again. He had a coughing attack and I helped him take another drink. We all moved closer to hear him.

"I have to start at the beginning. Elena texted me after we interviewed her. Said she needed to talk to me. I told her I was going to the Ag Fair with my family. She said a guy would meet me there, and he did. He said he feared for her life and needed someone to fly her to DR. That if I took her, she would tell me the whole Eddy story when we got there, that she knew everything." He lifted just his fingers off the bed, making tiny quotes when he said, "knew everything."

I knew it. I knew he'd lied to me about the man at the Ag Fair. I felt the first hot flush in my cheeks.

Relax, girl.

"I agreed," Nick continued. "We set a time for the next morning. So I snuck off St. Marcos and took Elena and her mother to Punta Cana, but first they asked me to stop in San Juan and pick up that same guy I met at the Ag Fair. His name is Jorge Gomez, and he is, or was, a Petro-Mex employee on St. Marcos, too." He stopped for more Gatorade. His sips were getting bigger and he seemed to grow stronger with every swallow. Or maybe it was his story that was energizing him.

"And a few hours later, some goons poured rum in your gas tanks," Kurt said.

"That's what it was, huh? I knew it was no damn coincidence that my engines failed. Man, I'll bet they picked up my trail in San Juan. It was a mistake to tell the tower there I was bound for Punta Cana. Bastards."

Nick wiped his chapped lips with his hand. I had smeared Carmex on them and was itching to do it again, but I restrained myself and let him go on.

"So Elena kept her word and told me the story. Gomez and Elena were lovers. They met when Elena moved to St. Marcos to marry Eddy. She said that when Eddy died, she had no idea if it was suicide or not. But she told people it had to be murder, because she didn't want people to find out about her with Gomez and say Eddy killed himself because of their affair. Then she got a visit from a guy who made her change her story. She said he was local muscle, a mafioso type."

I helped him drink again. His lips bled this time, so I put the Carmex on anyway, and he tolerated it.

"The guy told her he would kill her unless she said Eddy committed suicide. She was terrified. Her old boyfriend in Mexico is a tough guy with the Chihuahua cartel, so, thinking he could help her, she called him. Wrong move. It turned out that her mafioso visitor was with the Chihuahua cartel, too, and the old boyfriend knew all about what was happening. In fact, he was part of it. He laughed at her, told her that the cartel had gone to Eddy and demanded he help them, or they'd kill Elena. So Eddy did." Nick stopped to rest. His sips had turned into long gulps.

"Nice people," I said.

"Scary people," Nick said.

"What did the cartel want Eddy to do for them?" Collin asked.

"They made Eddy help them with the plans for a terrorist attack on the St. Marcos refinery. Remember that article I showed you, Katie? They're feuding over payola for a pipeline in Mexico, so the Chihuahuas wanted to shut down Petro-Mex's pipeline here, so to speak. The harbor."

"Why Eddy?" I asked.

"He had access to the information they needed. Eddy worked in Terminal Operations, the part of the refinery that moves crude off and products like gasoline onto the ships. His group also took care of the tank farm, that giant storage facility they have."

Now the printouts of maps and shipping schedules Nick had left in our office made sense.

"So Eddy was helping terrorists," I said. And the cartel murdered their informant outside my home. Yuck. Too close.

"Emphasis on 'was.' The ex-boyfriend told Elena that Eddy had found out about her sleeping with Gomez. Eddy refused to cooperate with the cartel anymore. He told them to kill her if they wanted to. They killed him instead."

"Why did Jiménez show up at Elena's house and insist Eddy was murdered? Is Jiménez a local stooge for the cartel, too?" I asked.

"Actually, no. You'll get a kick out of this, I think. Jiménez was paying Mexican women to marry the refinery employees. He paid Elena to come marry Eddy. No one else at Petro-Mex knows, and he was trying to keep it a secret. Elena said Jiménez was afraid she would tell us, or that we'd find something about it on Eddy's computer," Nick said.

I couldn't close my mouth. "What? But why?" Tutein was right. Petro-Mex had given Elena to Eddy as a retention bonus.

"Jiménez is the human resources guy. He had a terrible problem with employee turnover. The refinery employees couldn't keep their women from Mexico and the states on the island. The women hated St. Marcos—they were far from their families, they couldn't get jobs, they didn't like living next to the refinery. When the women left, the men left. So, to get the men to stay, Jiménez needed women who would stay. Women that were paid not to leave."

Wow. Just wow. "Is that even legal?"

"Not if the women were from the U.S. But even if he wasn't breaking any laws, Jiménez wanted to keep it a secret so he wouldn't look bad."

Made sense. "By the way, Ramirez fired us. Or you, rather. Because Elena begged him to call off the investigation."

"Figures," Nick said.

"So wrap it up for me: why don't you want the Coast Guard to let anyone know you're alive?" Kurt asked.

"For more reasons than the cartel thinks I'm dead, and I think they sent people to kill me?" Nick asked. His voice rose.

"There's no 'think' to it, babe. They definitely tried to kill you," I said. "And they followed us and killed one of the witnesses we talked to."

"What?" Nick said. "Are they still following us? Don't underestimate their reach."

Collin said, "They found us in San Juan, but we shook them. No sign of them since, and I've been vigilant. I know them well from New Mexico drug operations."

"They think you flew toward Mexico," I added. And then I remembered the boat. "Kurt, what was the deal with the boat that pulled up to *Kate* earlier?"

"Tourists. Drunk," Kurt said.

Maybe. "What did you tell them?"

"I told them I was a charter captain, and that my clients were scuba diving at Monito. They took a picture of themselves with *Kate* in the background, and then said they were going to check out Mona."

I hoped that was all they were going to do.

"We've really got to be careful." Nick shook his head. "There's just a little more to the story, and then I'm going to pass out. Gomez and Elena were scared to death after she talked to the cartel ex-boyfriend. So the two of them ransacked Eddy's stuff. And they learned that the cartel was very close, is very close, to attacking the refinery. They found the plans. So I want to work with Petro-Mex and the authorities to stop the cartel, and not end up dead."

Mere hours after we had scooped his limp body off a rock, Nick was preparing to go to battle.

"Yup. I see," Kurt said. "Do you know how they plan to attack?"

"Through the harbor. They plan to destroy the harbor and blow up the tank fields. To cripple the pipeline out of St. Marcos," Nick replied.

Kurt finally seemed to have heard what he needed. He was on his feet now, headed for the satellite phone.

"One more thing," Nick called after him. "Their plan is to stage a diversion, an emergency that seems legitimate, to draw the attention of all the refinery's personnel and resources away from their attack zone."

Kurt nodded and then disappeared from view. Nick fell back onto his pillow. If it were possible for a sunburned olive-skinned man to be deathly pale, he was. Time to intervene.

I held up my scissors. "I need to finish cutting you out of your clothes, put you in a shower, and then slather aloe vera over your whole body. Scat, Collin."

"Yeah, this is not something I want to see." He leaned down and squeezed Nick's shoulder. "Good to have you back with us, Nick."

Nick put his hand on Collin's. "Thank you, Collin. Thank all of you for coming for me."

"Katie's the one that found you, but you're welcome," Collin said, and he followed Kurt out.

"So you're the one who figured out where I was?" Nick asked.

I nodded. "I had lot of help, though. And I had dreams. Dreams where you talked to me and gave me clues. Annalise even gave me clues." I picked up my blue spiral notebook from the bedside table and handed it to him.

His eyes softened. He rubbed his palm against the cover of the notebook, and then flipped its pages, nodding his approval. "Did you dream about a rubber dinghy full of presents?"

I moved my face down to his, nose barely touching nose. "I did. And I dreamed about the *Wild Irish Kate*, and much more. Were you really there?"

His nose rubbed up and down against mine as he nodded. "I guess I was. I dreamed about you, too, that I was talking to you, but I didn't realize until just now that, well, they were more than dreams. But nothing surprises me anymore."

"Nor me."

He studied my face. "You are gorgeous, you know." His eyes swept my body. "And really thin."

In only days, I'd lost the rest of the baby fat. I remembered what Kurt told me, that Nick was worried about my weight. My husband and I were going to have a very unpleasant conversation when he was strong enough to live through my temper. About a lot more than my weight. About his subterfuge, his outright dishonesty. About cutting me out of the Petro-Mex case. I snuffed the wick as my temper flared. For now, I would just enjoy having him back alive.

"And you are a sight for sore eyes," I replied.

Nick puckered, hinting. I leaned in and kissed him.

He winced. "Hurts so good," he said.

I wiped his blood from my lips and smiled at him.

"How are the kids?" he asked.

A long story that would wait. "Great," I said. I left off "I hope."

"Good. I miss them so much. I want to call everyone myself soon." Kurt had called Julie already, as soon as we found Nick. "Um, Katie, I need a favor."

Uh oh. "Maybe," I said.

"After I ask for the favor, I want you to tell me all about what has happened since I left."

"That part sounds fine," I said. "Just keep drinking."

Nick took a sip. He folded his lips in and inhaled, then said in a headmaster voice, "I want to go straight back to St. Marcos. I don't want to go to the hospital."

I glared at him.

"Seriously, I'm fine," he said. "So I'm a little hungry and thirsty. I floated in a life raft for a day. I got a little dinged up on some rocks."

"You were in a plane crash, too!"

"It was really more like a rough landing, that's all."

"And you don't have any clothes," I said. I knew this was a weak argument, but it was all I had left.

"I can wear some of Dad's."

"Nick," I started to protest.

"Katie, I know you'll take care of me, and I just want to get back to St. Marcos, quickly and quietly. More people are going to die if we don't stop the cartel. And then all we've been through will be meaningless. Let's finish this. Let's do some good."

I thought of the young busboy, dead because he had helped me. Of the man I'd never known who died outside my driveway. I sighed. The long-suffering sigh of a woman who knows her husband well and is certain she has no prayer of winning the argument.

He didn't even need to wait for a yes to know my answer."

Chapter Twenty-seven

After I had Nick cleaned up, I deposited him back into the safari room on the zebra sheets. His eyes were already closing, his words slurry whispers. I tucked the leopard spread around him and walked to the door.

"Aren't you going to stay with me?" Nick asked.

"I'll be back in five, love. I just have to take care of something," I said.

"Hurry," he mumbled.

I had fudged my answer a little. I needed a powwow with the guys up top. I climbed the ladder and stepped onto the flybridge.

"Yoo hoo," I said, startling them. "We have a change of plans that I need to run by you guys."

Bill said, "This mission is defined by changes."

"By George, I think this man understands my motto now," Collin said.

"What's that?" Bill asked.

"Flexibility is the key to air power," Collin said.

I rolled my eyes. "Your fiancée's motto. When you're done, if you don't mind?"

"The floor is yours, sis."

"Nick feels good. Well, he feels fine, anyway, relatively speaking. He just needs rest and fluids. I promised we wouldn't take him to a hospital. He feels responsible for finishing this thing with the refinery, probably in part to flip the bird at the bad guys who tried to kill him, but also because he is Nick."

Kurt liked this plan. "Good, no need to waste time with doctors." I should have guessed he would say that. Mainers.

Collin didn't disagree either. "So, what's next?"

"We can catch a plane home from Rincón," I suggested.

Bill piped in. "My boss isn't due back for another week. Nick is my friend. And I can get you home just as fast and keep Nick in an air-conditioned bedroom. Let's just fuel up in Rincón and keep going."

His answer shouldn't have surprised me by now, but it did. Collin shrugged.

"Are we still follower-free?" I asked.

Kurt said, "Yup. Nothing out here but us."

"Good," I said. "Keeps our names off airline manifests and out of customs logs, too. Fine by me."

Bill added, "Plus, I'm having fun and Kurt's teaching me a lot of great stuff."

Kurt said, "I'm keeping him off the booze is more like it. Amazing what you pick up when you're sober."

Collin and I laughed.

Bill said, "That reminds me how much I'd love a rum and cranberry juice."

"Noooo," we all chorused.

"So, Rincón, fuel, and Bill plots the fastest course back to St. Marcos. What did the Coast Guard say, Kurt?" I asked.

He ticked the points off on his fingers. "They're notifying Petro-Mex of a potential terrorist plot by the Chihuahuas, and they'll increase surveillance around the harbor. The threat level will go up at the refinery. And they agreed not to release information about Nick's rescue."

Nick really couldn't ask for more.

I said, "Nick wants to call his mom and the kids when he wakes up. But for now, I'm going to help him stay asleep for as long as possible. If we don't come out when we get to Rincón, buy lots of Gatorade and food for my patient. And some more aloe vera and antibiotic cream."

I went below and slipped into bed with Nick, my entire body sighing "ahhhhh" as it touched his. He mumbled and flipped over, pulling me to him with one arm with all the gentleness of a dockworker throwing bags of cement into a cargo hold.

"Welcome home," I whispered.

I nestled close and we drifted off together.

Six hours later, I woke up with Nick still snoring beside me. I wriggled out from under his arm and was nearly strangled by his "don't go" reflex. I headed up top, from the dark of night to the lighted bridge.

"Hi, Red," Bill said from the helm. "We're almost to Ponce. Last fuel stop before St. Marcos."

Kurt and Collin didn't register my presence. They sat at the table, engaged in a heated battle.

"You cheat," Kurt said to Collin, pushing his backgammon marker forward.

"I do not, and besides, you can't prove it," Collin replied.

Boys.

"Whoa-oa-oa. What's this?" Bill shouted. "Hey, Kurt, come take a look." His head craned toward the gauges on his dashboard.

Kurt lumbered over for a look-see, moving like he had ingested a few of Bill's rum and cranberry juices. The rosy liquid in the two glasses by the backgammon set supported my theory. Kurt looked at the gauges and flicked his finger at one. It didn't seem to change the reading, because he stood back and scrubbed his hand through his hair.

"She's starting to overheat in the starboard engine," Kurt said.

Bill pushed a button that slowed *Kate* down abruptly. "Can you run down to the engine room and take a look?" he asked.

"Yup," Kurt said over his shoulder. He was already weaving toward the stairs.

"I'll come with you," Collin said. Which came out as "wischoo." Oh, my.

I stared at the gauges until I found Temperature. The dial had inched into the red zone, that much I could tell. My limited mechanical knowledge exhausted, I fretted. That, I excelled at.

"Is this a problem?" I asked Bill, pointing at the gauge.

"Well, it could be. I carry spare parts for the easy stuff. Let's see what Kurt says."

"Why did we slow down?"

"I cut the engine so it won't damage itself. We can run on one, just not as fast."

Kurt's salt and pepper head appeared, then the rest of him, without Collin. Odds favored Collin lying prone and snoring in bed by now.

"No leaks, belts are good. Engine room checks out fine." His speech was much clearer than Collin's had been.

"That eliminates the things we can fix on the fly. Unless you can think of something else?"

"Nope. I think we need a mechanic to look under the hood," Kurt replied.

I nudged my fretting up a notch.

"Yeah, that's what I think, too. Well, Ponce has a big marina. We'll find someone. I'm gonna run down and check her exhaust pipes, though. Take the wheel?"

"Yup."

Now Bill's sun-streaked head disappeared down the stairs. Out of an abundance of caution, I decided to stand beside my tipsy father-in-law. Although I was sure he'd captain a boat stumbling drunk better than I could sober. I'd driven boats, just not a lot. But I could take over if he passed out.

My visions of Nick waking the kids up with snuggles in the morning evaporated and were replaced by an image of a slowly limping *Kate* overtaken by a fast, sleek black boat. I shook it out of my head and searched the night sea for boat lights.

Bill was back fast. "It's too dark. I can't see a thing."

Kurt said, "Well, we can still hope that's what it is because otherwise . . ."

"You'll be seeking alternate transportation," Bill said, finishing Kurt's sentence.

Chapter Twenty-eight

"Hello, guys? Can you explain what's going on?" I asked.

They looked at me like I'd just stepped off the short bus. Kurt nodded at Bill, granting permission for his junior officer to take the lead.

Bill's enthusiasm level rose as he talked about "his" boat. "Sometimes *Kate* sucks up junk—seaweed, usually—in her seawater intake. It gets wrapped around the impeller."

"What's an impeller?"

"It's a propeller that pushes seawater instead of air."

That actually made sense. "Why is it important?"

He sounded a lot less like Spicoli on this subject. "The seawater keeps the engine cool. So if the impeller's not working, the engine overheats. And if the engine overheats, we can't use it. *Kate* has two engines, and you saw me turn the hot one off. We can keep going at this speed for as long as we want, but if we lose the other engine, we're dead in the water."

I knew this was bad news. Now I was imagining *Kate* surrounded by multiple sleek black boats filled with armed terrorists. Still, understanding this made me a little bit excited. As in, "I'm not a completely hopeless idiot about boat mechanics."

Bill continued. "The impeller is just made of rubber. It tears itself up trying to turn with the junk wrapped around it. *Kate's* had it happen before. A mechanic can fix it in a few hours. The other possibilities left after we rule out the impeller, leaks, and broken belts are major problems. Problems that would keep *Kate* in Ponce for days."

I sure as heck understood what that meant. "And us on a plane. Which would put Nick back on the grid where the cartel could find him, and us," I said. "Very bad."

"Exactly," Bill agreed.

Bill reached for his radio and clicked it to life. He hailed the marina and started talking boat-speak to someone. Ten minutes later, we had secured the services of an overpriced mechanic who swore he was an unparalleled expert on the sixty-foot Hatteras. He promised to meet us on the dock.

We entered the marina and Kurt eased back on the throttles for the no-wake zone. I took in the town of Ponce, whose lights were just beginning to twinkle against a backdrop of mountainous rainforest. Pretty. I preferred sleepy beach villages with goats tied up under palm trees, myself, but anywhere with a live-and-healthy Nick looked wonderful to me tonight.

"I'm going to roust Nick," I said, and scurried below.

The view in the safari room did far more for me than the view of Ponce had. Nick lay sprawled across the bed, snoring softly with zebra-striped sheets wrapped around his lower leg and his arms akimbo beneath his pillow. I dropped in beside him and kissed his cheek in front of his ear.

He stretched in protest. "Whaddyawannawakemeupfor?"

"We're overnighting in Ponce. Boat issues. We're paying an after-hours mechanic an arm and a leg to work on *Kate*. We just entered the marina."

He yawned and slung his arms around me. "Damn. That slows us down."

"Yes, and it gets worse. If this isn't a quick fix, we have to fly home."

"Sumbitch," he mumbled into my neck.

"There is better news, though. Kurt already has the Feds working with Petro-Mex on security issues and threat level. Don't worry, they won't announce your rescue, either."

"That part sounds good," he said. He sat up and dragged himself from the bed and I helped him dress. He looked gaunt, especially in the clothes I'd gotten from Kurt, who was about forty pounds heavier than his son. Nick stood up and took a few cautious steps toward the door, where he leaned against the frame.

"Can I have my watch?" he asked.

I retrieved it from my pocket, clipped the chain in place, and handed it to him. He rubbed his thumb over the cover, then tucked it into his pocket. My heart swelled.

"We'll grab dinner, take real showers, sleep in full-sized beds, and leave whenever the mechanic calls with news, one way or another." I grasped his hand and tugged him along behind me. "We'll Skype with the kids and your mother. Let them see you alive and well." And let me see them alive and well.

This made him shuffle faster. "I'm thirsty like a camel."

"Come along, then, there's a cure for that condition."

Nick and I joined the others above deck, where Bill and the mechanic, whose clothes and hands were in need of a proper degreasing, were discussing repairs.

"You guys go. I'm staying on *Kate*," he told us. "She's my responsibility, and I have everything I need here."

"We'll keep in touch by cell," I replied.

"We're docked at La Guancha Boardwalk," Bill said. "It's got it all—food, music, and local color—so have some fun for me."

So, off we went to Ponce, which locals called the Pearl of the South. It was the second largest city in Puerto Rico, but a distant second, less than two hundred thousand people, compared to San Juan's four hundred thousand plus.

Kurt and Collin were sleepy after their afternoon rum party, and Nick was moving like a zombie too, so I walked them to the end of the boardwalk and grabbed a taxi for the hotel the mechanic had recommended, a Howard Johnson. HoJo's was cheap enough to pay for in cash, a must to avoid the reach of the cartel. It was nearby and had a restaurant, which made it perfect. So much for local color. We'd have to catch the views of the Cardona Island Lighthouse and Coffin Island next visit.

At the restaurant, we ordered plantains, rice, beans, and fried fish, and Nick devoured all of his food and most of mine. Kurt and Collin ate, too, but mostly they refreshed their rum buzz. While Kurt had a good influence on Bill, Collin had a terrible one on Kurt.

After dinner, we settled into our hotel room. The décor in HoJo's Ponce was identical to the décor in any location of HoJo's U.S.A.: nondescript green comforter with yellow and purple stripes, green squeaky carpet. Our window looked out onto the parking lot instead of the courtyard pool and gardens, but it was clean. After I'd shanghaied Nick into a recumbent position, Kurt and Collin weaved over to our room and we connected the laptop to the Annalise crew.

I pulled the desk closer to the bed and angled the laptop to catch Nick's face. Our screen filled not just with the faces of Julie and the kids but with Ruth, Rashidi, and Ava, too. So many voices pealed at once, we sounded like a street full of New York cabs.

I held Nick's hand and basked in his glow as his friends and family peppered him with questions and welcomed him home. Nick looked good now, compared to earlier. Which was still pretty awful.

"Hi, Daddy," one voice trumpeted over the rest.

"Hi, Taylor. How are you, little man?" Nick's voice cracked, but Taylor didn't notice.

"I'm good. Are you done with your work trip? Gramma's happy you're coming home. Did you bring me a present?"

Good job, Gramma.

"I did, I got presents for everybody, but I dropped them in the water. Can you believe how silly I am?"

"Silly Daddy."

"Next time, buddy. How are your baby sisters?"

"They cried a lot today. Gramma said they're teasing."

"Teasing?"

Julie said, "Teething."

We laughed. How simple and settled we could feel, just by talking to Taylor. Chihuahua cartel, who?

"'Lise said welcome home, Daddy," Taylor said.

"Did she? When did she tell you that?" Nick asked.

"At lunch."

"Annalise can't talk," I said.

Taylor cocked his head. "Yes she can. She talks to me. And Oso." He looked to his left. "Bye bye, Daddy. Oso wants me to go play."

Well. That would give me something to think about. I knew Annalise felt a special bond to Taylor, but talking to him? Surely that was just his imagination. Understandable, though, for a boy who lived in a jumbie house. But maybe, maybe.

"Bye, Taylor. I love you," Nick said.

"Love you, too," Taylor said, and his head disappeared as he climbed off the kitchen barstool.

I listened to his bare feet slapping the porcelain tile as he ran off. When he was gone, I asked, "How did it go with the attorney about DPNR, guys?"

Rashidi answered. "Good. We all going in to meet the director tomorrow at 9:30. The attorney got some great ideas. And we haven't had any more visitors up here at Annalise."

"Excellent news all around," I said.

Nick raised one eyebrow and whispered, "Tell me about this later?" I nodded and patted his knee.

"I'm so glad you're all right, son," Julie said. "I've been very careful what I say and how I act in front of Taylor, but I've been praying twenty-four hours a day since you disappeared, and I am thankful to God that you are alive. I love you."

"Thank God, Katie, Kurt, Bill, Collin, and Annalise, Mom. I love you, too."

"Annalise?" Julie asked.

"We can't wait to get home and tell you all about it," Nick said.

We ended the call and Kurt and Collin headed off to sleep. Alone with Nick again, I found myself fighting my anxiety about *Kate* and the fact that I was the only able-bodied, right-minded person in our party. I was losing the battle.

Nick watched me get ready for bed, his eyes glazed with exhaustion. "I thought about you all the time, you know. While I was on that island."

I willed the creases I felt between my eyebrows to ease. I didn't need to pass my stress on to him. I lay down on my side facing him and held up my head above my bent elbow to listen to him.

"I was so optimistic at first. I was scared when the plane's engines stopped, of course. But I knew how to land it. I had my raft, my paddles, my survival kit. I could see an island in the distance."

I laid my free hand on his chest.

"I put the Malibu down perfectly. I got out in plenty of time and into my raft before the plane sank. I thought I'd be on land and looking for help by nightfall. But it was so much harder to get there than I thought it would be. That current was strong. I fell asleep during the night, and when I woke up, I was farther away than when I started. So I decided I would by God row until I got there. I made it around dusk, and by that time it had been thirty-six hours, I was out of water, and my arms felt like bricks. And the island was a giant jagged-ass rock. It was getting dark and I had to get out of the water, but I couldn't find a decent place to land. It took all my strength to crawl up to where you guys found me. I lost my raft. I was stuck. The next day I was starting to feel alone. Scared. Sunburned. Thirsty. Hungry."

"It sounds awful," I said. I would have flipped out.

He said, "I knew you were mad at me, too. And I knew why."

"Yes, I was mad." *Am mad.* Less than before, but still angry nonetheless. I was tired of being the emotional pinball caught between flipper and bumper.

He rolled his head toward me. "I'm sorry, Katie. I thought I was protecting you by keeping you out of the details."

"And how do you think that worked out for you?" I said, involuntarily sarcastic.

"Not good. Don't you see I had to, though?" he asked.

Wrong thing to say. I counted to ten, but it didn't work. "Had to? Like someone held a gun to your head and said they'd kill the kids if you didn't lie to me? No, I don't see that, Nick. I see you firing me from a case that you needed my help on. I see you texting your fingertips bloody and pretending you're not. I see you lying to me about meeting with Jorge. And flying to another country with Elena, not telling me one damn thing about it. I see a man who didn't treat his wife like a partner, or his partner like a wife." I was getting louder with each point I made. My last words punched into the walls like fists.

Nick's eyes widened. "You really are mad, aren't you?" he said.

I looked at my husband. We had rescued him only twelve hours ago. I was picking on a man who had dry-roasted in the tropical sun for four days. Could I save this for a better time and place? Maybe. I could try.

"Yes, I really am. Let's put it this way. For a while I wasn't sure whether I'd kill you myself when we found you. I still ping pong from joy to fury in between heartbeats."

"I wanted to keep you safe."

"Lying made everything worse, Nick. Everything." I exhaled forcibly.

Nick put his hand on my leg. His eyes had started drooping. "I know. I know it did. I knew that even when I was stuck on that island. At one point, I looked around for a way to climb the damn rocks, and I managed to scrape myself up pretty good." My eyes traced a few of his cuts and bruises. "But I was locked in. I wished I had told you what I was doing, where I was going. All I could do was hope you'd come for me. Or someone would come for me. But it was you I counted on."

"You didn't count on me before you left. You should have known. You should have known you can always count on me."

"I know." His eyes closed. They didn't reopen.

I chewed the inside of my cheek. His regret over lying to me was that it kept me from rescuing him sooner. No mention of the impact on me. Not a real apology.

Later.

The time for reckoning would be later. I let the exhausted man sleep and lay there listening for the phone, hoping for good news.

Chapter Twenty-nine

Bill called at 3:30 to let us know *Kate* would leave the dock in a half hour. Nothing like an early start from a last-second warning, but it was good news. Collin and Kurt appeared at our door seconds after I hung up the phone.

"Bad news, sports fans. We have watchers," Collin announced.

"What?" I sputtered. Where had they come from? "How could they have found us? I thought that's why we paid in cash."

"We did pay for our rooms in cash. But remember dinner?" Collin asked.

I thought back. I hadn't paid, but I couldn't remember who did. I looked at Nick and he lifted his shoulders in a "Dunno" sort of way.

Kurt mumbled something.

"What, Dad?" Nick asked.

"I said, 'Shit,'" Kurt said. "I slipped the waiter my credit card to make sure I beat you guys to the bill. I was tired. I drank too many cocktails. Damn, I just forgot."

"Blame it on the a-a-a-a-a-al-co-hol," Collin sang, imitating Usher poorly. "Here's the deal. One of our goons is in the lobby. But there are more of them, one in a car by each exit. So, unless someone comes up with a better idea, I think slipping out the front door makes the most sense."

"What? Just walk right past the guy sitting out there?" I said in a sharp voice.

"Well, I do think we should stage a diversion."

"Like what?" Kurt asked.

"Like Kurt goes to the front desk and asks the clerk in a very loud whisper to send a taxi to the back door for his party."

"Collin, you're confusing me. I thought you said you think we should go out the front door," I said.

"And so we shall, as soon as the lobby watcher leaves his post for the back door," he said.

"Which we will know how?" I asked. Collin's plan was giving me a headache.

"Because I will call the clerk two minutes later and order a taxi for the front door, and I will nonchalantly ask if my yellow-shirted friend is still waiting for me in the lobby."

Ahhhhh.

"It all sounds good except for one thing. I'll go to the lobby. I'm the most recognizable member of our group," I said. "We need to be sure the watcher sees and hears us."

No one disagreed.

I won't pretend my heart wasn't in my throat, or rather, pretty much all the way up my nasal passages and into my cranium. But I sashayed my tall red-haired American self into the lobby like I owned it, channeling the energy I used every time I went onstage. I wanted rent-a-thug to be unable to tear his eyes from me, to strain to hear my every syllable.

In my best slow Texas accent, I over-enunciated terrible Spanish to the clerk. "Par-doh-nuh-may, señor. I need a taxi, um, I mean, Yo necesito uno taxi por favor, en cinco minutos? Did I say 'five minutes' right?" The clerk nodded. "Now how do I say 'to the back door?' Um, puerta posterior? By our room?"

Out of the corner of my eye, I saw a burly man in a yellow shirt stand up and stretch. Bingo.

"Sí, un taxi, puerta posterior. A taxi to the rear door. You are checking out?" the clerk responded.

"Sí, checking out." I gave him our room numbers and a vapid grin. "Dónde está el aeropuerto?"

"It's OK, I speak English," the poor guy said. His ears were probably bleeding. "Your taxi driver should know the way to the airport, but here's a map." He handed me a map and a receipt for our rooms.

"Gracias, señor," I said, but it came out more like "grassy ass." *My work here is done.*

"Safe travels," he said.

"Adios." Addy-ose.

I felt the eyes of Yellow Shirt following me as I continued my performance down the hall and back to my first floor room. I fumbled my room key on purpose so I could get another look at him. He was talking into a cell phone and had moved to the end of lobby nearest me. *Take the bait, sucker, take the bait.*

I slipped into the room.

"Well?" Collin asked.

I pretended to put out the fire on my smoking hot hand. "No problem. He appeared to be rounding up his buddies on his cell phone and heading toward the back door."

Collin grunted, which I took to mean "Wow, sis, you rock." "Let me go make the call for the taxi from the other room, so they won't think it's related to you."

One minute later, he knocked and beckoned us out into the hallway. I held my breath and Nick's hand. We humped our packs on tiptoe through the lobby and out into the tropical night, where we found Ponce still awake around us. Puerto Ricans partied every night, which meant cabs were always available. We ducked into the one waiting for us, which was a tight squeeze with four passengers, our bags, and my hatted head. The cab appeared to have had a spray-paint makeover, and patches of yellow were still visible through the uneven sky-blue paint job. If I had seen it on the street, I would have walked.

Kurt got in the back seat last. As he shut his door and settled in, though, he said, "Uh oh."

I didn't like uh oh.

"Señor, how fast can you get us to La Guancha dock?" Collin asked. "There's $100 US for you if you lose him." Collin pointed to Yellow Shirt, who stood in the hotel entrance speaking into a cell phone and looking at us.

The young driver said, "Sí, señor," and stomped the gas like in the movies, only harder.

I closed my eyes. Horns blared and brakes squealed as the taxi bounced into the street and fishtailed through a right turn. We accelerated like a drag racer and cornered on two wheels, or as close to it as I ever wanted to come.

"What if we don't lose them?" I asked.

No one answered me.

After we had gone about three blocks, the cab driver stepped on the brakes. Revelers were spilling into the street from a bar that looked closed. Music blasted from a boom box and people were dancing on the sidewalk.

"We could get there faster on foot! Let's run through that alley," I said, pointing at a narrow opening on the far side of the bar.

Collin said, "Whoa, good idea, sis. But we need to throw the bloodhounds off our scent."

He rolled down his window and held out a handful of hundred-dollar bills. "Who wants to make some money?" he yelled. A cry went up among the people nearest the cab. "Stop the car," Collin said. He turned to the driver. "Here's a hundred bucks to drive these folks to the airport, and there's another hundred for you when you get back. Go when I tell you to." He turned to the three of us crowded in the back seat. "Don't wait for me. Run like mad. I'll meet you in the alley where it ends at the dock. Stay hidden until I get there. Everyone out."

We barreled out of the car one at a time. Collin got out and smiled at his new friends. "I need two men—you and you—and one woman—you." He handed them each two hundred dollars. The trio cheered. "All you have to do is ride to the airport and back in this taxi. We're trying to get away from her husband, so we can have some fun," he said, pointing at me.

The crowd cheered.

"And wear this," I said, snatching off my straw hat and jamming it onto the drunk woman's head. She giggled and put her hand to the back of her head to hold it on.

The partiers clambered into the taxi, waving goodbye to their friends. Collin noticed we were still there and shouted, "Go, go, go, what are you waiting for?"

We took off, running into the pitch black of the alley.

The last thing I heard was Collin's hand slapping the roof of the car as he yelled, "Now," and the taxi's tires peeling out.

We kept running. Nick had grabbed our duffel bag, but as weak as he still was, I kept up with him easily. I couldn't see his face in the dark, but I could hear him breathing and he sounded as bad as I felt. Kurt pulled ahead of us.

And then the ankle strap on one of my gladiator sandals broke in two. I hadn't packed for a track meet. Next time I chased a lost husband across the Caribbean I would know better what to wear. While I ripped the shoe off my foot, Nick caught his breath.

Ahead of us, Kurt yelled in a whisper, "The dock is across the street. We wait here."

Behind us, I heard a splash—someone's foot in a puddle. I yelped.

A second later, Collin's hand clamped around my arm. "Move it, sis. We haven't got all night."

"Did we lose them?" I asked as I started my careful one-shoed run, scanning for broken glass.

"Last I saw, they'd picked up the taxi and were following it. But we have to hurry. They could figure out our switch any second."

He led the way across the street, which was eerily devoid of partiers. Collin appeared relaxed, but the rest of us swiveled our heads back and forth, scared of the long night shadows. We sprinted for *Kate* down a dock that seemed to pull an Alice in Wonderland and stretch longer with each step. The hairs at the back of my neck tingled like hot needles. I wouldn't relax until we were at sea with no other boats in sight.

Bill shouted a cheery "hallo" at our approach. He stood ready to untie lines with *Kate's* engines running. Kurt dropped his bags and went straight for the helm.

Collin said, "Make haste. We have a tail."

Bill patted *Kate's* side and replied, "Sounds good, my friend. See that boat over there?" He indicated a Hatteras one hundred feet away, identical to ours. "Our mechanic borrowed her impeller and a few other odds and ends, and he asked me to remove the evidence as quickly as possible." He high-fived Collin. "We are simpático."

Nice. Now we were knowingly transporting stolen property. Wait, no, as soon as we put *Kate* in gear, we were the thieves. Even better. I tried to clear my mind of things best not considered.

Collin stayed to help Bill with the lines. Nick tried, too, but Bill and Collin waved him off.

"Goldbricking ends tomorrow. Live it up while you can," Collin told him.

I settled Nick on the couch in the salon. So far, no men with guns were running down the dock. I decided to think positive and stay busy, so during our rapid disembarkation, I made breakfast for the crew: scrambled eggs, toast, and little smokie sausages with a big pot of extra-dark-roast Colombian coffee. My hands were still shaking as I loaded the plates. I dropped one off with Nick and headed to the flying bridge with the others. I passed them out as we exited the harbor.

"No followers?" I asked.

"None," Kurt said. He turned up the corners of his mouth ever so slightly.

"Thank God," I replied.

"Thanks for the grub, Red. I'd slap you on the ass for good measure, but now that Nick's restored to good health, I think I'd better not," Bill said.

"There's a man who has a way with women," Collin said.

All Bill needed was Collin backing him up. "Not a good idea," I said, "no matter how Nick feels. You've noticed the color of my hair, but I take it you haven't figured out its significance yet."

"Are you a natural redhead?"

It appeared that Bill had kept himself hydrated during our absence. I changed the subject to everyone's favorite topic, our new plan, and then slipped away when I'd heard enough. It took a lot more than a drunken sailor to offend me, especially one who had helped rescue my husband. Still, best not to let him test my patience.

Nick held up his empty plate as I came back into the salon. His sunburn had started to peel, but still, somehow, his color looked better. His eyes were brighter, his movements stronger, and his appetite endless. I brought him seconds and curled up against him with my coffee.

"Bill said the plan is to drop us off on the dock around 10:30 on the west end of St. Marcos. He remembers it from dropping you there two years ago after Hurricane Ira."

Nick chewed in exaggerated motions to show he wanted to speak when he finished his bite. "That was a wild trip. What do you think of Bill?"

"Childlike, endearing, irritating, drunk, and generous. Oh, and totally en-thralled with your father and loyal to you like a brother."

Nick speared a smokie, but waited to pop it in his mouth. "That about sums him up. He's a great person, and he's not afraid to be himself, even if no one else approves of him. He covers up the fact that he is highly competent at what he does pretty effectively with that surfer attitude, but the truth is, he's sharp and he isn't afraid of anything."

Nice to be unafraid. I was afraid of a lot of things. Like Chihuahuas and their hired help. I was afraid of something happening to Nick and the kids. Of losing what I had with Nick. Of Tutein.

I owed Nick an enormous update about Annalise, the kids, and the bones.

I took his paper plate and plastic cutlery to the trash. "We've still got over six hours until we land. Want to go below?"

"Are you propositioning me, Mrs. Kovacs?"

"I would never take advantage of an invalid," I said, glad to let last night's tension go.

"I was thinking you could be the nurse, I could be your patient, and we'd take it from there. Besides, didn't you ever see *Raiders of the Lost Ark*, in the scene where Indy shows Marion all the places that don't hurt too bad for her to kiss?"

"As I recall, Indy falls asleep. And I forgot to bring my white satin nightgown."

Nick sighed a long, beleaguered sigh. "Try to be prepared next time." He walked past me and slapped me on the behind. I followed him down the stairs and swatted his behind right back.

With no disparagement intended toward my husband, who was dehydrated and tired after all, the extent of our Indy/Marion adventure consisted of me pulling back the covers and kissing the tip of his nose as he got in bed.

"Now that I've taken care of all your needs, are you ready for a bedtime story?"

"Are we going to sleep?"

"I sure as heck hope so. It's not even six a.m."

"OK, lay it on me," Nick said, and he slipped his arms behind his head.

"Once upon a time, a very bad man lived on St. Marcos," I began. I proceeded to tell him about Tutein, every last gory detail.

I had trouble getting the story out, because Nick kept interrupting me with angry questions every fifteen seconds, but I didn't blame him. I was mad, too.

He balled his fists, and I reached out for his hands. He let me hold them.

"Katie, I'm not going to sleep anymore. I feel the need to plan Tutein's immediate demise with Collin."

I knew he was only partially kidding on the demise part. I also knew that the combination of Collin and Nick could lead to dangerous results. But I'd rather make it OK for him to discuss it with Collin in front of me than have any more secrets or half-truths out of him. Just the thought of that raised my blood pressure. Last night's apology had not helped, and I was far from over it.

We joined the others on the bridge after a quick shower in the guest head. The shower wasn't big enough for two, but the other party to my twosome wasn't in the mood to play anyway. While he was in the water, he muttered the whole time about people who messed with his wife and his mom, not to mention his kids. I think he threw in the dogs, too.

By the time he and Collin started talking, Nick was frothing at the mouth. I kept my distance and let him spew. Bill joined in enthusiastically, and Kurt urged them to talk where he could hear them. Soon, all four men were shouting and pounding their fists. I sat with my arms around my knees in the corner seat, half-listening and half-asleep, wholly done with stress for now, happy to pass the burden to them.

At 9:05 a.m., the satellite phone rang near my head. Where had the last two hours gone? My first impulse was to rub sleep from my eyes. Ah, a clue. The next was to lift my head from Nick's warm lap. Another. Collin and Bill stood beside Kurt, drinking coffee. Kurt passed the helm to Bill and answered the sat phone.

After a short hello, he listened for a long moment.

"Slow down, Julie. I couldn't understand you. Repeat that," Kurt said.

Fast-talking calls to a satellite phone usually meant problems. More problems. Please, not the kids.

"All right. I'm going to hand the phone to Nick so Rashidi can tell him about it."

Nick said, "Hello, Rashidi?" He listened for a few moments. "So it just flipped right in front of you and exploded?" Pause. "What did the guy look like?" Another pause. "Did you get out and take a look?" Short pause. "No? OK, what's happening there now?" Longer pause. "You guys are all OK, right?" Barely a pause. "Well, I'm very glad you called. Good luck with the DPNR director, and thank you again."

Nick turned off the phone and ran his hand through his hair. It stood on end. He sat motionless, staring at the tabletop for a fraction of a second, and then exploded.

"It's on, it's happening, it's happening right now," he said, jumping to his feet.

"What is?" I asked.

"The cartel. The Chihuahuas. The terrorist attack on Petro-Mex. The diversion." He turned to his father. "How do I get hold of your Coast Guard contact, Dad?"

Oh my God.

We hit a bigger wave than normal, and everything from the table bounced onto the floor. I grabbed for coffee cups, dice, and backgammon chips as they rolled in all directions.

"Whoa, son, tell me what's going on first," Kurt said, a voice calling for reason in a situation rapidly developing without any.

Nick bristled, then spoke rapid-fire. "A jet fuel tanker flipped and exploded in front of the refinery, right outside the fence by their housing compound and a day care. Mom had Rashidi, Laura, Rob, and Ava with her in the car, and they had just driven past there to make their 9:30 appointment with their attorney and the DPNR. Rashidi was sitting in the front seat, turned around talking to people in the backseat, so he saw it happen. He said a man threw something in the road in front of the tanker truck, and that the truck lost control going around the corner. It flipped over and burst into flames. Then Rashidi said the same man ran back into the road and picked some things up and drove away in an unmarked police car."

Collin broke in. "An unmarked? Sounds like he threw down road jacks to puncture the tires. A police officer. Not good."

"So you think this is the diversion the cartel planned to stage before the real attack?" Kurt asked, still holding the satellite phone.

Nick looked ready to pounce on his father if Kurt didn't hurry up. "Yes, Dad, and we have to report it immediately and get the right people involved. Come *on*."

Kurt finally dialed, handed the phone to Nick, and said, "You'll be speaking to Ralph Tate. He's up to date on everything except the tanker flipping."

Nick spoke rapidly into the phone. The conversation was short, and when he hung up, he said, "Good man. He's reporting to the other authorities and mobilizing on the harbor."

"Who else should we call?" I asked. "What about Petro-Mex?"

"Ralph said he would call them, but I don't think it hurts for us to tell Ramirez ourselves. While I do that, Katie, can you run get me some more Gatorade? I am out of my mind thirsty again."

I nodded and he kissed my cheek without making eye contact. I had a bad feeling he was moving me out of the way. Again.

He turned to the others. "Let me make a call, and then we need to discuss a change in plans, guys."

Bill said, "Hey man, no problem. Flexibility is the key to air power."

He slapped Collin on the shoulder and Kurt actually laughed. They were all pumped full of adrenaline and testosterone. Nick ignored them. Lava began to boil deep inside me.

Collin said, "I owe the Chihuahuas for my partner and his family. I'm in."

This really didn't bode well. I made for the galley and Gatorade as fast as I could.

I heard Nick speaking to Ramirez on the satellite phone even before I got back to the stairs. I returned, out of breath, as Nick was hanging up the phone.

"As expected, the refinery has its hands full just dealing with the explosion and the leaking jet fuel. The Coast Guard was on the other line by the time we hung up." He turned to Bill. "Now for the change of plans."

Bill said, "I'd expect nothing less, old buddy."

"We need to set course for the refinery's harbor," Nick said.

Kurt lifted his hands in the air, ceding the helm to Bill.

"No problem, mon," Bill said, and he whipped the wheel to the right. "Get me a map, Kurt."

Kurt pawed through the maps and laid one out for Bill. One hand on the wheel and both eyes on the map, Bill traced his finger along it, and then tapped the spot where his finger stopped.

"How far away are we?" Nick asked.

Bill pointed to St. Marcos, which was now in sight. "We were an hour ahead of schedule already since the ocean is flat today. We would have docked on the west side of the island in about twenty-five minutes or so. With this great water, it will only take about another twenty to get all the way around and into the mouth of the harbor. Call it forty-five minutes total."

"This may sound like a stupid question, but why are we headed to the refinery?" I asked.

"We talked about this, Katie," Nick responded. "People's lives are at stake."

My line of sight narrowed and I felt my emotions creeping toward the precipice. "We talked about you needing to warn the refinery about a terrorist attack before the cartel found out you had survived. We didn't talk about taking an unarmed pleasure boat and going up against terrorists with both parents of our children on board." I was yelling now.

This jarred Nick, although not in the way I hoped. "Bill, what do we have in the way of weapons on board? Flare guns? Spear guns? Anything more lethal?"

Collin was all over this idea. "How about knives, sharp things, anything that will hurl projectiles, anything explosive?"

"Yeah, man, all of that, plus one big gun, too," Bill said. "The owner keeps it in case of pirates."

"Guys!" I yelled, louder this time. No one listened to me. Mutiny.

Bill gave Nick and Collin directions and they ran off to ransack the boat for weapons.

"Kurt, this is just not the right way to handle this. You see that, don't you?" I pleaded. "We could sink this boat. We could get in the way of the appropriate, trained, well-armed authorities."

"Yup, not ideal. Have to play this one out, though. We can scuttle our plan at the eleventh hour if it looks bad."

"What plan?" I asked. "We have no plan. We're just charging in there with no idea what we're doing."

"Nick and Collin both have experience with this type of thing, Katie. Everything came out all right when they rescued us from Taylor's father, didn't it? I have faith in them. You should, too."

The satellite phone rang and he answered it, ending our conversation.

Without much hope, I turned to Bill. "You could get fired, you know. *Kate* could sink. We could all die."

"We're going to be fine. No problem, mon." Bill's eyes reminded me of a greyhound I had once seen right before a race. I'd hated the dog track, and I hated this. I couldn't stop these guys any more than I could have stopped that greyhound from chasing a rabbit around the track.

Collin and Nick returned. Collin had a 12-gauge shotgun and a box of shells. They had at least brought life jackets, which assured me that they could still access some small part of their rational brains that wasn't overrun with Fight Club mentality. Nick had stuffed an unimpressive cache of makeshift weaponry into my large overnight duffel; a couple of spear and flare guns, some fish-filleting knives, grill lighters, and heavy link chain. It looked like a Unabomber-wannabe scavenger hunt.

Great. They dumped my lady clothes on the floor to make a gun bag for the macho men.

"That's it?" I asked.

Nick said, "Oh, no. We left the scuba tanks downstairs."

He'd either missed or ignored the message in my tone.

"Scuba tanks?" I yelled. "What the hell do you need scuba tanks for?"

"Didn't you see the final scene in *Jaws*?" Nick said. He took a closer look at my face and added, "Just kidding. No scuba tanks." He turned back to the guys. "Bill, thanks, man. How far away are we?"

"Ten minutes."

Collin motioned for us to gather near Bill. "We need a plan."

This was the first acknowledgement that we hadn't had one before, even though we were less than ten minutes away from real, live terrorists. Killers.

"If we didn't have a plan, there'd be nothing to change," Bill said, and pounded the dashboard like a bongo. Ba-dum-dum.

"Well, really, we just need to refine the one we have," Collin amended.

I'm not seeing the funny here.

Now that we were near the island, boat traffic had increased. Each boat I saw behind us tightened the thumbscrews to my temples. Right now I had my eye on a cigarette boat coming up on us like a cheetah after a wounded wildebeest. Not good.

Kurt interrupted with a Coast Guard update before I could bring up the cheetah. "Good news, bad news. That was Ralph. All their sea power, the boats in range, are converging on the harbor. They've coordinated with the local FBI, and they're mobilizing and probably already at the gates of the refinery. Petro-Mex is cooperating. But the Coasties were on the far side of the island apprehending some drug runners. They dropped what they were doing and got on their way, top speed. But we'll still get there before them. A good five or ten minutes before them."

Mother of God. What a horrible idea.

"This just confirms that we're doing the right thing," Nick said. "Somebody has to stop these bastards. Collin, what do you think? I defer to you for the details."

Collin took over. "Bill, do you have any handheld radios?"

Bill pointed with his toe. "In that cabinet." Kurt retrieved them and started passing out radios. Of course, there were enough to outfit a boatload of guests. Or a small army. "Test them for charge," Bill added.

Collin went on. "Kurt and Nick, how about one of you each take a side post. Find a way to strap in, wedge in, or hold on. We can't stop for a man overboard. I'll take the stern."

"Got it," Nick said. He scooped up a flare gun and a spear gun. Kurt handed him a radio and followed suit.

"What about me?" I asked.

"Stay out of the way," Collin said. He sounded like Nick about the Petro-Mex job.

My ears burned and my eyes watered. I rose on my tiptoes so we were eye to eye and shouted, "You guys cannot drag me into this and then treat me like Penelope Pitstop. I won't sit here powerless to have a role in our survival." *You need one person in full control of her faculties.*

"Fine. You'll be our runner. If anyone needs anything, Katie will bring it to you." He handed me one of the radios. "Let's move everything down to deck level. Bill, enter the harbor like a bat out of hell, OK? We're looking for anything that doesn't belong on the dock in a refinery. Or on the water. If it runs, we chase it. If it chases us, get us in position to fight back."

He was acting like we had AK-47s mounted on every side of the boat, but really, we were charging into this battle like Yosemite Sam. *What in tarnation is goin' on?*

I positioned myself just inside the salon's sliding glass door, leaving it open. I was scared out of my mind—more scared than when Tutein had dragged me into the woods. We had no business doing this. It was probably even against the law. And yet, if I were forced to do so, I'd admit that I couldn't imagine the men in my life handling it any other way. I would just have to hold the operation together.

From my post, I had an unobstructed view off the stern. The cigarette boat had cut the distance between us in half. It looked like it was only a quarter mile behind us now.

"Is anyone else worried about the boat on our butt?" I said, trying out the radio.

I took the collective lack of an answer as a no.

The guys moved into their appointed spots. I watched Collin contort himself thirty-six different ways as he tried to wedge his body in so he wouldn't fly out of the boat. He tucked the flare gun into his waistband and held the pump-action shotgun down at his side.

"You want binoculars?" I asked, proud of myself for thinking of them.

"Yeah," he said, and I rounded them up and passed them out.

As I slipped the strap for Nick's over his head, he touched my cheek with his fingertips. "I love you, Katie. Everything will be fine."

Maybe.

"Try not to get yourself killed," I said, and I let him kiss me just in case he did, once quickly on the lips. I ran back to the galley.

The cigarette boat had pulled within a hundred yards.

We turned to the port side and entered the harbor at breakneck speed, *Kate* steady under my feet in the smooth water protected by land on three sides. I had never gotten close enough to this entrance to the refinery for a good look, as the entire area was restricted access. I'd heard stories from the old days, pre-global terrorism, when locals would fish its waters in their motorboats, dwarfed by the giant tankers at the dock. Rashidi said the concrete pylons that crowded the shore on each side made the perfect hiding place for lobster. He and his pals used to gather them by the boatload. But those kinds of escapades would land you in jail these days.

The waterway was a quarter mile wide and split down the middle by a dock that stretched a mile into the sea. Monster-sized ships lined up on either side of the dock like the inverted teeth of a zipper. Next to them, the harbor vessels looked like water bugs. All these diesel engines meant fumes, and fumes meant hateful odors. My nose curled. Behind and above it all, the refinery loomed, the dark backdrop to the drama playing out in front of us.

Who was I kidding? As close as we were now, it was no longer in front of us—we were onstage.

I had just started the Lord's Prayer again when Nick yelled, "FBI on the dock! Sirens, lights, agents everywhere."

Yes! Let them handle it.

I had no view of the action, but I imagined agents yelling, doors slamming, sirens screaming. *Kate's* engine and the rush of water blocked out the sounds, but in my head, it was like listening to "Ave Maria," a song so beautiful it made me want to weep.

Nick relayed an update. "Looks like they've already cuffed a few people and are putting them in cars."

I pictured an FBI agent in a blue windbreaker with big yellow letters, his hand on a suspect's head as he pushed him into the backseat of a black Ford Explorer like the ones I'd seen local agents driving around the island.

Bill eased off the throttle and we coasted up the mouth of the harbor closer to the melee. I could hear the sirens now, too. *OK, let's go now. Turn the boat around. The good guys are winning.*

"Are we done here, fellas?" I shouted.

No answer.

I stood up and looked out the back of the cabin. How odd. A little boat was cruising around one of the tankers. It didn't look like FBI to me.

I clicked the talk button on my radio. "I see something. Back out toward the mouth of the harbor. There's a little inflatable by the last ship."

What I didn't see anymore was the cigarette boat. Had it kept going? Maybe I had succumbed to hysterical paranoia, if there was such a thing.

Seconds ticked by.

"I see them!" Nick yelled.

And then Collin was shouting into his radio from his post at the stern. "The FBI missed some of the bad guys. They're in a little inflatable with a big motor."

"Copy that," Kurt said into his radio.

"I'm on it," came from Bill.

The tiny, low-profile boat was slinking from tanker to tanker, shielded from the eyes of the FBI agents above by the looming ships. And then they pulled close to the side of a ship and stopped, and a man stood up and leaned toward it. I was trying to figure out what he was doing when Bill's voice boomed out from the flybridge.

"Well, what do you know. Looks like they got them a getaway vehicle, out by the little island past the mouth of the harbor."

I swung my head and binoculars around for a look. The boat Bill saw was all the way out of the harbor, but trolling, almost like it was whistling with its hands behind its back looking skyward. "Who, me?" it seemed to ask. It was the cigarette boat I'd seen earlier.

Collin's voice crackled over the radio. "Oh crap, they're planting explosives on the hull of the tanker. We've got to stop them. Swing her around, Bill."

Once again, I spun around to see, but we were already too late. The man who had stood up seconds ago—planting a bomb?—sat back down, and the boat shot up the waterway.

Chapter Thirty

Bill spun *Kate* 180 degrees and pushed her throttles forward. She responded, but at the lumbering rate of a sixty-foot yacht. When the inflatable's driver caught sight of us, he hit the gas, too. *Kate* strained to increase speed but the nimble inflatable outpaced her.

From my handgrip on the back of the cabin, port side, I could see three men. We weren't close enough for me to see their faces, but through my binoculars, two looked Latino and the other appeared local. That surprised me, although it shouldn't have. Lord knows they'd hired local every step of the way.

Kate roared up the harbor. She had planed out and her body rode high above the water. We had the intercept angle on the inflatable as they raced for the mouth of the harbor. As we got closer, Kate's bow started to shimmy slightly in their wake. I slipped back into the cabin and stood on the white leather couch with my nose against the glass. I would apologize to the owner if I ever met him for putting my dirty feet on his upholstery.

Collin moved around from the stern to the walkway behind Kurt, both of them inches away from me on the other side of the window. His voice through my radio was muffled by the wind as we flew toward the terrorists. "Bill, bring us in for a shot from the side. Nick, be ready in case they make a tricky move. Kurt and I will unload as we get closer."

Unload?

"Ten-four, good buddy," Bill said. Bill was having way too much fun with this.

I crept out of the galley again and peered around the side to see what Collin and Kurt were doing. We bore down on the little boat, but the occupants were ready. Two muzzles appeared above the sides of the boat, aimed back at *Kate*.

"Guns, they're pointing guns at us!" I shrieked. I bounded back into the cabin and flattened myself on the sofa as shots rang out and bullets slammed into *Kate's* hull. My three favorite men hit the deck almost simultaneously. But *Kate* lurched to port and lost speed as she made a crazy left-hand turn, digging deep into the water.

"Bill, what the heck's going on up there?" Collin yelled over the radio.

I sprinted for the stairs. Something was very wrong. I took them two at a time and bounded over the top and onto the bridge. Bill lay on his side clutching his thigh. Blood seeped through his shorts and down his leg. *Thank God, it's only his leg.*

"Are you all right?" I crouched beside him.

"Grab the wheel, Katie. I'm shot, but I'm fine. Grab the wheel," he yelled.

I leapt up and put both hands on the helm.

"Straighten us out and put us back on course. You be my eyes and hands. I'll tell you what to do," Bill said in a voice that sounded much calmer than I felt.

"These black knobs on the right are the throttles, correct?"

"You got it."

I didn't stop to think. I turned the wheel until I had *Kate* pointed back toward the inflatable. *Kate* struggled to get higher in the water.

Collin's voice came through clearly on our radios. "What the hell happened, Bill? Make sure you're aiming for intercept, now, not catch-up, and don't back off the throttles. Nick, stay low and come around to our side at the stern. We can't shoot until we're right on them. You guys aim for the side of the boat. I'm shooting to disable the driver. Let's put a few spears in that spare tire with a motor."

There was no time to tell them I was captain now. I pushed the throttles all the way forward and aimed in front of the inflatable at an angle. I had done this before in vehicles. Land vehicles. But not at top speed, and not in a boat.

Bill dragged himself up on the settee so he could see where we were going. Red blood all over white cushions. Not good.

More shots rang out. Our guys stayed low. I tried to look invisible and wished I could lie down on the floor, but I held steady.

We barreled even closer. The men stayed down.

More shots.

Closer.

More.

Closer still.

"Now," Collin cried, and one shotgun and two spear guns shifted over *Kate's* side below me and released in the direction of the inflatable. Collin's gun blast blocked out every other sound, and he pulled the barrel back, cha-chook, and shot again and again. Seconds later, three men disappeared, and I hoped they had dived into the cabin.

More shots rang out and thudded into the hull. The damage to *Kate* was going to cost us a fortune if we lived to pay for it. I had the sensation of bees swarming the bridge and I realized it was the sound of bullets whizzing past me.

"Get down, Bill," I screamed.

All this—but had we hit the inflatable? The suspense plugged my lungs with cement at the same time as it poured accelerant into my heart. But then I saw it, and I jumped into the air and yelped.

I pulled the throttles back and keyed the radio. "You got it! The inflatable is collapsing on one side." I thought for a moment, then spoke into it again. "Um, also, Bill is shot in the thigh."

I heard Collin pumping his shotgun, and then a boom.

"Don't let them get away, Bill!" Nick screamed into the radio.

Either he hadn't heard me or he thought Bill was Superman. I looked into the distance and saw the cigarette boat fleeing. I rammed the throttles forward on *Kate*, ignoring Bill's groans about her engines. *Kate* came to speed and shot out of the harbor after the getaway boat.

Nick and Kurt stood together on the port side, spear guns reloaded and aimed. Collin was one step in front of them, pumping and firing, but the boat was pulling away. Again, I aimed in front of them for an interception, but we made up no ground.

And then the U.S. Coast Guard arrived, appearing suddenly because the island had blocked sight of its approach, and we erupted in a cheer. Their cutter intercepted the cartel boat from the front while I closed in on it from behind and it dropped speed. There was no escape. A barrier island hemmed it in on the right, and an exposed reef crowded it from the left. The terrorists lifted their hands in the air in surrender, weapons pointed down. Another Coast Guard cutter arrived and replaced us on point.

I pulled back on the throttles and *Kate* hummed her way to coasting speed.

"Turn her around, Bill, and let's make sure the inflatable stayed put," Collin ordered.

I spun *Kate* around, back toward the inflatable, which was now half submerged. I brought her to trolling speed and stationed her between it and the other apprehended vessel.

Just then a third and a fourth Coast Guard boat appeared.

Bill said, "Hand me the radio, Katie," and I passed it over.

He said, "Attention, all passengers. The Coasties are pulling into the harbor, and they have their guns sighted on the bad guys and us. Put away the weapons, everyone, and adjust your halos."

Now that her engine was quieter, we could hear the Coast Guard over their loud speakers. One of the boats had pulled alongside the inflatable, and the other by us.

"Cut your engines and drop your weapons immediately. Prepare to be boarded. This is the U.S. Coast Guard."

Three heads appeared at the top of the steps, one after another, as Kurt, Nick, and Collin joined us on the bridge.

"Bill!" Kurt said.

"They got me in the leg. I'm fine," Bill said. He had tied his shirt around his thigh and was pressing the cloth into his leg. Most of the bleeding had stopped. "Well, it hurts like hell, but I'll live."

"So who drove the boat?" Kurt asked.

Bill pointed at me. Now that the action was over, I was trembling, but I gripped the helm behind my back to hide it.

"You drove the boat?" Nick said. But he was grinning at me, a lot of white teeth against his sunburned skin.

"What? You think I can't drive a boat? Or investigate a death case? Or find a lost husband?" I asked, smiling, too.

"Don't burst his bubble, Katie," Collin said.

"You're amazing," Nick said. "Badass, Katie."

"I'll bet you never fire me from another case, Nick Kovacs," I said.

"Scout's honor, I won't," he said.

"Is everyone else all right?" I asked the other three men.

"I'm pretty sure Nick peed himself, but other than that we're good," Collin said.

"That coming from the pro whose shot missed by a mile. Luckily I came over to your side and saved the day," Nick said. "You're welcome."

"You both missed. That's my spear in the side of that boat. Wisdom and experience beat youthful bravado every time," Kurt said.

They appeared to be completely fine.

"Is it safe to leave the bridge?" I asked.

"Yeah, somebody needs to make me a drink," Bill said.

"Hang tight a little longer," Collin said.

I moved over to Nick, who took my hand. I felt his heart beating in his fingers. His pupils were still dilated and looking for the enemy. Seconds stretched into minutes until a shout came from over the side. *Kate* rocked as a smaller Coast Guard craft bumped us. "Everyone OK here?"

Five voices called, "Yes, sir."

"We need to come aboard and confirm the absence of unfriendlies. Is that all right, Captain?"

Kurt restrained himself and Bill said, "Yes sir, and welcome aboard."

The Coastie threw a line and Kurt went down to secure their vessel. The rest of us went down the steps, Collin helping Bill, and stationed ourselves outside the cabin door, clear of where the Coasties would board. A younger man and his heavier partner climbed over a few seconds later.

"Good morning, gentlemen," the heavier one said, and then saw me. "And ma'am."

I ducked my head in acknowledgement as the guys all said, "Morning, sir."

He spoke again, to Kurt. "Permission to search your vessel, Captain."

Kurt gestured toward Bill, and Bill pointed at me. I curtsied, and the guys all laughed. The Coasties registered mild surprise. Bill grinned and lifted the arm he'd been using to apply pressure to his wound with a beach towel. He waved it and the bloody towel at our visitors. "Be our guest."

Again, surprise. "You're injured, sir?"

Bill relished the moment. "Just a flesh wound. I'm fine." He'd take a thousand bullets to live a day like this one.

The Coasties commenced their duties. When they returned, the younger one said, "Nice boat. Commodore Ralph Tate called ahead to let us know to expect you. Thanks for hobbling the terrorists until we could get here."

"No problem," Kurt said.

The jauntily uniformed Coasties shook hands all around. "We'll need statements later."

We gave them our contact information and agreed to meet them at three p.m. at the FBI offices in the Federal Building in town.

The heavier one spoke again. "You guys are free to go for now. I understand one of you has had a long week?"

Nick raised his hand. After a beat, Kurt and I raised ours, too. The Coasties both laughed as they went back over the side to their boat.

Kurt turned to Bill and said, "Captain, if you would please allow me the honor of fetching you that drink."

Bill saluted Kurt.

I moved to the side walkway for a better view of the real action. The bad guys in the inflatable had their hands up. Their boat listed badly but was still floating, one side of it limp and sinking. I turned to rejoin the others.

Wait a second.

I walked to the bow and lifted the binocs to my eyes again. What the hell? Detective Tutein was in that boat. In profile, but clearly recognizable. What was he doing here with the Feds?

I looked closer.

His wrists were behind his back in silver bracelets. Was Detective Tutein the local I had seen in the boat with the two Mexicans?

Impossible.

I counted heads in the boat. Three men. Two Mexicans. One local. The same as during the chase. And the only local in the boat—a local wearing handcuffs—was Detective Tutein.

I punched the talk button on my radio. "Nick, do you see who that is in the terrorists' boat?"

Nick came up beside me to take a look. I felt his large, warm hand on my shoulder, moist breath on my neck, and his binoculars protruding past my face.

"Holy Mother Goose and Grimm. It's Tutein. It is, isn't it?" he asked, as incredulous as me.

I smiled. "Yes, it is Tu-friggin-tein. And you without your spear gun."

Chapter Thirty-one

Returning home felt like a huge gulp of fresh cool air. We pulled into our driveway at lunchtime or thereabouts with Bill, who'd refused medical treatment, telling Nick he'd "be fine if you'll just let your good-looking wife clean it and stick a bandage on it," referring to the wound on his upper thigh.

To my chagrin, Nick had cheerfully agreed.

"You live here? This is your house?" Bill asked.

Annalise always shined brightest for visitors. Her yellow stucco dazzled the eye and bright bougainvillea reached up to her as if she were the sun. She glowed like Monet's "Woman with a Parasol."

Hello, old friend.

"We live here, but we've come to realize we belong to the house more than she belongs to us," I said.

"Huh?"

"Long story," I said.

"Does this have anything to do with your wife hearing voices?" Bill asked Nick.

Nick slapped him on the shoulder and said, "That's not even the half of it."

Five dogs circled our parked car, yelping, barking, and growling. Oso defied certain punishment and put his front paws on the door to stick his long nose through the open window. This started a trend, and soon six paws were on the door and three noses in the car. Bill shrank back. Oso grinned, showing his teeth and dripping drool onto Bill's lap.

"Are the dogs vicious?" he asked.

"Not if you feed them raw meat. You brought some, didn't you?" Nick said.

Everyone laughed except Bill.

We'd been trying to call Julie ever since we made it off the boat, but all we got was voicemail. Her car wasn't home, either. Ruth was here, though, and she ran out to greet us. I had only seen Ruth run once before, and that time she had thought Taylor was drowning in the pool. Which he kind of was, but not really, because Annalise had saved him. Ruth ran straight for Nick today.

He opened his arms wide. She hugged him and wailed like a baby.

"Don't you ever go scaring us like that again, Nick Kovacs, or I whup you, and whup you good. Shame on you," she said when she had calmed down enough to speak.

Nick laid his head on hers and then lifted her up and twirled her around.

She squealed. "Put me down. I too old for nonsense, put me down." She swatted him and he set her down, but she held on for a little while longer anyway.

A small body worked its way through the long legs of the grown people.

"Hi, Daddy! Hi, Mommy," Taylor said, and I gave him the same treatment Nick gave Ruth.

Nick released Ruth and wrapped his boy in a bear hug, rubbing his cheek against Taylor's wavy hair. I saw him wipe his eyes, but I kept it our secret.

"Where are the babies?" I asked Ruth.

"I put the girls dem down to nap, just after they lunch. They still sleeping," she said.

Julie's car pulled up behind ours in the driveway, and the process of hug, twirl, and squeeze was repeated a few more times. Julie grabbed Nick and Kurt together and somehow managed to get her arms around both men, as small as she was. Then she hugged me tight and whispered, "Thank you for bringing him home, Katie."

We all trundled bags into the house and congregated in a noisy throng in the kitchen. We made a big group, which immediately threw Julie into a frenzy of hostessing. She made drinks and passed them out to everyone: the DPNR team of Ava, Rashidi, Rob, Laura, and the attorney, Vince Robinson, and the *Kate* crew of Collin, Bill, Kurt, Nick, and me. Nick and I sprinted upstairs to look in on our sleeping girls for a few sweet moments, then rejoined the party.

"Boy, do we have a lot to tell you about our day," Julie said.

"Boy, do we have a lot to tell you about ours," I replied.

"You first," she said.

"No, you," I said.

"You."

Nick put up his dukes. "Ladies. Are you going to fight for it?"

"OK. You win," Julie said to me. "We go first." She swept her hand toward Rashidi.

"First, to tell the story right, I got to introduce you to Rob and Laura," he said.

Rob bowed, and Laura curtsied. He slipped his arm around her waist. I would have pegged Rob as gay had I not seen him with the wife for whom he had obvious physical affection. Laura, though not a beautiful woman, was twinkly, from her eyes, to her voice, to her mannerisms.

"So tell the people what you find," Rashidi prompted.

Rob rubbed his chin and cleared his throat. "OK, I try to make this long story short and give proper credit. My brilliant wife and U.V.I. librarian, Laura, find a diary entry written by a young slave girl a hundred and fifty years or so ago, about a plantation owner who bury her mother on top of a hill overlooking the valley of the mangoes. The plantation, it turns out, named Estate Annalise. Good job, honey."

He held both arms toward her as if she were on display. Laura walked around the kitchen like a model. These two were fun. We clapped. "Hear, hear," Rashidi said.

Rob continued. "I look back through all the old maps of the area I could find through the museum. No graveyards, no cemeteries, no burial grounds. But I did notice something in one of them. The word 'Uxolo' printed on a hilltop, a hilltop overlooking the house we standing in now."

I got goose bumps. I looked around and saw that he had the rapt attention of everyone in the room, even Taylor.

Rob kept going. "I flip back through the others, and I find another reference to Uxolo. No other detail. Same hilltop, though. About this time, Ava tell us that Tutein and the DPNR breathing down Julie's neck, so Rashidi and Ava meet us up here." He unfurled a weathered paper map and we all leaned in close.

He pointed to the word Uxolo on a hilltop to the northwest, with nothing but a smooth downward slope to where Annalise now stood. A collective "ah" escaped our mouths.

I stood closest to the map, and I touched the word. *Uxolo*. The feel of the slightly raised ink on grainy paper raised the hairs on my neck. But that wasn't all that it raised.

I heard a hum growing around us within Annalise's walls. The noise came on so gradually that it was hard to identify, but I knew it well. The attorney kept looking over his shoulder, his eyes wide and nervous. He'd heard it, too.

"She's hanging on your every word, Rob," I said.

"Who?" he asked.

I gestured all around me. "Annalise."

Everyone in the kitchen fell silent. Without their background noise, Annalise's hum vibrated the air around us. Nick slipped an arm around my shoulders.

Vince dropped his glass. The hard plastic bounced once, twice, three times on the kitchen floor before he moved to scoop it up. We all listened to the spirit of the house as she sang out her approval.

"Oh my God, I hear it," Laura said. She clutched her throat with one hand.

"Go on, Rob," I said. "Don't be frightened. She just wants to hear your story."

"Are things always this exciting around you guys?" Rob asked.

Everyone but Nick and I shouted, "Yes," and laughed.

"I hope I get the story right, since it appear one of us might have been present for the real thing. This a new one for me." Rob cleared his throat. "OK, where was I? We drive up to the spot marked Uxolo in a jeep, with machetes, very National Geographic, you know. Rashidi hack us through the forest, and let me tell you, that forest dense. We make it up to the hilltop, which really nothing more than one of those narrow ridges, but there a small flat area where we park. Laura pack us a lovely picnic lunch, chicken paninis with pesto and organic tomatoes, and the view fabulous."

"Robbbbbb," Laura said. "Tell the story." She nudged his shoulder with hers.

"Oh, well, while we eat lunch, Rashidi whack down all the bush on the hilltop. One place already been cleared and freshly turned dirt all around it. Like an exhumed grave. That strike us as pretty strange. Then we do our best amateur imitation of an archaeological grid search. And we find this."

Laura walked in front of us like Vanna White, holding over her head a battered wooden marker with the words "Uxolo Cemetery" carved into it. I sucked in my breath, my eyes wide. I wanted to hold Annalise's hand; the air felt like it would cry at any second.

Rob continued. "So then we notice the rocks. Piles of rocks. Some fallen and scattered a bit, but the spacing look right. And there a few more old wooden markers, but none with carvings that clear enough to read. We know we hit the cemetery jackpot." He grinned, so obviously enjoying this adventure outside his academic life. It was far less pleasant for us, but I didn't begrudge him his excitement.

"We really careful not to mess anything up and cause more DPNR trouble. Because if we don't cause any new trouble, Uxolo solve the old trouble."

"I don't completely understand," I said. Partly because I didn't, and partly because Rob seemed to hope for this question.

Rob said, "Because Uxolo on the edge of your property, far away from Annalise. And there definitely bodies there, in the marked graves, and also as explained in the diary."

"But that doesn't mean there wasn't a body under Annalise," I said. "Or more than one. Couldn't they have washed down from Uxolo?"

"Good point. That's what we wonder, too. But stay with me. Rashidi walk the hilltop, and he say the natural slope create a drain, if you will, that lead down to Annalise. Which don't sound good."

"Except for one thing," Ava said. She had restrained herself for quite some time, but she loved a good drama. "Look out the window." We did. "There a cut in the land around Annalise. A deep, natural cut between Annalise and the base of the hill. It even on the old map."

Rob pointed to the ravine indicated on the map.

Ava continued. "There no way anything wash down that hill and land up where we now stand. It would stop, down there." She swept her arm toward the ravine. "So if, hypothetically speaking, some remains wash down the hill, they don't come up this one." She lapsed into thickened local dialect. "There ain't no way the bodies dem under the ground where Annalise now standing."

Now the attorney took over the story. "When I heard all this," Vince said, "I advised taking it to the DPNR directly. The director is married to my second cousin's husband's mother. He's a reasonable man."

"Yah, he reasonable after he make us wait in the lobby two hour," Ava said. She was a hybrid; born on the island, but went to college in the states and sang in New York for a few years before returning to her roots.

The attorney was a stateside-educated local, too. "Well, yah, he do that." He switched back to Yank. "But we just came from our meeting with him. He agrees it's unlikely anyone that was buried in Uxolo ended up under Annalise, or that there's another completely unrecorded burial site under her. He also agrees we're talking about a report of old, old bones, and not some recent burial, so he thought our research on the maps that led us to Uxolo made sense. He just needs some kind of concession to make this go away."

A concession. Of course. Because, after all, we were in the islands.

"What kind of concession?" I asked, hands on my hips.

"He made some hints, but in the end he asked us to come back with a proposal," Vince said.

Julie spoke up for the first time. "We came up with a great idea we think will work."

Ava said, "We think he agree to let this go for a permanent right of way up to the site, and a deed carving off the half acre on the hilltop."

Rashidi spoke next. "The plot it sit on can't be used for anything else. It too narrow. That probably why the plantation master let the slaves use it for their graves back then anyway. And that ridge mark the edge of your property. It won't even make a hole in the middle."

Vince said, "Let the government decide what to do with it, whether to make it into a historical park, or nothing at all. They get to put a notice in the paper that you've conceded the land to them after they received the report of the bones. That's really all they want."

So simple. I liked it, especially now that Tutein was handcuffed to a chair in the Federal Building. I decided to leave it up to my house.

What do you think, Annalise?

The open kitchen door creaked as it slowly swung closed with a firm click. I looked at Nick, and he smiled. That sealed it for me.

I said, "Guys, this is just magnificent. You did so well, I don't know what to say, except thank you."

Nick had commandeered my cell phone earlier to warn Petro-Mex about the diversion from the real attack. It rang now. He pulled it out and read the number displayed. "Hold on, everyone, this is Ramirez at Petro-Mex." He walked outside to take the call.

Kurt took the opportunity to tell everyone about our morning. The celebratory mood shifted to one of absolute shock. Jaws gaped.

"All that happen here on this island since we last talk to you? Here?" Laura said, her voice squeaking. "Actual terrorists from an honest-to-God Mexican drug cartel?"

"Yup, but we stopped them," Kurt said. And gave one of his rare Kurt-beams.

Laura turned to me. "I don't know how you do it. Your life so dangerous. Dead bodies and terrorists. How you stand it? I mean, no offense—I sure it great for you, it just not for me."

"No, that's fine," I said, and realized she had spoken my recurring thought aloud.

My life was out of control.

That's why I'd been mad at Nick before he disappeared. And look at all that had happened since.

A cry interrupted us, followed by another. Two little girls waking up from their afternoon nap. Ruth and I walked up the stairs together while Julie said, "Now who's ready for some peace and quiet and a little lunch?"

I was ready for a large serving of the peace.

Chapter Thirty-two

Ruth and I worked side by side on wet diapers and new outfits. I crooned to my beautiful girls. I had lost four days with them and risked my life in the process. What would they do if they had to grow up without a mother? Like Taylor almost did? He shouldn't have to lose another. My mind took off down a trail best left untraveled, and my ebullient spirits deserted me.

Ruth lifted Jess and asked, "You coming?" as she headed for the door.

"No, I think I'll just stay here and rock Liv, keep her all to myself for a little while." I felt an irrational, ugly mood swing coming on. Maybe rocking would help me.

"She gonna want the bottle in the mini-fridge, there," she said.

"Yes, you're right," I said, and pulled a bottle of formula out. I sat down in the glider between my girls' cribs and rocked my daughter, crooning "Hush little baby" to her as she looked at me with expressive green eyes and tugged down the formula like a newborn calf.

"I missed you," I said, and touched her tiny nose with the tip of my finger. She released the nipple and smiled around it. It made a drawn-out noise and vibrated against her lips, then she went back to the business of sucking. I studied her sweet face. Bless this child's heart. If I wasn't mistaken, she had the makings of Nick's nose. Distinctive. Strong. But hopefully in a feminine way.

"Here you are," Nick said. He was standing in the doorway, one hand on the jamb. "Ooooh, baby girl." He walked to me and held out his arms. "May I hold her?"

My irritation bubbled up inside me, but I just held her up to him and switched places. As I handed him the bottle, my motions felt jerky and uncoordinated.

"Ooooo, so sweet, I love you Livvy," he said.

And then I recognized it, and I let it in. The unexpressed anger I'd been tamping down since Nick had disappeared. Covered up by fear, then elation, relief, and fear again. If he loved us so much, why had he taken these risks? Why did he lie and shut me out? Why did he disappear with no explanation?

I bit my tongue. If I could stall myself long enough, maybe this would go away. I didn't want to spoil the harmony, the celebration. I did love him. I could light into him later, after everyone was gone.

But I was pissed off, deep inside where I held on to the dark stuff, like my husband not telling me he was flying to Punta Cana.

Stop.

Nick was singing to Liv now. "You are my sunshine, my only sunshine."

I turned to go.

"Wait, Katie, stay with us," Nick said. "Liv, say, 'Mommy, don't go.'"

I stopped in the doorway, a copy of his pose a few moments ago. I didn't trust myself to speak. I tried to hide the ugliness inside me.

Nick said, "That call from Ramirez was very good news."

I waited for him to go on; he waited for me to respond. I won.

He continued. "Did I ever tell you about the reward Petro-Mex gives for information leading to the apprehension of terrorists?"

I nodded. He didn't see me. I gave in. "Yes, you did."

"Petro-Mex wants to present Stingray with a check for a hundred thousand dollars. Plus our fees for the investigation work." He looked up and grinned. "That's more than enough money to pay for the delta between the insurance payout and a replacement airplane."

His joke, if it was a joke, fell flat. And that's when I lost it.

"God forbid you wouldn't have the means to run out of the country without telling me. Hurry—buy that airplane, Nick, hurry! I just hope you have enough money left to ship me off to a fat farm, too, so you don't have to look at your fat wife anymore."

And then I ran.

Not just out of the room. I ran down the stairs and out the door, past the noisy party full of happy people in the kitchen. I ran down our driveway like a madwoman with all five dogs behind me. I ran until I found the fresh-crushed bush where Rashidi had driven a jeep up to the hilltop overlooking the valley of the mangoes. I ran until I was out of breath, wishing I was in shape, wishing I would learn to wear sensible shoes, trying not to think about that squishy feeling between the toes on my left foot, and then I trotted, and finally I gave up and walked, but fast, fast up the trail Rashidi had cut.

Paradise. I was run-walking up a trail in the middle of flippin' paradise, or at least that's what it looked like from the outside. "Oh, Katie lives in the Virgin Islands with her perfect husband and their three beautiful children. Their house is a mansion in the rainforest. Oooooooooh."

Bullshit. It was paradise until you threw in dead people and a husband who says he loves you more than anything, but who loves his freedom more. I stopped, huffing. Nick loved me. I knew he loved me. But he sure did love being able to lie to me, to omit the truth, to go where he wanted and be accountable to no one. And if he loved me more, why did he choose those other things over me? Ipso facto.

I ran again, slower this time, thinking about the fallacy of paradise. For God's sake, I was running to a graveyard on my property. Because of this place, this Uxolo Cemetery, I'd had a crazy man show up on my doorstep telling me about skeletons, and a crooked police officer drag me into the bush to make threats against my kids and me. And the house was nuts, anyway. What kinds of families lived in houses that threw pictures and knocked down tackle boxes? That hummed to the guests in the kitchen? Nuts! All of it was nuts, not paradise. Nothing was what it seemed.

I reached the hilltop. I crossed Rashidi's rough and tumble clearing job with ease and saw a pile of fresh dirt and the rocks Rob had described, the plot of graves that was discernible if you closed your eyes and imagined it a hundred and fifty years ago. I saw a large rock on the edge of the clearing, and I perched on it, holding my knees up to my chest. Sitting where a young girl may well have mourned her mother and written in her diary. I looked out to the view she would have seen from this spot.

The Caribbean Sea rolled out in intoxicating blue waves. Three miles below me, where the sea met the land, was my favorite spot in the world, the Baths, my peaceful place. It was filled with millions of small rocks through which the ocean rushed in and out, creating a visceral sound that washed my soul clean. She had probably visited that place, too. I listened for it now.

I heard something. It may have been the wind in and out of the trees between that place and me, but it served the same purpose. I let it fill me up; I let it empty me out.

I heard another sound. A vehicle. Of course.

I waited until I heard feet crushing the cuttings on the forest floor. No words were spoken, but as my husband entered my sensory range, I smelled his unique and wonderful scent, and I felt him. I always felt him. The cosmic energy between us wouldn't allow otherwise.

He sat beside me on the big-enough-for-two surface of the rock and we watched the sea together for a while.

I kept breathing, in rhythm with the waves.

He put his hand over mine.

I didn't pull it away.

"I'm sorry," he said. He didn't elaborate.

The harsh lashing my tongue would have delivered fifteen minutes before was gone with the wind, gone with the sea. All that was left were the memories of my very real emotions.

"I can't ask a bird not to fly, because then it wouldn't be a bird," I said. *I hope you don't think that made sense, Katie.* I started to try again, but he interrupted me.

"You can ask a bird to tell you where it is flying off to, and to fly a little closer to the ground," he said.

"Birds can't talk. So it wouldn't do any good."

"So, say it in bird language, sing like a bird, tweet, quack, however you have to say it. The bird loves you."

"The bird told his father I was fat. Daddy-bird squawked."

"What? No, I never said that."

"That's not what your father says. Did you know that Tutein tried to convince me you ran off with Elena to Mexico? And that your father said we couldn't rule it out because you *really* wanted me to lose all of this baby weight." I didn't dare look at him.

He was silent, then exhaled. "I never told him that. The only thing I ever said that comes close to that was when Mom asked me what to make for dinner one night, and I said to take it easy on the fattening stuff because you were struggling to get your baby weight off. I was trying to help you because you were always talking about it. I didn't say I thought you were fat."

His explanation was plausible.

"Really?"

"Really. You're beautiful. All the time. I'm sorry Dad said that, Katie. I'm sorry he hurt your feelings. It wasn't how I felt. But why would you ever think I'd leave you?"

How to explain?

"I didn't believe it. I fought against it. But you didn't make it easy. You texted Elena the second we left her house. You lied to me about her. All signs pointed toward you, her, and Mexico. Tutein swore Monroe killed himself in our driveway on purpose. As a message to you."

Nick pursed his lips. "I understand. I hate it, but I understand."

I nodded. I hated it, too.

He put his arm around my waist. I let it stay there. "You know what Uxolo means?" he asked.

"Is it a real word?"

"So says Rashidi. He followed me out to the car when you made your jailbreak."

"I'm not ready to laugh at your jokes yet."

"Fair enough. He said it's a Zulu word, which makes sense. The slaves here came from Africa." He kissed my hair, right above my ear, and then stayed there, the movement of his lips rubbing my hair against my scalp. "It means grace. As in 'by the grace of God we live, and by His grace we die,' I suppose."

"I like that."

"I hoped you would." He squeezed my waist. "I'm asking for some. A little grace, for me, from you. For flying too high without telling you. For falling short of perfection. For bringing the Chihuahuas into our life and lying to you. For not being here to protect you and the kids from Tutein because I left without telling you. I'm disturbingly human, it turns out. I make mistakes. But I am sorry. And I love you—" he took me by the shoulders and shook me lightly, "more than anything."

Grace. I could use some, too. For lacking faith, for general bitchiness at times, for my inflexibility. For my addiction to Clorox wipes. For a lot of things. "I'm sorry, Nick. I'm sorry I ran out. I'm not mad at you anymore." I turned my face into his neck and breathed him in.

"Don't be sorry. Just love me," he said.

We held each other for several minutes, silent, reconnecting at a level deeper than words. The invisible vines that grew from my heart to his—the ones I had machete-chopped apart to make my flight—grew back faster than bamboo reaching for the sun. My mother's mother's wedding ring felt molten, like a warm, approving embrace.

I lifted my head and faced him, nose to nose, in exactly the position I loved best.

"Hey, you know what I just remembered?"

He Eskimo-kissed me. "No, what?"

"The very first time I saw Annalise, with Rashidi, I Googled her. To see what Annalise meant. Because I have a thing about that."

"I know you do. That's why I knew I could make some headway by telling you what Uxolo meant."

"Manipulator. Anyhow, Annalise means grace in Hebrew. Which I think is pretty cool, considering."

He put a hand on either side of my face and leaned back to look into my eyes. "It's cooler than you think."

"Why?"

"Cue the *Twilight Zone* theme music. When I was stuck on Hornito—"

"The island is called Monito."

"Huh? I thought it was Hornito. Like the tequila."

I tried not to laugh. "No, it's not."

"Well, I like Hornito better."

I sighed. But in an accepting way.

"When I was on that fricking island not knowing if I'd ever get off, I would swear I talked to Annalise."

"You told me that in a dream. That she talked to you."

"See? OK. I feel a little less crazy remembering it, then. But she wasn't a house. She was a person. She was the person that is who we think of as Annalise."

"Oh. My. God," I said. "Seriously? Really? Our Annalise?"

"Our Annalise."

"Tell me about her."

"She was a young slave girl. She worked at the plantation at Estate Annalise. She died in childbirth when she was sixteen. When things went bad, the
owner wouldn't call for a doctor. Her name was—"

But I already knew, just like I knew her face.

"Grace," I said.

"Yes."

"And her daughter lived, and went on to write a diary. That Laura found.
That led us here."

"Precisely."

Uxolo, Grace, Annalise, us.

I felt Nick move closer. His free arm wrapped around me from behind and
he leaned his head forward to press his nose and cheek against my face. His
breath caressed my lips, and as he moved his head back slowly into my hair, I
felt that same breath on my eyes, my temple, and my ear. He landed a kiss into
the shy triangle between my collarbone, shoulder, and neck.

That's when it rocked me. It, the same thing as a thousand times before
with him. My heart thumped open with a sonic boom, and all its contents flew
straight and true for my husband. His met mine somewhere in the middle, and
the intense connection threw off heat and a rainbow of colors that shot into the
air like a Roman candle. I heard a crashing "thwack thwack" way off in the
distance, and I didn't have to see it to know that Annalise had thrown her
stately mahogany doors wide open.

Subtle, girl. Real subtle. But I'm with you.

The End

Now that you have finished *Finding Harmony*, won't you please consider
writing an honest review and leaving it on Amazon and/or Goodreads, or any
other online sales channel of your preference? Reviews are the best way readers
discover great new books. I would truly appreciate it.

About the Author

Pamela Fagan Hutchins holds nothing back and writes award-winning and bestselling mysterious women's fiction and relationship humor, from Texas, where she lives with her husband Eric and their blended family of three dogs, one cat, two ducks, four goats, and the youngest few of their five offspring. She is the author of many books, including *Saving Grace, Leaving Annalise, Finding Harmony, How To Screw Up Your Kids, Hot Flashes and Half Ironmans,* and *What Kind of Loser Indie Publishes?* to name just a few.

Pamela spends her non-writing time as a workplace investigator, employment attorney, and human resources professional, and she is the co-founder of a human resources consulting company. You can often find her hiking, running, bicycling, and enjoying the great outdoors.

For more information, visit http://pamelahutchins.com, or email her at pamela@pamelahutchins.com. To hear about new releases first, sign up for her newsletter at http://eepurl.com/iITR.

You can buy Pamela's books at most online retailers and "brick and mortar" stores. You can also order them directly from SkipJack Publishing: http://SkipJackPublishing.com. If your bookstore or library doesn't carry a book you want, by Pamela or any other author, ask them to order it for you.

Books By the Author

Fiction from SkipJack Publishing:
Saving Grace (Katie & Annalise #1)
Leaving Annalise (Katie & Annalise #2)
Finding Harmony (Katie & Annalise #3)
Going for Kona coming Fall 2014

Nonfiction from SkipJack Publishing:
The Clark Kent Chronicles: A Mother's Tale Of Life With Her ADHD/Asperger's Son
Hot Flashes and Half Ironmans: Middle-Aged Endurance Athletics Meets the Hormonally Challenged
How to Screw Up Your Kids: Blended Families, Blendered Style
How to Screw Up Your Marriage: Do-Over Tips for First-Time Failures
Puppalicious and Beyond: Life Outside The Center Of The Universe
What Kind of Loser Indie Publishes, and How Can I Be One, Too?

Other Books By the Author:
OMG - That Woman! (anthology) Aakenbaaken & Kent
Ghosts (anthology), Aakenbaaken & Kent
Easy to Love, But Hard to Raise (2012) and *Easy to Love, But Hard to Teach* (coming soon) (anthologies), DRT Press, edited by Kay Marner & Adrienne Ehlert Bashista
Prevent Workplace Harassment, Prentice Hall, with the Employment Practices Solutions attorneys

Audiobook versions of the author's books are available on Audible, iTunes, and Amazon. The *Katie & Annalise* books are narrated by Ashley Ulery, http://ashleyulery.com.